The Tulip Terror

The Tulip Terror

A LILY LIST MYSTERY

C.L. BAUER

For information contact:

www.clbauer.com

ISBN: 978-1-7363460-5-1

First Edition: October 2018
Second Edition: March 2021

10 9 8 7 6 5 4 3

The Lily List
Mystery Series

The Poppy Drop
The Hibiscus Heist
The Tulip Terror
The Sweet Pea Secret

Dedication

Thank you to all the women of my family and to the men who choose to live with all of us! My mom would be devouring these books, but she'd be wishing they were westerns. My one sister would be showing anyone in an airport that her little sister wrote this book. From my "Sister, Sister" who listens to me recite plot lines over and over; to Scarecrow and her little lovelies and to the Metro Buddies and the girls and boys to come...I thank you all for what you have brought to my writing.

We will always have Paris!

Prologue

Today was Ed and Helen's day. Well, it was *supposed* to be Ed and Helen's big day, but Vic and Lily kept drawing all the attention. Vic's little brother was getting married today and he wanted, he needed everything to be absolutely perfect. Lily, his wife, just wanted this day over. There was just too many Schmidt family members buzzing around for her taste. Her husband's family had been her family for many years now, but with all of them hovering, pecking away at her sanity with their questions and comments was just too much. Besides, she desperately needed a drink.

Vic checked Ed's bow tie one more time. He brushed off his shoulders, removing the imaginary pieces of lint.

"You good, Ed? You have enough money for the honeymoon?"

"Yes, Vic. I've been planning for this for a long time." Ed smiled. He couldn't wait to be Helen French's husband. He couldn't wait to have a family with her and to see where this life led them. He hoped and prayed they would be happier than his older brother and his wife.

Lily and Vic had hit a rough patch, but Ed knew better. They were careening over a cliff, a very high cliff adorned with jagged rocks and ocean below. Lily had run her family's flower shop before she met her husband. When Vic and she met, a passionate fire erupted into an inferno that everyone around them could see. They were a couple from the day they set eyes on each other. Lately--well for a few years now--that inferno had been doused with a dam of water. Vic disagreed with Lily's business decisions; Lily didn't want to stay home at night. The only embers of love burning now were their tempers. God help you if you ended up in the middle of one of their arguments.

Yet here they were making sure that Ed Schmidt had a beautiful wedding. Vic had arranged everything from the photographer to the church hall decorations. He'd found his favorite cake lady and the family had provided the food for the morning brunch and for the reception this evening. That's what family did, at least this German family did.

Lily was being Lily. She had one of her famously large chic hats on the top of her perfectly coiffed hair. Everything matched, including her clutch bag and shoes. She'd picked the ensemble up in Chicago last month. Her hair and makeup was perfect as usual. She'd tried Elizabeth Arden for her lipstick, discovering a shade of red that soon became her favorite. Her fragrance was Chanel No. 5. It was pricey, but she deserved it. All the movie stars were wearing it. She was a fashion icon in Kansas City. She had to maintain the aura of what little celebrity she had acquired over the years.

Lily Schmidt was the wedding florist queen. Everyone who was anyone came to her for their flowers. It wasn't that she was the best florist in town, but her personal care was what most clients wanted. Besides, many just wanted to watch the woman set up a wedding in those high heels. Even her own husband couldn't understand how she could walk all day in those dangerous shoes. But the heels had to be high; they showed off her long shapely legs.

As the wedding time was nearing, Lily was at the back of the church with her soon-to-be sister-in-law Helen. The bride was more than ready to walk down the long church aisle.

Only minutes later the priest began the ceremony. Ed nervously waited as the four bridesmaids walked slowly down the aisle. The music became louder, the congregation stood. Helen and her father began the long walk to her new life. Ed smiled. He wasn't nervous anymore as soon as he saw her glowing face. Her simple smile erased all his fears of today and the future to come.

Helen French had fallen in love with Ed Schmidt on their second date. He had taken her out for ice cream. She'd dropped the cone down the front of her dress. He ran for more napkins and quickly began to dab at her dress, not realizing what pieces of anatomy he was touching. When he suddenly understood why everyone was watching him, it was too late. Helen and he shared the same exact shade of red face.

He winked at her and whispered, "Guess I'll have to marry you now."

She surprised herself when she answered, "Yes, you will."

That was only four short months ago. Helen was shaking a little, but her father steadied her hand on his arm. She carried a small bouquet of lavender and purple Cattleya orchids with cascading blooms of white stephanotis knotted onto slender satin ribbon. Each delicate flower had a pearl within its bloom. It was a "Lily Special", carried by just about every one of the shop's brides that year. It was perfect.

Helen's eyes met Ed's. She loved the man standing in front of her. She couldn't think of anyone she'd rather spend her life and future with than Ed Schmidt. He was her everything.

When her father gave her a quick kiss beneath her veil and handed her to Ed, her stomach growled. Her future husband smiled.

"Just an hour or so more. I made you a ham sandwich and it's at the back of the church in a cooler. I knew you'd be hungry."

"And that's why I love you," she whispered. The priest coughed and they turned their attention to the task at hand.

It was only the beginning for them. Eventually, the couple became a family of five. The youngest daughter was named Lily, after an aunt she never knew and a shop she eventually inherited.

This Lily Schmidt was not a prisoner to fashion or celebrity. Her attire was mostly black in color so dirt and flower stains didn't show. She loathed dry clean clothes because she rarely took the time to drop them off and remember to pick them up. She only wore make-up occasionally; her hair frizzed in the Kansas City summer humidity.

She had her own style in flower design, but she still held fast to her family's tradition of personal attention. She loved her clients and they loved her. Clients became friends; families used her shop for generations of weddings and funerals. Lily would hand deliver plants to customers she hadn't seen in awhile just to stay in touch.

Lily was highly organized, preferring to make lists to keep herself on target. She used so many post-it notes she should have bought stock in the little devils. Lists were her life. Her life was her work until that fateful day when a handsome DEA agent walked through her door. He ended up protecting her; he ended up loving her.

1. Get bid on new phone lines for shop
2. Make sure Neal brought in the pink tulips
3. Dog food for Mort
4. Call bride for Saturday
5. Check on delivery times for the week
6. Talk to Abby

Chapter One

*L*ily Schmidt's hands were full physically and metaphorically. Her work bag and purse hung on one shoulder, keys and coffee cup in one hand, a bag with lunches for Abby and her in her other hand as she climbed out of her car. As soon as she shoved the car door closed with her shoulder, she grimaced. She uttered a German cuss word out loud.

It had been only a few weeks since Garrett Notte had grabbed her wrist and twisted her shoulder. He'd intended on killing her too. The sociopathic drug dealer from a very good Kansas City family blamed the wedding florist for every problem he had. Oh, it really wasn't her fault that he was in a federal prison waiting for a trial date. He was there for international drug trafficking and attempted murder of a federal agent. His own father was on the run from the DEA and perhaps some South American cartel. The Notte men owed the bad guys millions of dollars. The federal agents couldn't really pin any crime on Bernard Notte, the father, but they sure wanted to talk to him. The cartel that he and his son had been involved with probably wanted to know where their money went. It was rumored the elder Mr. Notte had gone to Europe, and many of those countries had very weak extradition laws. The Notte family was old money and perhaps he could con someone over there to take him in. And all of this nonsense began because Lily, the owner of Lily's Flower Shop, had received a mistaken drug shipment instead of her hydrangeas for a wedding. Of course she had received one other little thing from the very special agent who had been on the case.

Lily juggled all her packages and locked the car. Her hand, specifically the new engagement ring on her left hand, caught her attention. She giggled. "Holy Moly, I'm a fiancée."

That was a unique concept for Lily, one she never thought she would ever have to get used to but was doing very well at enjoying. Dev had styled the ring with a jeweler friend in Alexandria, Virginia. He'd bought the large blue sapphire planted in the middle when he was stationed in Afghanistan. She loved the sentiment behind the twelve diamonds that surrounded it. There was one diamond for every month Devlin Pierce was away from her. Lily had done the math on one very boring day last week and yep, he was probably correct. The man had been away almost a year out of their two-year relationship.

But despite his absence, the constant in and out of her life, they were making a commitment of some kind, to be planned at a later date. She found herself humming, almost non-stop. It was beginning to irritate poor Abby who had to work with her almost six days a week. Lily giggled again as she thought about the man she loved. In fact, she was humming as she walked to the shop's door. She could hear Abby's raised voice as she came closer. *This does not sound good. Abby never yells.*

As she approached the door to go inside, she stopped. Now Jeremy, Abby's boyfriend, was talking. His voice was lower, softer. Apparently, he was the one in trouble. Lily had her hand on the door when she decided to go back to the car, but it was too late. *Get out of here, Lily.* Abby had spotted her and was motioning her inside.

"Crud," Lily muttered out loud. Abby was pushing past her boyfriend, coming toward her like a steam engine, its smoke furling from its stack, racing to its destination.

Lily thought she could ignore the quarreling couple; pretend she didn't hear anything. "Oh hello you two. What's up?" *Seriously, Lily. What's up? You know what's up, they're arguing and they never do that.*

"You won't believe what he's done now," Abby said as she pointed back to Jeremy. She helped Lily with her bags. Her boss was hoping to avert eye contact. Avoidance, escaping, and pretending nothing was going on apparently wasn't going to work.

"Oh, Abs, I'm sure it's not all that bad."

"So, you're taking his side? Of course you would. It's partly your fault."

Lily stopped at her desk and shoved her purse under. Abby had followed her and was standing next to the desk. It appeared that Jeremy was positioning himself behind Lily for protection. *Now, what had she done?*

"Enough. What is my fault? What is Jeremy doing?" She turned around and physically moved Jeremy to the side. "Hello Jeremy."

He waved innocently in her direction. "Hey, Lily."

"This, this nitwit," Abby stammered. She always stammered when she was utterly and completely out of control. "He has been training. He's been making plans without me. He's been planning our future."

Lily stifled a laugh and tried as hard as she could to retain a stoic face. *What was wrong with making a few plans?* She stopped her own thoughts. *Ah, he was doing it without her.*

Lily completely understood the outrage. Her own fiancé had tried to do that to her and for her. So, she'd listen to Abby's outrage until she discovered what the nitwit was actually planning. If he was going on an adventure in the Himalayas to discover any shared DNA with an alpaca then Lily might have to agree with her assistant. If he was actually getting a job that offered a six-figure salary with health care benefits, then Abby would have to take a chill pill. *Gosh, this day just keeps getting better.* Lily would have healthcare for the first time in years when she married Dev. There would actually be a retirement account. As a small business owner those perks were like golden tickets.

"What has he been planning?" Lily watched Jeremy move his body into the corner of the adjacent wall, perhaps his attempt at invisibility.

"Well, you're to blame because," Abby took a deep breath before continuing, looking straight at her boss for emphasis, "he is leaving to join the FBI."

Lily put on her shocked face, but this time it really was her shocked face. She looked at Abby and then toward the invisible Jeremy. He just shrugged his shoulders and held his head down like a naughty puppy. *Speaking of puppies, where was Mort?*

Her dog, an inventive gift from Dev, had gone to live happily with Jeremy and Abby, but she still helped out with treats and dog food. She'd ask later, after all this drama was finished.

"Tell her Jeremy, just tell her." Abby pointed at her boss. Lily still couldn't figure out how all this was her fault.

Jeremy's head raised. "I have been accepted into Georgetown for my master's. I'll be undertaking an internship in the FBI, training, volunteering with one of the police departments, and going to school. I go to Washington, D. C. next week to get it all settled."

Now, Lily's mouth dropped onto the floor. Before she could ask how, why or when, Abby continued her attack, an accusatory finger pointed at Jeremy and then at Lily.

"See...see, he's...he's, you...you," she stammered in an art-like fashion. There were tears forming in her eyes. Lily brought out her desk chair and led Abby to it.

"Sit down and listen to the man. I for one would like to know how and when this all happened." Lily sat on the edge of the desk, holding her assistant's shaking hand in hers. "Spill, Jeremy. You didn't just come up with this on your own."

"I took an aptitude test last year. I knew I was good in computer information compilation. Then when my other skills for languages and games were assessed, well there were a few professions that came up."

Lily's eyes were crossing. *Holy Moly. Who was this man and where did the nitwit go?* The boy who only cared about video games and sports suddenly was a man thinking in multisyllabic words.

"It was kind of ironic actually," Jeremy admitted, a slim smile now on his face to his girlfriend's consternation. "The next day this guy from the FBI came to talk to us. You remember that dude from the hotel when you got that free night? Tom Fullerton? He's really part of the FBI. He's in charge of the field office here in Kansas City. I didn't even know the FBI was even here, did you?"

And the nitwit had been resurrected. "Yes, Jeremy. I knew he was with the FBI and that they were here. You remember, he helped with all that stuff that happened here at the shop, right?"

"Well, yah, we had a long talk about that. That was pretty cool now that I know some of the details, and we had that free night at the hotel. The television in that place and the food was the best ever."

"Jeremy," Lily said, waving her hand in front of his face. "Get to the part where you start being an adult."

"Yah, well. I've been talking to him for several months. I started running and doing weights, really trying to physically take it up a notch. I've even started watching what I eat. I never have done that. He got me a job with a security firm that helps out with some of the banks in the area. I go through surveillance footage, online stuff and when there's something that doesn't add up, I go in and figure out the problem. I have a knack for finding anomalies and algorithms."

Ah, Lily thought. He has special skills. *Imagine, Jeremy was special.*

"Oh and I'm proficient in Russian, Chinese, and a few other languages."

Lily and Abby looked at each other, asking the same question in silence. When did all this happen?

Lily had to discover how he learned a couple of the hardest languages in the world. "Jeremy, you really know Russian and Chinese, how and when?"

"Actually, Mandarin. Schezwan is a little harder for me. Not the food. I love those little dumplings, but I'm not sure what province they are from. I learned the languages online. I'm self-taught. I also played a lot of competitive video games with this guy in Hangzhou. My mom knows

Mandarin too. She says I get my aptitude from her. My dad only knows three languages."

"So," Lily interrupted, "obviously you are very talented in some skills the FBI really needs. It's a great career choice and it seems like you've thought this out." Lily looked over at the now crying Abby. "Why didn't you share all this with her?"

"I didn't think she'd approve."

Dev had surprised Lily with a dog, Mort last Thanksgiving. Her surprise was his attempt at protecting her while he was away. He had thought it through, but her reception of said gift was underwhelming and frankly, cold. When you didn't share "the plan" and someone was left out of the decision making process, the reception meter didn't rise too high. Jeremy had obviously thought this out, with Tom's help. His surprise was intended for good not the chaos he was creating. Lily would make a note later to talk to her old buddy Tom. Why hadn't he mentioned Jeremy?

Of course, it was all that covert indoctrination. DEA agents didn't divulge and FBI agents didn't elaborate, both sets of law enforcers didn't share with the ones they loved. But that was for another day.

Abby was still crying and Jeremy was still standing there like a lost soul. "Jeremy, you have a scholarship at Georgetown. You have a job for experience and you'll be working with the FBI. Then what? Where does Abby fit in with all this? You haven't asked her. You thought she'd disapprove."

Abby looked up and added, "Yes, what Lily said."

"The FBI sounds so conservative and I know she's such a free spirit. I just knew she wouldn't like me working for the MAN."

Lily laughed. "Jeremy, this isn't the sixties. The MAN is part of the federal government and they protect us. I'm sure Abby would've thought this was all pretty cool."

"No," Abby screamed out. "That's where it's your fault, Lily. You brought all this agent stuff around. Jeremy could be shot like Dev was just a few weeks ago. Heck, you were hurt too. I don't want my baby hurt."

"I won't be, Abs. I'll be in some van or office building in some basement. I won't be actually fighting the bad guys, well at least they won't know I am." Jeremy finally moved from his safe space and kneeled in front of his girlfriend. "I love you Abby, and I want us to have a good life. I'm really good at this, and I want to help get the bad people around the world. I can't do it without you. You can come visit, and we can visit those Georgetown coffee shops. There's this little French café right beside one of the historic canals. It's so cool. We can go to the art galleries, maybe take in a show at the National Theatre. It's right by the White House. I'll have some time off during the week, and you could come up and be back for weddings on the weekend. I know you like the weddings."

And Abby nodded. The crisis was over. Lily would wait until later to talk to Abby about another plan she had developed.

He held her hands in his and added, "I'm so sorry, Abby. I should've told you. I should've trusted you. Abigail?"

Lily held her breath. *Oh, Lord, is he really going to ask her right now? That could be a dangerous move.* As if in slow motion, he held her left hand and began to fiddle with something in his pocket.

"Will you marry me? I mean, if you want to, if that's cool with you?" He held out a small gold ring. A small diamond was the bloom within gold petals. Etched into the side of the band were delicate leaves.

Lily shut her eyes and smiled when Abby finally stammered out a positive response. Life was certainly going to change around here.

Chapter Two

After almost a full hour of kissing, hand holding and words of love, Jeremy finally left the shop. Lily found Mort. The poor dog was hiding out in the backroom until the shouting had concluded. Abby and she went through orders and had their lunch. It was almost two in the afternoon when Lily had finished today's part of her list.

"Abs, are we caught up on everything back there?"

"As far as I know. We don't have any deliveries until tomorrow, and I thought I'd take them. There's a couple downtown and then the midtown funeral chapel."

"Great, come and sit down."

Abby had already become proficient in walking and looking at her engagement ring. It had taken Lily almost a week to obtain that little known talent. She grabbed a chair from up front and brought it to sit near Lily at the desk. Lily removed her glasses and smiled.

"You're firing me."

"No, silly. We need to talk."

"You're giving me a raise?" Abby smiled sweetly with all her teeth showing.

Lily laughed. "No, silly."

"Then what's up?"

"You really do love working here, don't you?"

Abby eyed Lily suspiciously. What was her boss up to?

"Yes, more than anything."

Lily sighed, grateful for the correct answer. "You know, eventually Dev and I will get married, and I'm not sure how we are handling anything yet. I was wondering if you could take on managing the place when I'm out. If I am out."

Abby nodded an enthusiastic yes. "I would love that. I know I can do it, Lily. I can even do some of the weddings by myself."

"I know you can. You've been doing more and more. I really have appreciated it. So, after today, I'd like to put you down as the manager of Lily's Flower Shop."

"Do I get business cards? I've always wanted those little suckers. I don't really know why, but I'd love that. I could even pay for them." She clapped gleefully at the thought.

"I'll get them. I'll do it tonight. I'm so happy you're excited and now that's all settled. With all this with Jeremy," Lily stopped talking. Abby was crying, full out ugly tears. "Abs, what's wrong now?"

"I have to be out of our apartment by the fifteenth. I can't afford to stay there with him gone." Terror was in her voice. It was one thing to be uncertain about your future, it was another to be homeless.

Lily gulped. Dev had to marry her now after what she was going to ask. Even if she only lived with him just part of the time in his Alexandria, Virginia townhouse it would be fine. She could do this and this would be the right thing to do. Maybe not the smartest, but the best for all of them. She gulped again.

"Abby, come live with me. You can pay me, and I won't charge you as much as your half of the apartment rent. Then, if I do live for months with Dev, you can pay me the rent money and still be able to have a nice place to live."

"Can I buy your house?" Abby had sat straight up in the chair in anticipation. Her tears had suddenly ceased.

Lily was shocked at first. "Well, let's think about that. The rent money could go toward the purchase of that house, if it eventually comes to that. How about that? No guarantees, but a tentative agreement?"

Abby extended her hand out and Lily took it. "I'm good with that. Mort will have the yard back then. I won't be lonely without Jeremy. We will be one little happy family."

"Yes." Lily answered tentatively. She had a few doubts, but this was the right thing to do. She'd have to live with that for now. Besides, she was prepared. She had plenty of wine, and the liquor store was just a mile away.

"Oh no," Abby exclaimed.

Lily was confused. "What? I thought everything was good."

"Not you silly, but that?" She pointed in the direction of the sidewalk and peering through the big shop window was Gretchen Malloy, premier wedding coordinator and planner, delusional sidekick and lusty pain in the you know where. "Your bestie is here and I'll be in the backroom." Abby quickly ran from Lily's side.

"Coward," Lily yelled after her as Gretchen arrived into the shop. *Could this day get any weirder? Yes, it could and it just did.*

"Bestie," she yelled as she sauntered into the consultation area. She didn't just walk, her hips swayed and heels clicked on the wood floor. Gretchen seemingly always made an entrance. Her entrances made some, like the cowardly Abby, perform hasty exits. "I want to see that ring."

How did she know? Who told her? Lily never understood how Gretchen knew everything and everyone in Kansas City. That annoying sing-song speech pattern was patently Gretchen speak.

Gretchen grabbed Lily's left hand without permission and pulled out a jeweler's loupe from her pocket. *What the heck?* Lily just shook her head. The woman surprised her at every turn. Gretchen continued to make small noises, mostly in approval.

"Why white gold?" she asked as she plopped down in the open chair, placing her loupe back in her pocket.

"It's not white gold. It's platinum. With all the hand work I do, he went with that."

Gretchen agreed. "You need a manicure if you're going to wear that beauty. Mr. Delicious did very well. Those diamonds are so fine and that sapphire is unbelievable. That set him back a pretty penny."

"He had it made for me. He designed it with a jeweler he knows." Lily smiled as she looked down at her hand. Gretchen was right. Her work- hardened nails were in direct contrast to the delicate beauty of that ring.

"And didn't I tell you he was the one for you? You can thank me." Gretchen was serious. Lily couldn't stand her egotistical, condescending manner. Damn, she had been right.

"I'm not thanking you for anything, but you did say we fit together." She should've thanked her, but she just couldn't. Gretchen had reprimanded her for not having enough confidence to go after him; to think she could have him. Lily had listened and taken in the good advice. The silliness was thrown out like bad garbage. The overly-made-up wedding coordinator was still calling her Dev Mr. Delicious!

"Where will we have the wedding? Now, let's see, his family and yours are on the east coast. Where's his brother? Nevermind, he can travel. The Bahamas are a short hop, so is Bermuda. Oh, Bermuda! I had a wonderful time there with a certain gentleman. It was my thirtieth birthday, and he gave me some gift!"

Lily rolled her eyes. She leaned her head back, closed her eyes and began to pray as Gretchen continued with her memories of Bermuda. The man had been a captain of a luxury cruiser. He'd only been in port for a week. *Lord, please give her laryngitis. Lord, you aren't listening because you can't stand to listen to this either, can you? What? What did she just say? The palm tree did what when they…*

"And then he just sailed away. But you better believe he was still removing that chocolate for days."

Lily opened her eyes. It was best to ignore her story. "What are you doing here?"

"I have this client. The couple is very particular and I'm sure they want to do a church wedding. Is your little church nice?"

Lily blinked. Gretchen was asking her opinion? "Yes, it's nice. It doesn't need any decorating. When we do a wedding there, maybe we do something on the pews. If it's an afternoon wedding, maybe an arrangement in the foyer. They have a large table there. If it's an evening ceremony, I'd use their candelabra and really decorate them."

"And the bride is a lot like you. Where would you have a reception?"

Lily smiled softly. Her eyes sparkled at the thought of a wedding.

Gretchen Malloy caught the softening of Lily Schmidt. The little wedding florist apparently knew the exact place that made her happy. "Well, where? Some barn?"

"No, but there are some great barns, snobby Gretchen." She stuck her tongue out. "No, I'd love the hotel off the Country Club Plaza. At night, even if it wasn't the holidays, all the lights on the buildings just sparkle from that penthouse room. It has that cocktail area on one side that is very New York chic, and then the full ballroom on the other. You could do tons of candles in both areas. Maybe low arrangements everywhere, vines, ivy, soft petals. Now if the couple is younger, then somewhere else."

Gretchen howled. "No, they're verging on elderly."

"Well, then the beauty of that hotel is you can do your magic and get them a block of rooms. They have the reception and the guests take the elevator down to their rooms. It's perfect."

"It's an idea. I'm hoping they pick some island."

"When is the wedding? Who's doing the flowers?" Lily really didn't want to work with Gretchen, but as the owner of a flower shop she thought it was mandatory to ask that question. The client would probably go with one of Gretchen's outrageously expensive florists who could also provide the tablecloths, the fabric hanging from the ceiling, the disco ball. Lily laughed at that thought.

"Something funny?"

"No. So, when and who?"

"I'm not sure. They're trying to clear their schedules. Sorry, honey, but I think I'm going with this new florist. I know you have your hands full with Mr. Delicious."

Whew, that was a close one. "Gretchen, could you please stop calling my Dev that. He has a name."

Gretchen rose slowly, almost seductively up from the chair. Lily just shook her head. There was no one to impress with her sexuality in this room, yet she still oozed seduction. She just couldn't help herself.

"See you, bestie. I have to keep calling him that for now. Gorgeous seems so provincial and Hercules has been taken for a long time. Tootles." Her ring laden hand waved behind her as she departed the shop.

Seconds later, Abby stuck her head out. "Is she really gone?"

Lily threw her hands up in the air. "If you mean gone as in left the building, yes Gretchen and Elvis have left the building. If you mean gone as in lost her mind completely, yes she is absolutely bonkers."

"And she's your bestie!" Abby ducked before the flying magazine glanced by her leg. "Nice throw, boss."

By the end of Lily's day, hours and miles away, a man walked quickly to his meeting spot in Les Halles. Cave people of the catacombs, those who enjoyed the vampire and werewolf lifestyles escaped their dens and roamed. This was not the world of light and runways. Paris was different at night; the shadows seemed longer, filled with intrigue or romance. There was nothing else but those two dangerous ingredients when the clock of a nearby medieval church chimed midnight. His Gucci shoes made no noise on the cobbled street. He saw his contact near a corner café. The cloaked form leaned against the building, the only light provided by the window. Only a few patrons were sipping wine inside the establishment. The drizzle prevented others from sitting outside.

"Bernard Notte, it has been way too long, *mon ami*. Do you have it?"

He slid the small brown paper wrapped parcel from the inside of his raincoat. With his hat pulled down to his eyes and his attire, he resembled a cold war spy, not a cultured man from a good family. He definitely did not have the appearance of a criminal, a man possibly wanted in the United States. The framed artwork was small but worth the price he was to be paid.

"Yes, and you have my package?" He held his hand out and it was filled with a black velvet pouch. "If you don't mind, I'll take a quick peek."

Even in the darkness of a rainy night in Paris, the dim light exposed the shimmering diamonds. Yes, this would do for now. "*Merci.*"

"You were a couple of weeks off this time."

Bernard shook his head. He'd had a few problems. "I was delayed this time but it shouldn't be a problem now."

"Your delay was because of your government? They want you returned to answer their questions. Lucky for you

France has a very weak extradition policy for your crimes. That mess with your son will not do. *Mon Dieu.*"

Bernard nodded. "He had his demons. He fell in with riff raff. I don't associate with people like that. I only worry if there is too little champagne at a party." And he definitely didn't plan on returning to the United States or to his hometown of Kansas City. That life was in the past. Now he was only running to his future, perhaps a little villa in Eze on the Côte d'Azur, maybe a wealthy socialite attending to his every need, arriving on the red carpet annually at the film festival. He nervously pulled his coat tighter to his body and shoved his hands in his pockets. His left one wrapped tightly around the pouch.

"So, we will return to our regular schedule now that you are settled?"

"You'll know where to find me either here, Brussels, or Zurich. My apartment in the sixth arrondissement is rather nice. You should stop by sometime. I'd love to show you some things I've picked up along the way."

His contact stifled a laugh. "Maybe. You never know with me, but you have someone looking for you. He wants to do business with you."

"And do you have a name?"

"*Oui,* I have met him many times. I know him intimately, and we can trust him to help us with our little project. Will you be able to have our little bowl in Paris for the gala?"

"I told you I will. Do I need to meet your contact before I leave for Turkey? And what is his name?"

His contact was turning to leave, to disappear into the darkness and anonymity. It was a preferred and necessary talent.

"And his name?"

"Pierce. He will contact you. *Bonsoir,* Bernard."

Chapter Three

"Abs, just put the bouquet box over there." Lily directed her assistant as they brought four more boxes into the church. It was a church she knew very well. It was her church. Just a couple of weeks ago, she'd celebrated Holy Week and Easter in her favorite back pew. Dev was unable to visit, but he'd be in Kansas City soon. But she did miss him during this church season. During her favorite church service on Holy Thursday, she sat alone this year, but she was comforted by the memory of the Holy Thursday night he had shown up, sat beside her and then kissed her in the parking lot. That kiss had begun everything.

Soon, the florists were decorating the aisle with long ivory satin bows and touches of greenery. Abby remarked that a few of the Easter lilies belonged in the trash and not around the altar. She looked up to see the pastor at the back of the church.

"I'm going to check with Father about these lilies, Lily," Abby snorted with laughter. "Get it, lilies, Lily?"

Lily shook her head. Sarcastically, she answered. "I've never heard that one, Abs. After you do that, could you begin checking the bouquets?"

"Sure thing, boss." Abby was still amused at her modest joke as she headed to the back.

Finally, and officially, spring was here. The church was still decorated from the Easter celebrations. Lily fluffed the last bow on the aisle and met Abby. She was lifting out the first bouquet, examining every bloom and pulling off the outer guard rose petals. The guard petals protected the beauty of the rose and they usually pulled them off after transport.

"Father said we could move things around. His wedding coordinator won't be here today. She's on a cruise."

Lily sat down next to the flower boxes and watched Abby work. "I'll check with the bride when she arrives about how she wants it to look." Lily paused to watch her helper. She was mesmerized by the soft look on Abby's face and her dedication to perfection. "You really love doing that, don't you?"

"I guess I do. I never thought I'd still be doing this. When I walked into your shop that day, almost four years now, I just thought it would be a summer job."

"And yet, here you are," Lily remarked softly. "Abby, I've already made you a manager and now--"

Abby looked up suddenly from her work. "You've reconsidered?" Lily could hear the panic in her voice.

"Oh no. You are still the manager. I'm just wondering if maybe, maybe you might want to take over some day."

Abby smiled and began on another bouquet. "I haven't thought about it. Really, I think it should always be Lily's and you should own it. I like the title of manager. Did you get my business cards yet?"

Lily smiled. There were times when she did forget to do one or two items on her list, and those business cards had been neglected for two weeks. "I'm sorry. They should be here next week and then you can start passing them out all over town."

"I thought I'd start at my old high school. There's a few teachers who thought I'd never do anything except ask if you wanted your salad to come first or with your meal. I could've made great tip money as a server, but this is way better. I want to wave a business card right under their noses."

Lily's eyes widened. *Memo to self, do not underestimate Abs, ever.* Actually, there wasn't a week that went by when Abby didn't surpass expectations. She was a force; maybe not a hurricane, but she was definitely a water spout.

The bridal party began to enter the church, and Lily went to work pinning on boutonnieres and corsages. Everyone was congregating for a few photos before the ceremony. Father McKenzie had returned to joke with the men about the Royals' baseball game last night. The bridal party had attended the game as had many of their guests including their officiant. He was a close friend of the groom's father. Apparently, the Royals' mascot had abducted the bride for a tour of the stadium. She left in the third inning and returned in the fifth. The groom hadn't even noticed she was missing.

Between the conversation and laughing, the sound in the foyer was deafening. Lily and Abby stepped outside to wait for the bride. It was a beautiful spring day and the only sound came from the warbling birds. And then the sirens down the street. Originally, they'd heard them when they were delivering the last boxes into the sanctuary.

"That must mean a big crash or something that it took them that long to clean up," Abby said. She was sitting on one of the large concrete pillars on the edge of the steps. "Maybe they had to cut somebody out."

"Well, that's a grim thought," Lily reprimanded. Abby just shrugged her shoulders.

"It might have been a fire?"

"Let's hope that whatever doesn't goof up the traffic to get here. We are still missing a bride and a couple of family members."

Abby agreed. "You know, both moms and dads are missing, the bride, and a couple of the bridesmaids."

"As soon as the bride gets here, we need to check with her if she wants us to move some of those Easter lilies. Then, we will be done for the day. Getting up early and decorating the club at eight in the morning gives us almost an entire day off." Lily was beginning to want Saturdays off. She wasn't in the best business to continue that behavior.

"Does Father Mac really need us to stay?" Abby really didn't want to; she was ready to get out of her work clothes and into a pair of shorts for the first time in months. It had been a long, dreary, cold, nasty winter. Although Lily liked the cold, she preferred to sweat and didn't mind it one bit.

Father McKenzie popped his head out. "Any sign of the

rest of them? The groom is a little worried, and rightly so. She was angry at that boy last night." The priest couldn't contain his laughter. He pointed at the two women. "Young love, don't either one of you do it."

"Too late, Father," Lily admitted. Abby and she flashed their engagement rings in front of his face.

"Dog gone. You both had a busy winter, didn't you? Do I get to meet these men?" He took both of their left hands in his and studied the tokens of love.

"Probably not," Abby admitted. "He's at Georgetown getting his masters, and then he is on his way to the FBI."

"Wow, I'm impressed."

"Oh, don't be," Abby commented. "Ask her what hers does."

"I'll bite. My little florist, what does yours do, and do I get to meet him?" He freed both of their hands and hugged Lily.

"He's a DEA agent. Some day, I want you to meet him." *Preferably on our wedding day.*

The priest looked over toward Abby and winked. "I think he does win."

"And he is an undercover one," Abby added. "He seems like a very dangerous dude, but he's actually a big dork."

He kissed the top of Lily's head. "I'm so happy you found your dork. Hopefully, you'll be married here?"

"Not sure, Father. His schedule, my schedule makes it very difficult to pin down a date. Sometimes it's hard just talking to each other. He says it will be better this summer."

Father Mac held her a little tighter. "Just let me know. I can be ready on a moment's notice just to get you married, finally." He emphasized the last word. Lily playfully hit him in the rib cage. "So where is our bride? Ah, there's the limo and a couple of cars."

You know when you just know that something is very wrong? Lily had that feeling as soon as she saw the bride depart the limousine. Her flowing satin and tulle emerged before she did, helped by the two missing bridesmaids. Her face was sullen, all color drained. One of the maids was crying freely. She wiped the tears with the backside of her hand. No makeup remained. The other maid was propping her up and attempting to assist the bride.

The other cars had parked and sets of parents were headed toward the church.

"Something is very wrong," the priest murmured. He headed over to the bride and hugged her in his arms.

"What do you think it is?" Abby questioned. She stood closer to Lily. She was terrified, but her boss was calm.

Lily saw both sets of parents and a few other family members. They all gathered around the bride and the one crying bridesmaid. Father was explaining something to them and then their heads bowed in prayer.

"Christ," Lily whispered. It was more of a prayer, but it came out of her mouth as profanity. "This is bad."

After the prayer, they came toward the door and the two florists stepped aside. Now was not the time to ask anything. They dropped to the back and entered the church last. Father Mac had everyone come into the sanctuary, sitting in the first two pews. He talked briefly with the couple and their parents. There were slight nods to whatever was agreed upon. The photographer was nervously pacing back and forth. He wanted to get his photos started. The pastor motioned him to sit down and everyone else took their seats. Even Lily and Abby held hands as they sat by silently.

Father Mac began to speak softly. He held the teary-eyed bridesmaid in his embrace, his arm bolstering her from behind. "Natalie wants me to tell you about what has happened. I know we've all heard the sirens. There's a one-way street a couple of blocks east of the church. Her husband Danny, the groom's brother-in-law, was headed north taking a shortcut to get to the bride's townhouse. Another driver was headed south, but he was in Danny's lane and hit him head on. It seems like the driver was intoxicated."

The priest stopped and Lily's heart sunk. She knew what was coming. She knew the tone, the words. She gulped to steel herself from emotion. It wasn't going to work. "Everyone, Danny has passed away."

The gasp from those who didn't know was louder than some congregants' responses at an early morning service when you're half asleep and soon to be asleep from a lengthy sermon. The groom, sitting next to his bride and his parents, slumped into her arms. Tissues were passed out. The front pews always had them for the mothers during a wedding, but today they were used for a totally different reason. And now what to do?

"We've all discussed what to do. Obviously, the bride and groom and their parents are very distressed, but folks we are going to go ahead with the wedding." Father McKenzie led Natalie to the front pew where her mother cradled her distraught daughter.

"First, a prayer. Everyone, please bow your heads. Heavenly Father, we need your help. On such a happy occasion we are filled with sorrow on the loss of Danny. An accident like this on a day like today cannot be soothed. Our hearts are breaking; our eyes are crying; our soul is screaming for your healing touch. We are going ahead with this sacrament of love and unification. Today we will celebrate as we can. Tomorrow we will grieve as we most certainly will. We are leaving Danny in your arms today and forever. We beseech you to look over all of us as we go forward with love, compassion and the dedication to the life you offer us, your faithful servants. Amen."

"This is so hard," Abby whispered. "How can they go on with this?"

Lily had shut her eyes. The tears were rolling down her cheeks. All she saw was a man in a hospital room, her future husband. She couldn't take it that day when she saw him, bruised and battered with his arm immobilized from a gunshot. She'd almost given up and walked away. She learned that love brought pain at times. If you didn't love so much, it didn't hurt so much. This hurt so much and so many were hurting.

"They'll lose everything if they cancel now. The reception is ready. People are on their way. Most of them won't know. I'm not sure if there is a right answer." Lily heard the church doors opening and shutting. She looked back to see the singers and musicians. "I'm going back to tell them what is going on. Stay here in case someone needs help."

Lily nodded toward the priest as she left the pew. He seemed to understand where she was headed. Plainly speaking, Lily detailed the dilemma taking place at the front of the sanctuary. She knew the singer; he was also a parishioner at Lily's church.

"Lily, we need to practice just a little," Peter Court admitted. "If we wait about fifteen minutes, do you think that would be good?"

"I think that would work. I know the photographer is antsy, but I'm not sure he is going to get anything you'd want to use in a book to remember your wedding day. The man's wife is in the bridal party."

"This is awful. We will try to be as respectful as possible."

"Thanks, Peter." Lily hugged the man. His beautiful voice would sound like salve for the wounded soul on a day like today. The group was dispersing at the front of the church. She had never heard a more quiet group of people on a wedding day. Somehow, the photographer was gently choraling them, setting up a photo of the bride. Abby and Lily rushed the bouquets to the girls and asked about the lilies surrounding the altar. The bride gave them carte blanche to work their magic.

Father Mac assured Abby and Lily he would handle the processional. The helpful florists could go on and enjoy the day. "You know, ladies, there is never a right answer when it comes to cancelling or going on with a wedding."

"You hate to think it comes down to money, but Father, it is a small fortune to have a wedding these days. Abby and I have the reception ready to go. The club has all the food and the servers are arriving for work. What do you do?" Lily honestly wanted an answer.

"You pray, Lily. That's all you can do. We will take care of Danny tomorrow, but we can't do anything for him today. It's days like these where you have to have faith. We can do this." The priest turned and began to walk away.

Abby swayed nervously back and forth as she watched the priest. She needed out of this church. *Please, Lily, don't offer to stay.*

"You're sure you don't need us?" Abby heard her boss ask. *Crud.*

Thankfully, Father Mac shook his head no. His gaze was fixed on the front of the church where the photographer had the entire bridal party posing for a group shot. Even Danny's wife was standing unassisted, attempting as much happiness for her brother as possible. Someone had cleaned her face up and added some fresh makeup. She offered a lame attempt at a smile.

The musicians and Peter began to practice.

> *"Oh Danny boy, the pipes, the pipes are calling...*
> *From glen to glen, and down the mountain side.*
> *The summer's gone, and all the roses falling...*
> *It's you, it's you must go and I must bide."*

Abby burst into tears and sprinted for the door. "I can't stay, Lily, I just can't."

Lily stood in shock and watched the disintegration of any semblance of calm. It was a portrait of grief; a tableau of ironic everyday coincidence. In other words, it was life in all its ugliness. Father Mac, usually a pillar of strength wiped at his eyes. "I'll go check on her." Even he needed to escape.

But Lily stayed and watched. Her voyeuristic spirit made her stay as if she experienced it she would become immune to it, to the tragedy. She watched as Danny's wife ran from the church. Two other women sped after her, as fast as their high heels would allow. The bride reached over to hug her groom, comforting him in this awful time.

"Blessed are those who mourn, for they shall be comforted," Lily said out loud. Peter couldn't possibly know how hurtful his song was to those below the choir loft.

> *"But when ye come, and all the flowers are dying.*
> *If I am dead, as dead I well may be,*
> *You'll come and find the place where I am lying,*
> *And kneel and say an Ave there for me.*
> *And I shall hear, though soft you tread above me,*
> *And all my grave will warmer, sweeter be,*
> *For you will bend and tell me that you love me,*
> *And I shall sleep in peace until you come to me!"*

Lily bowed her head and said an amen. It was time to go home and leave a message for Dev. It would be a short one telling him she loved him. She was learning day by day that attempts at controlling life or fate was futile. There wasn't a list long enough to prepare for everything. She'd noticed she wasn't using as many post-it notes. Today you celebrated; tomorrow you grieved. It was life and one little wedding florist couldn't stop the future, no matter how good or bad, from happening. Yes, it was time to go home. Soon, very soon, that home might not be here.

Chapter Four

*I*t was only two in the afternoon on a Saturday, yet Lily felt like it was closer to midnight. She was done. She was done in by today's wedding, well today's death. She was parked in her own driveway, her head resting on the steering wheel. She was exhausted by depression. She'd already texted Dev that she loved him. He didn't need to hear that she missed him. He was off doing whatever he did. Besides, he knew she missed him.

"What was that all about today, Lord?" she asked out loud in the privacy of the car. Her eyes were shut to concentrate on a divine answer. "Just give me an answer."

"What did you say?"

Lily's head shot up. *Was it the voice of God?* At her driver's side window, Gretchen Malloy stood. It was not a divine being. However, it was not of this world. *Really, Lord? Now?*

"Get out of the car, Lily."

What if she just stayed there, started the car and backed out like a bat out of hell, speeding away, away from Gretchen? Lily made a sound like a defeated, broken horse and opened the door to depart the vehicle.

"What are you doing here, Gretchen?"

"I'm here to visit my bestie."

Lily headed quickly up the sidewalk and opened her front door. She could hear Gretchen's heels clicking away on the concrete. *Did the woman own a pair of sneakers, any flats?*

Lily groaned as she entered her home, the unwanted visitor passing by her in a flash. Gretchen made her way to the sofa, sat and spread her arms over the top of the piece of furniture, draping the object like a naked model posing for an art class.

"How many times do I have to tell you we are not besties? I dislike that word immensely." Lily dropped her bags on the desk and kicked her shoes off. She turned to face Gretchen. "Why are you here?"

"I heard about your bad day." The woman really DID know everything that happened in Kansas City.

Placing her hands on her hips, Lily was defiant. "It just happened. You can't know. How do you know?"

"The photographer texted me, and I texted my reporter friend at the newspaper."

"Gretchen, that is just awful. The man died right before the wedding."

Gretchen began to look over the magazines on the coffee table. "It was news, dearie. People love to read about other people's misfortune. It makes them feel better about themselves and their lives."

Lily sighed in despair. Of course, the demented wedding coordinator was right, but what an awful world this was that it was true. "Do you want something to drink? I know I need something."

"That would be lovely. I usually like a vodka on the rocks with a lime twist. A shot of Perrier would be divine."

"How about a glass of water on the rocks?"

Gretchen looked up to see Lily's face. She was slightly afraid of the little florist. The look on her face was indescribable, perhaps between a jilted lover and an angry mother baboon.

"I suppose that would do." It was best not to irritate. Lily probably wouldn't have the good vodka anyway.

Lily returned in a few minutes with two glasses of water filled with ice. She placed them on the table in front of Gretchen. She left again and returned with a bottle of very good vodka. Gretchen was impressed.

"Drink the water first and then you can pour the vodka over the ice. I'm not going back to the kitchen for another glass."

Gretchen eyed the bottle. The girl had taste. "Yes, mother. Thank you, mother."

Lily heard the tone and understood it's meaning. Surprisingly, she wasn't afraid of Gretchen's power in the wedding world any longer. She was just a woman, not a demigod. Gretchen couldn't hurt her. Actually, she could hurt her business, but Lily just didn't care anymore, not on a day like today.

"Gretchen, you came over here. I didn't ask you. It's been a long, awful day as you well know and have spread all over the city by now. What are you doing here?" Lily had already downed her water and was pouring the good stuff over the ice.

"I thought you might need to talk to someone. That's it." Gretchen continued to drink her water, her eyes peering at Lily over the rim of the glass.

Now Lily was completely suspicious. She squinted to see a woman who seemed concerned. "It was strange today, but why would I need someone to talk to?"

Gretchen set her glass down and poured the vodka. She took a sip and sat back on the sofa. She kicked her stilettos off under the table and lifted her legs up to get more comfortable. The woman was flexible, Lily thought. She knew Gretchen talked about yoga, but maybe she did actually go to a class or two.

"I remember a few years ago you had a wedding at Loose Park. You didn't get back in time before your dad died. I just thought you might want someone to talk to tonight. I figured Dev was out, wherever out is."

Again, the woman really did know everything that happened. Lily saw a softer version of the wedding coordinator terrorist. She was just a woman sitting across from her, emanating her own form of compassion. It was a new look for Gretchen, one that Lily didn't quite understand or believe.

"It's only the afternoon, Gretchen. You won't be here until tonight." Lily took a very large drink and finished the vodka.

"I have time. Have you talked to Mr. Delicious?" And she was back.

"I texted him, but he didn't need to know what happened. Abby was really upset."

"And you went into boss lady mode, good in a panic situation, didn't you?"

Lily reached for the bottle once more. She usually didn't drink this much, especially vodka. Gretchen did make her drink over the years. Usually it was over some insane demand she placed on her the day of a client's wedding. Today was completely different. Actually, Lily didn't know what to think.

"Everything was moving along as well as they could until Peter Court began singing *Danny Boy*. The man who died was named Dan. Everyone lost it. Of course, his wife ran out; Abby escaped from the church and even Father McKenzie was having a hard time. It was absolutely awful. Not like when Dad died. I mean, my client didn't even know he was ill. I just don't tell the brides that kind of stuff."

"Always little Miss Professional. That's what I like about you," Gretchen admitted.

This day just kept getting weirder and weirder. "So, what are you really doing here, Gretchen Malloy?"

Now Gretchen was the one taking a rather large drink and refilling her glass. At this rate, the two women were going to need food soon.

"I was having a bad day," Gretchen said softly. "I didn't know who to talk to, and I didn't want to go back to an empty apartment. Satisfied?" She pursed her lips smugly.

"So, you thought of me? Nice; weird, but nice." Lily could see the room spinning. Darn, she'd forgotten to each lunch. Now she didn't want to eat; she was very thirsty. "What happened to you?"

"My sister died."

Lily sat up in her chair, looking straight at Gretchen. She'd said it so calmly. What was wrong with that woman?

"Good God. Were you at the hospital? Is she out of town? How? Why?"

"Always the caring person, aren't you? You just can't turn it off, can you? What is that man going to do with someone like you? You really can't be that good," Gretchen said calmly then added, "Or maybe you can?"

She studied Lily's face. The woman didn't have a wrinkle anywhere. The woman worried about each and every detail, but she had no worry lines. Lily was the consummate good girl. Perhaps she was for real. No, Gretchen thought. No one could ever be that nice, that good. But there was something about her.

"Your sister, what about her?" Deflection seemed to work very well with Gretchen.

"She didn't die today. It's the anniversary of her death. It's been years, but today when I heard what happened at the wedding, well, she died the same way."

"Car accident?"

"Yes, on a one-way street and a drunk driver was going the wrong way. But you see, my baby sister was headed to her own wedding. It was a beautiful day, just like today. When I heard about your wedding--" Gretchen's voice trailed off.

Lily's hand was across her mouth, stifling a very loud gasp. "On her way to her own wedding? Good heavens, Gretchen, I'm so sorry." *How did the woman go to all those weddings, plan all of them with those kind of memories?*

"You see, Lily, I know what I am. I'm over the top, lascivious, and very loud, and egotistical at times." Lily narrowed her eyes in disbelief. "Alright, most of the time, but I plan those weddings for my sister. I plan the wedding she never had. Although it is difficult for that couple today, I'm happy they went forward and didn't allow death to triumph over love." Gretchen drained the vodka bottle of its last drops of liquid. "I didn't want to be alone, Lily. I didn't want you to be alone. Dearie, we need a bigger bottle."

And Lily laughed, straight out loud until she snorted. "Is that kind of like Dallas, we have a problem?"

Gretchen laughed out loud. A hiccup surprised her. Both women were laughing together. "It's Houston, Lily, not Dallas."

Lily grabbed her head in an attempt to stop the spinning. "I need food. I'm ordering pizza. What toppings do you want?"

"Pizza? I haven't eaten pizza since Clinton was in the White House. Order what you like. Do they have carb-free?"

Lily stumbled over to her cell phone on the desk. "There is no such thing, well I guess you could have cauliflower crust, but when you eat pizza, you eat pizza. I'm getting everything on it."

Gretchen toasted her. "To everything! Do they deliver vodka too?"

Chapter Five

"Who's cute little boy are you?" Gretchen asked as she answered the door. She examined the unsuspecting teenager as a shark looks at a tarpon right before the animal devours the other. "Lily, did you order me a man, well a young, young man?"

Lily ran from the kitchen but not quick enough. Gretchen had the young pizza delivery boy by the hand, leading him into the living room. "Drop the nice boy, Gretchen. Drop his arm right now and step away." Geez, it was like entertaining Mort again. The dog used to bring muddy squeak toys into the house. It was a challenge to stop her before she reached the wood floors and Lily's favorite rug. She'd yell drop it, but many times it took a full hug around the dog's ample body to make her behave. Hopefully, it wouldn't come to that with Gretchen.

"He's young, but they all have the same anatomy."

Lily pushed Gretchen out of the way. She handed the

money to the confused young man and sent him on his way. Shutting the door she leaned against it with the pizza box in hand. "You scared him. The poor boy may be traumatized for the rest of his life. Same anatomy, really Gretchen?"

"I prefer to think that he'll have pleasant dreams of a slightly older woman who thought he was an attractive man."

Lily's eyes were getting over-exercised; eye rolls were an hourly occurrence while in the presence of Ms. Malloy. *Was there an Olympic event for eye rolling?*

"You keep telling yourself that. Come on, we both need to eat something."

Lily set the box on the coffee table and gathered up two plates and napkins. Gretchen looked at the set up and then at Lily. "You want me to eat without a knife or fork?"

"It won't kill you. Fine, I'll get you utensils." Lily proceeded to the kitchen, again. "The woman has to have a knife and fork," she muttered, scrunching her nose in disgust. "Geez, she's not the queen."

Lily turned around right into Gretchen's ample bosom. She was eye level at them, a sight she could've gone without today, heck for her lifetime. "What?"

"It's Italian. I must have wine."

Lily leaned her head back on her shoulders. "You must not. We've already downed one bottle of vodka, and we are into our second. It's not even dinner time yet. You don't need wine."

It was too late. Gretchen was searching through Dev's stash of red wines in the corner of the open cabinet. "This will do." She presented it to Lily. "Open."

Maybe Gretchen was the queen. She certainly acted like it. "You'll have to explain to Dev why this bottle is missing. I don't drink reds." She reluctantly took the bottle, opening and pouring one glass of it for her unwelcome guest.

Gretchen, wine in hand, sauntered back into the living room. "Oh, I'll explain it to that delicious man."

Lily finally took a bite of pizza. Now this was a taste that was intoxicating. She'd ordered everything on it, including any and all meats. She savored every bite.

"Why do you call him delicious? Pizza is delicious. Doughnuts are delicious. So many other food items are delicious, but Dev is not."

Gretchen was now savoring a food she hadn't enjoyed in many years. She lifted sauce from her face and then licked her finger. "Yes he is."

Lily shook her head. *I'm never winning against Gretchen.*

"I'm not going to argue with you. Do you notice him, really look at that man? His hair is phenomenal, full and healthy. His skin isn't weathered. He must have used sunscreen in the Army. Teeth are good, shoulders are dynamite. Oops, forgot those eyes. I mean, really, Lily, those eyes!"

Lily smiled shyly. "They are nice, aren't they?"

"Do you want me to continue?"

"No, I can imagine what you're going to say about his body."

Gretchen laughed loudly. It was time for another drink of wine. "Well, what part do you like the most and don't tell me his darn personality."

"His laugh?"

Gretchen threw a napkin in her direction. "Spill. What is it? What have I missed?"

"I am fond of those shoulders but that chest." Lily sat silent for a few minutes.

After all the action was finished in Key West earlier this year, and Garrett Notte was finally arrested thanks to her actions, Lily and Dev had stayed a few days in Miami. After her special DEA agent was debriefed, they had just spent time together, but Lily's favorite time, which she would not admit to anyone, was watching Devlin Pierce swimming and laying by the pool. Sweaty or wet, her future husband was a sight to behold. She would never tell Kansas City's number one gossip anything about that trip

"Ah hah. I knew there was a little lust in your heart. I can see you are thinking about that rather nice chest. I remember the day I dropped in on you two playing house, when he was mowing the lawn and he was all sweaty."

It was Gretchen's time to be speechless. "I'm sure he has a great personality."

Lily's self-induced trance was broken. "Yes, and he's very smart. Gretchen, I have to tell you that we laugh so much together. His best trait is his thoughtfulness, his heart. He could look like the nicest nerd in the world and I would still love him."

Gretchen's brow rose. "But isn't it a bonus that all that goodness is housed in a nice package, and you get to play house with it?"

"I'm not complaining. I don't understand it, but I'm not going to throw him away."

"If you do, throw him in my direction. And if you ever do, I will wonder what in the world is wrong with you."

Lily reached for another piece of pizza. "I was going to walk away just a few weeks ago."

That statement made Gretchen set her wine glass on the table. "Shut up. You did not."

"I did."

"Details, my little child who doesn't know a good thing when she has it."

Obviously, Lily couldn't tell Gretchen all the details, but after an hour of back and forth questions, arguments and storytelling, the wedding coordinator was painting a clearer picture of Lily Schmidt in her mind.

"Let me get this straight, Lily, you didn't think you were good enough for him *still?*" Gretchen emphasized the last word of the question.

In between all the storytelling, Gretchen had wandered into the kitchen and returned with a bottle of red wine. She'd explain it to Dev later. She needed it right now, actually, she didn't need the liquid as much as she needed to straighten out the curly-haired wedding florist. Humidity really did a number on her hair! Something must be done about that.

"Yes."

Gretchen's mouth gaped open. "You aren't going to deny it? Lily, what an unmitigated idiot you are. I told you before that he loved you and that ring is certainly no small indicator that I was completely correct."

"I know, and now I know that this is for real. We're still

not sure how or when we will live together, but I know he loves me and I know how I feel so I'm trying to get over that little insecurity."

"Little?" Gretchen muttered into her glass. She took her drink and then reached for one more piece of pizza. "And I'd be figuring out how I was going to live with that man, the sooner the better, before some other woman figures it out."

"I know but --"

"Don't but me," she snickered. "That was funny, don't but me." She composed herself and continued. "Don't tell me you have to be married first."

Lily grimaced.

Gretchen threw her hands up. "Lord, Lily, morality be damned."

"I don't think it works like that, Gretchen."

"Well, then we better get you married. What do I need to do to make sure you both end up sleeping under the same roof, preferably in the same bed?"

At that point, Lily needed more alcohol. She might not make it to church tomorrow morning and it would all be Gretchen's fault. She thought God would probably understand that excuse.

She headed into the kitchen and grabbed a half full bottle of white moscato. *Yikes, vodka with a sweet wine? How could Gretchen drink that red after what they'd already imbibed? Perhaps her stomach was larger and stronger than the ordinary human? She was indeed made of cast iron, except she thought she had heard empathy, compassion and sorrow when she spoke of her sister. Maybe Gretchen had a teeny, tiny heart like the*

Grinch? Maybe it could grow ten times larger in a pinch? Lily laughed to herself. She'd just rhymed.

When she rounded the corner, Gretchen was moving the pizza box over and grabbing the remote. "You have anything good on this thing?"

It depends. How long are you staying?"

"Long enough to figure out how to get you married."

Lily had a bad feeling. Gretchen might just be her bestie, God help her. She might never get rid of her.

"You have any porn on here?" Gretchen smiled as she looked up at her.

Before Lily could answer, her computer rang. It was a video call from Dev. Gretchen was like Mort. Her head was straight and questioning, looking at the direction of the sound. Daddy's here!

Lily hit the button and clenched her body around the screen so Gretchen couldn't see.

"Honey, I can only see your shirt. Pull back a little."

"Is that Devlin?" Gretchen managed to get up from the sofa and scoot Lily over on the chair. There really wasn't enough room for the two of them, but Lily couldn't move an immovable object, yet. The woman might end up on the floor.

"Hello, Dev, Mr. Delicious," she yelled at the computer.

Lily held her head with her left hand. He never called her when she wanted him, but this time his timing was way off. "Gretchen is here. Can you tell?"

She could tell that Dev was completely taken off guard. "Um, yes. Hello Gretchen. What are you doing there?"

"I'm spending time with my best girlfriend in the entire world, silly."

Dev smiled. Lily could tell he was trying to find the right words. Well, there just weren't any.

"I hope you ladies are having a good time." Now Lily smiled. Dev Pierce was utilizing one of his best traits, avoidance. Lily nudged Gretchen, thinking she'd topple onto the floor, but she was like a stiletto in a grate...stuck.

"How are you?" As soon as Lily asked the question, she realized Dev was dressed in fatigues or whatever they called them now. "And what are you doing?"

She heard an airplane flying overhead. It looked like he was in a hangar somewhere. The large door behind him was open and it was pitch black. She saw lights from a tower and a distant lit runway.

"I'm getting ready to fly out. I wanted to talk to you before I left. It's probably going to be awhile, maybe all summer before I'm back in the States."

Gretchen and Lily looked at each other. Surprisingly, Gretchen removed herself and headed to the kitchen.

"Are you in uniform?" Lily couldn't stop the cracking of emotion in her voice. *Darn. I get the guy, and he ships out.*

"Yes. I'm headed back, but just for a couple of months. You need me, call Dad. I couldn't put you down as the contact since we aren't married. I'm sorry. This is a bad way to tell you this, but I really had no choice. We have some intel we have to follow."

Speechless, Lily held back her tears. In the small hallway, Gretchen Malloy looked on. She pushed back her own tears trailing down her caked makeup. Gretchen's thoughts brought her back to her own memories of a man she loved; of a man who went away in the service of his country. She never saw him again. He was the one who got away, and she regretted it every day of her life. She wouldn't allow that to happen to Lily.

"Lily, I love you," Dev said softly. There was an alarm of some kind going off behind him. "That's our plane. I have to go."

"I love you too," she choked out.

Gretchen hurried up to the screen and put her arm around her friend's shoulder. "When is the wedding? Inquiring minds need to know, and buddy, there better be one real soon."

Dev shook his head and laughed. "Gretchen, you'll be the first one to know."

"Deal. I'm taking your word on that. I'm not fond of disappointment and I abhor liars. Just remember that."

He saluted her. "Yes, ma'am. I really have to go. Lily, I'll call as soon as I can. I love you, just remember that."

His screen cut out as she was nodding.

Lily remained sitting in the chair, looking at a blank screen. He was gone. She'd told him she had pushed him away the first time because he didn't know what he wanted and she wanted something, someone serious. She'd lied a little. She was afraid of being left behind, just like now. She had always thought she wouldn't marry. She just knew. Then two other men had come along and she had hoped. By the time Dev had come along, she'd given up hope. She'd always been afraid of the blank screen. She had steeled her heart and had formed a life that didn't require a man, a marriage. She'd given up on having children, a family to surround her on holidays. And she was fine with that. Until now. Again.

Gretchen was on the sofa, feet up on the table. Lily was missing Mort. At least the dog would go to her bed and only bother her to go outside. Gretchen had control of the remote again.

"So, where's the porn?"

Lily, never again to be intimidated by the wedding coordinator and new best friend, removed her slipper and threw it. Mort would've caught it.

Chapter Six

"Jack, how are you?" Lily just needed to hear Dev's dad's voice and everything would be normal, well a little bit more. She was discovering lately that her normal life didn't exist. In fact, it never had. Her life always revolved around the cyclical nature of the year. January she cleaned. February she didn't sleep until after Valentine's Day. March she prepared. April the wedding season began. May focused around Mother's Day. June was the beginning of weekly weddings. July was hot and sticky as was August. September was uniquely busy with outdoor weddings and always worrying about the weather. October brought cooler breezes and fall weddings. November the holidays began and by the time she reached New Year's Eve she was so tired she retreated to her sofa in sweats or pajamas and did absolutely nothing on New Year's Day. Her year, her life, revolved around her work. Having a love life had actually thrown a wrench in her plans, but it was very well worth it, until he left. She just needed reassurance that one day he would come back.

Jack Pierce could hear the uncertainty in her voice. Lily was pretty easy to read, although his son liked to study her habits and idiosyncrasies. It really wasn't necessary. He knew her, well he'd actually been married to someone much like her.

"I'm fine, but you don't sound too great, kiddo. What can I do for you? My therapy couch is unoccupied at the moment."

"Just wanted to check in with you."

He knew the translation of that statement. "No, I haven't heard from him either."

The man was as perceptive as his son. "Pat and I had a great time last night. She said you might visit Kansas City?"

"Yes, I'm thinking about July or August."

"When it's so hot? You should come in the fall."

"I don't think that's going to work. Maureen is getting so busy out at the vineyard that I made a commitment to her for the fall. That's why you should take her up on her offer and help her out."

Lily shook her head. The Pierce family, not necessarily the man who had asked to marry her, was determined to see her move to Virginia and assist on weddings at Dev's aunt's property. It would be a great business, but Lily had her own to run for now. "I'm pretty busy here with my own."

"But some day--"

"Some day," Lily repeated followed by a heavy sigh.

"Lily, this is just a small hiccup. Can you imagine what it was like when he was gone for years? Oh, he'd come home now and then for a couple of weeks at a time, and then he'd be gone for months. One time we didn't see him for over a year. You can do this. I'm sure he'll call when he can."

"I know." She did know, but there were so many reasons why this relationship wasn't working. As she continued to talk about nothing at all with his father, she examined her engagement ring. It was exciting and spectacular and that sapphire in the middle was so blue. So was she.

Chapter Seven

1. Make sure those peonies are red
2. Really make sure those peonies are red
3. Clean out my front hall closet
4. Clean out the guest room's closet
5. When will Abby move in?

"Where are my cookies?" Lily walked quickly back to her personal refrigerator and popped open the freezer compartment. Usually, this unit was being used for overflow of corsages and boutonnieres on really big weekends of multiple weddings or prom. She'd removed the small refrigerator by her desk at the beginning of this year when all their frozen meals defrosted overnight. The "overnight" had been the night before Valentine's Day. It had not been the best of times. They'd ordered pizza to be delivered, a very large one with everything. It lasted two days. The gas lasted for three.

She continued to look inside, moving other microwavable dinners. She didn't see any green boxes of magic. Urgent desperation was setting in.

"I need cookies, the thin mints, now. Abs, have you seen my thin mints?"

Lily only heard garbled words she couldn't understand.

There were those many times she didn't really understand Abby on a weekly basis, but that was on differences of opinion. It sounded like her mouth was full.

Lily slowly turned around toward the work table. Abby sat on her chair. Her hand was covering her mouth. Her full cheeks were evidence of a cookie crime. There was a strong scent of mint in the air. "Rnor."

"Rnor? Abby, those are my mint cookies, aren't they?" Lily stood with her hands on her hips, clear eyes viewing the obvious evidence. The green box was beside her assistant's elbow.

"You little nut. You took those out when I was talking to that crazy coordinator, didn't you? Instead of rescuing me, you stabbed me in the back. You've resorted to larceny!"

Abby finally gulped down her last bite. "I'm sorry. I knew it was going to be bad. I mean, that woman makes Gretchen look like Joan of Arc. I ran and grabbed the cookies so I couldn't hear you yell."

Lily shook her head. "I didn't yell at her. She yelled at me, but you are right about one thing. I'm going to yell at you. Hand over what's left." She threw out her open hand. "Now, Abby. I need those cookies."

Abby slowly reached for the box and handed them carefully to her boss, almost as though she was placing meat inside a lion's cage, careful, you might lose a hand.

The tired, defeated florist pulled up the other chair and opened the remaining foiled sleeve. The other roll was in Abby's left hand. They needed these therapy cookies.

"This is going to be a rough one," Lily admitted. She wished she had a tall glass of milk. Actually, she probably should only eat one cookie at a time. It would be almost another year before any scouts would wander into the shop with magic cookies.

"If these peonies aren't the exact shade, she is going to have a fit. Peonies are tricky, and that shade of red, well I'm going to have to go to church and pray for this miracle. She already informed me I work for her and the client and there will be hell to pay if I don't please her. I found out they've been just as difficult at the reception site. They brought in fifteen people to their tasting!"

"This is bad," Abby answered. The coordinator had been a shrew since the first day she'd arrived over thirty minutes late with the bride in tow. The bride expected everything, and she wasn't about to pay one cent more for her vision than she expected.

"Bad is not the word I would use," Lily murmured. She slowly ate one more cookie and then twisted the roll shut. "That's enough wallowing."

"Speaking of wallowing, have you heard from Dev?"

"Nope. No texts, no calls, no messages. He's somewhere and there's nothing I can do about it."

"So, are you worried?"

"Yes and no. I know he's good at his job, well at least I think he is. He seems to be." Lily stopped. Was he? Would he be fine? Could the odds finally catch up to him? "I can worry, but it really isn't going to do any good. Heck, I'd take a good old fashioned letter right about now."

"Mommy, what's a letter?"

Lily playfully threw the empty cookie box in Abby's direction. "Anything else, smart one?"

"Is this a good time for me to have self doubts? I mean, can both of us doubt at the same time or is that taboo?"

"What? You might as well say what you need to say." She could tell that Abby was concerned about something. "By the way, when are you moving in?"

"That's part of my doubts. Jeremy's parents have paid for the apartment until November. I thought I'd probably move in around Thanksgiving or the first week of December when we aren't so busy."

Lily nodded. "That's great. It gives me more time to clean out some things. So what are you doubting?"

"Me," Abby answered, taking a deep breath. "I don't know if I can do these weddings every weekend like you do."

"Then don't," her boss answered quickly. "You know your budget for the shop, and I gave you numbers on utilities for the house and rent. I'll still pick up the personal property on both locations. I thought you had this figured out and you thought you'd be great."

Abby was silent. Her eyes glanced down in humble embarrassment. "I want to, but I don't think I can."

Lily reached for her hand and held it in hers. "Honey, please, don't torture yourself. Don't do this out of loyalty. I've just learned that it is alright to move on. If I have to shut it down, I will. I won't live in "what if" anymore and I sure don't want you to do it. Understand?"

Abby nodded slowly. As she lifted her head, Lily saw the large pools of tears in her eyes. "But I do want to do it. I don't want this shop to close. I'm just scared that I will fail."

"Join the club," Lily whispered. "I'm so scared to what's ahead of me, Abs. It's exciting and different. I may be moving for the first time in my life. College doesn't count. I'll be living with a man whom I barely know. We know we love each other, but we sure haven't been together enough to prove it. I'll have to learn new streets, grocery stores, and find a new church."

"The worst is finding where you'll get your haircut and your nails done."

"You're right. That is the worst of it. But the best of it could be amazing."

"That's very enlightened of you," Abby laughed.

"And that's a very big word for you. Let's get to work. The red peony wedding is this Saturday and it has to be perfect."

Thankfully, the red peonies arrived the next day. They were the correct red, not the wrong red. Lily's other wedding for the weekend was as simple and sweet as any wedding could be. The bride wasn't picky about the delivery; she wasn't picky about the flowers or the colors. She just wanted something pretty and that's what she was going to get with a few extra blooms here and there because she had been the perfect client.

By Saturday, Lily and Abby never wanted to see red peonies again. Lily dropped off the other wedding to a very grateful bride and headed over to Abby at the reception site. Lily knew something was wrong from the second she took one step into the venue. Abby still had all the flowers for the tables lined up on the bar.

"Abby, what's up?"

Abby pointed toward the tables. Glasses, plate settings and cutlery were displayed perfectly on each guest table. The reception staff were huddled to the side of the room discussing something so seriously it must be about world peace.

"What am I looking at? I'm kind of tired by now, you know that, so spell it out for me."

"Look at what's crawling all over the tables." Lily followed Abby's pointing hand toward a slab of wood in the middle of each table. The coordinator and the bride had provided them. She walked closer. There was a strange design on the tablecloth. *Oh my dear Lord, some sort of bugs or ants were everywhere.*

"Have you called the coordinator?"

"Believe me, she's been called." The answer came from Kim, the reception site's coordinator. "After all the crap they've put us through and this happens. We can't set out anything and we're keeping the cake in the kitchen."

Lily walked closer to one of the tables to examine the debacle. "Are they from the slab?"

"Yes, but you need to know, they had all sorts of peonies in here earlier this morning. The bride's aunt had brought them in. I think the ants are from those and these little bugs are from the wood. They didn't treat it; they probably cut them from the aunt's tree in the backyard."

"Yikes." Lily stood back. She rubbed her forehead. Her stomach was sinking. She actually didn't know what to do. Every plate, charger, glass, tablecloth, knife, fork, spoon would have to be washed and how did you get rid of the little suckers?

The coordinator entered behind the women as they thought about a strategy.

"What is the problem with you people? Can't you do anything?"

Abby stepped back away from Lily and Kim as they both turned toward the woman.

"We've done our job," Lily spat back. "You are the one with the mess."

"The aunt and you brought in these wood slabs and some of her garden peonies this morning and now we have this mess," Kim said defiantly. Professionalism was out the window.

"Well maybe it's Lily's fault."

"The bugs came out to play almost four hours ago. I texted you," Kim answered. Lily retreated as Kim held the ground. The battle was waged.

"What do you want me to do?"

"You decide what you want done. We need to wash everything and I'm not sure how we are going to get this infestation out before the reception. If the health department hears about this, well, I'm not sure what we can do."

Lily studied the coordinator carefully. She was ready to blow. Not only would Lily make a mental note never to do another wedding with her, she would write it in big red letters in the backroom.

"If you can wash everything and reset it all then we can do that. I'll shake the tablecloths off outside."

"You get new ones," Kim demanded.

"Where am I going to get new ones? Everything is closed."

"We can rent you ours, but you'll explain to the bride why we didn't use these."

"Fine," she answered and turned to leave.

"Oh no," Lily exclaimed. "You are going to remove those wood pieces and those tablecloths and get them out of here. And you can't just shake them out near the building."

Before the woman could answered, Kim had another idea. "We have some bug spray you can have. You have some work ahead of you. I'll get you a cart, oh and come with me. I need your credit card, preferably a personal check or cash. There's an extra charge for all this work. We've taken time stamped photos so don't even think about denying this cost later."

As the two women headed to the back area of the venue to conduct business, Abby stepped on a very energetic pest. "He was almost to the bar. Here's another one. You know, I could invent my own termite tango if this keeps up."

"I'm afraid they won't be able to get rid of them all. They are going to have to get an exterminator in here tomorrow if they can."

"What were they thinking?"

Lily just shook her head. "They thought they knew better. I told her months ago they couldn't and shouldn't use those peonies from the yard. I didn't know about those wood slabs. You know, you can stick them in the freezer and that'll kill the little buggers?"

"Good to know, boss."

"I am very talented," Lily laughed as she stepped on another over-achieving pest.

They set the last arrangement as the first guest arrived. Abby and Lily continued to kill any bug they could as did the rest of the wait staff. It had become a game, a dance of death of the bugland variety. They'd stifled their laughter as the coordinator, hair undone and shoes off, had finished her work and was swiping off ants on her arms. She was utterly undone and miserable. A very small part of Lily felt for her, a very small part. Actually, she didn't feel sorry for her at all. The woman had played them for months and made every vendor miserable, every one of them. That was a record in the wedding industry. Yep, Gretchen was looking pretty good right about now.

As Abby and Lily finally finished their day, almost three hours later than planned, they headed back to the shop to unload.

"You want anything to eat, Abs? I'm paying."

"No, really after all that creepy crawly stuff, I'm going to grab something and take a nice long bath. Maybe I'll call Jeremy. You going to bill her extra for the time?"

Lily was depositing the last bucket into the backroom.

"You really think she'd pay me? I'm going to cut my losses and forget this day and this client existed."

"They really need to listen to the professionals."

Lily sighed. "Well, at the very least they shouldn't listen to some crazy coordinator or a headstrong aunt who just has to bring something from her yard."

Abby was laughing before she could get her words out.

"Oh, she did bring something from the yard alright." Lily joined her in the laughter until they both snorted and had tears in their eyes.

Lily headed home. Abby had a great idea. A bath would be the perfect way to end this day. She ate some cheese, brought her wine with her, and soaked until her skin was white and wrinkled like a Shar Pei dog. She shuffled the five feet from tub to the bed and drifted off to sleep. She'd cringe the next time a bride wanted red peonies.

Chapter Eight

1. Need milk, bread
2. Get Mort from Abby and let her play in yard
3. Pay bills
4. Get mail out of the box
5. Check in with Dev's dad

By the time Lily was in shorts and an old tee shirt, Mort was attempting to dig up something in the backyard. "Drop it. You know better."

The DEA drop out canine paid attention immediately and began to run circles in the grass. Mort was now Abby's dog and whatever discipline she had acquired was completely gone. She was a couch dog who loved potato chips. Weren't we all?

Lily grabbed the mail and sat down at the desk to write out bills. She shuffled through the mail and saw one unusual envelope. The post office box on the return address was in Germany. Her name was in Dev's handwriting. Finally.

She opened it carefully, several pages of handwritten papers were in her hand. She shook the envelope to make sure he hadn't sent sand. What was she thinking?

Honey, do you know that this is the first time I've ever written a letter home to the woman I love? I'm discovering

I'm not very good at this love letter stuff. You should be laughing now, I hope. I really miss you. It seems I enjoy your company. I miss our talks, laughing with you, eating out. I miss food, but really they feed us pretty well when we're in camp.

We are very successful at what we are doing, but I'm afraid we really will be here the entire summer. It's a little warm!

How are the weddings? The shop? Abby? How's Jeremy doing in DC? This is a very big step for him and the boy has some skills. Who knew that video games could get you a career in the FBI? He has a long road, but I think he'll be just fine.

Now, about you and me, I love you so much. Have you started planning our life together? Surely, you have some post-it notes somewhere with bedroom colors, how you want to decorate my office or maybe future addresses in Kansas City? I am willing to move. If there isn't an opening, we can commute until there is. I don't want you to think that you have to give up anything for me. I want to give to you. I want to give you the life you deserve and the love you need. You have always stepped up to the plate when we've faced challenges and I thank you for trusting me and bearing with all this uncertainty.

I'm sure Dad and you have been talking. He really loves you. I bet Aunt Pat and you are as thick as thieves.

I can't wait to see you again, to kiss and hold you. You know, when I couldn't get you out of my head, it was because you had already wiggled into my heart. Too sappy? I thought about it for a few minutes. Please appreciate it.

Tell Tom I said hello and that we had steak and lobster after one of our missions. He'll be jealous. Saw some kids I knew from years before, and they are now in the military here. I was very proud of them. Many of their friends are dead. They went another route, the wrong one.

Speaking of wrong, how is Mort? Is she being a good girl? Do we want a dog of our own? Also, are you sure you could care less about planning a wedding? Hopefully, you and your bestie, Gretchen, have everything planned. I do think we should get married as soon as we can, don't you?

I better sign off. I haven't written a letter in so long I hope it was up to your standards. Just take a red pen to it if you have to. You know you want to!

Dad can help you get word to me if you've run off with some other federal agent or if you are currently living on an island after your lottery win. I will join you on said island; if you are with the new guy, I still might join you. I could use a dip in the ocean right about now.

I love you and not a day goes by that I don't think about you and what you are doing. I know you clean on Monday, plan on Tuesday, buy flowers on Wednesday, begin work on Thursday and Friday, deliver on Saturday and go to church on Sunday. I'm so ready to be on your schedule.

Take care and I will see you soon. If you are with that other guy, make sure you get me my own room and my own case of beer. If you're on the island just waiting, I prefer a king bed and rum if the island is in the Caribbean.

Love,

Dev

And he was gone with that last word read.

Chapter Nine

1. Get through June
2. Meet Gretchen for dinner Wednesday
3. Put Starlight tickets in purse
4. Pray that Gretchen and I don't physically hurt each other

Going out to dinner and to Kansas City's outdoor theater, Starlight, was a true experience for Lily. What had she been thinking? Abby had taken a few days off to visit Jeremy in DC so her companion was unavailable and Dev was still MIA. His dad had called her one night to check in and to tell her Dev said hello. On Monday, a small package had arrived at the shop. Inside, three French soaps were packaged in the most perfect flower covered boxes. The simple note featured just his name. Obviously, he'd ordered it online, but at least he was thinking about her.

That package and the letter kept her going. She was planning and thinking constantly about what their future would or could be. She was scared spitless. And that's when she had thought it would be a good idea to take Gretchen to Starlight. Obviously, her defenses were down. It was like having the flu and someone brings you soup. You can't really appreciate how good the soup is, but you eat it anyway. It was so nice of the person to bring it to you, but you were going to throw it up within the next hour. But it was so thoughtful!

"You have good seats," Gretchen remarked as she settled into the metal chair. "Don't they have cushions?"

"You can rent them over there," Lily said as she pointed to the shop. She scanned the program for the sponsor sheet. If there was a gold star on the page, you won some sort of giveaway. "Darn, nothing."

"What?"

"Give me your program, and let's see if you won anything." Lily looked at the page and saw the star. "Are you kidding me? I have been coming here all my life and you get the giveaway. That is just wrong."

Gretchen swiped the coveted item from her hand. "I'm lucky, what can I say?"

Right before the show, *The Jersey Boys*, began, they asked for the winner to come up on the stage to receive the gift. Gretchen pranced, sashayed in all her glory to accept a $200 gift certificate from one of Lily's favorite local jewelers. Lily only laughed as Gretchen almost mauled the executive director, leaving a very large lipstick imprint on the side of his face. The crowd roared and Lily sunk into her chair as Gretchen returned to her seat and handed her the certificate.

"Use this on Dev's ring."

Lily was absolutely speechless. The crowd stood for the singing of the *Star Spangled Banner*, and Lily continued to look at the woman beside her rather than at the flag. Who was Gretchen Malloy? Had they really gotten her wrong all these years? No, she was still obnoxious, but there was a wonderful being underneath the layers of makeup and powder, the perfect hair, the long attached lashes, the large earrings that hung to her shoulders and the over-the-top clinging clothing. Perhaps she was a lost angel inside a retired Las Vegas showgirl's body?

Lily's usual little Starlight family weren't even there to see the act of generosity. On the other hand, it was safer for them. The men would have been in jeopardy when the lights went down. Apparently, they had exchanged their tickets for another night.

"Lily, the show is starting. Stop staring at me."

"But that was so kind of you."

"I can be nice now and then. Hush, the music is beginning. Did I tell you I met Frankie Valli once in Atlantic City? Oh, what a night. I believe it was late September. It was an amazing night."

Lily shook her head and rolled her eyes. She was becoming very talented in both exercises, especially and only when she was around Gretchen. Thankfully, the music began. The show was entertaining. Everything was going along just fine until "Frankie" began to sing *Can't Take My Eyes Off Of You* while strolling into the audience.

Lily began to panic as he came closer. *Please stay away, but no. What have I done, Lord?*

Of course, the actor came right over to Gretchen, spotlight engulfing them, as he sang the entire song to the mooning woman. Lily watched in suspense, with a held breath at Gretchen's restraint. She saw the coordinator's hand moving lower down the actor's back. Thankfully, "Frankie" finished his song before Gretchen could continue any lower. Dev had been such a better, well-behaved companion when she brought him as a guest to one of her favorite places in the city.

On the way back to Lily's house, Gretchen was humming. "Thanks for tonight. I really enjoyed it."

"I'm glad you could go." Lily continued to drive. It had been an enjoyable night, except for the wayward hand incident.

"I'm serious about the money. Use it to buy his ring."

"Alright, but we'll have to see if the certificate has an expiration date."

Gretchen stopped humming. "Are you ready for all this change? Really ready? Maybe moving?"

Lily sighed. She'd thought it over so many times but now saying it out loud would make it real.

"Yes. I am so ready."

"Then, when you get the chance, when you both are in the same place at the same time, marry the man. Have whatever life you can with him, will you? Please, don't wait a second longer because sometimes, that time is taken away from you."

Lily was at a stop, waiting for the light to turn green. Gretchen was no longer humming. Her face was turned toward the window. She suspected she wasn't looking at anything; she was seeing someone in the past, perhaps her sister or the man who got away? Could shallow Gretchen be deeper than an ocean of emotion?

"Gretchen, I really had a wonderful time tonight. Thanks for being there for me." Gretchen patted her shoulder. The moment was lovely and then Gretchen became Gretchen again.

"I think "Frankie" wanted to take me home, don't you bestie?"

Chapter Ten

1. Clean over the Fourth of July
2. Make sure Abby brings Mort's bed
3. Check in with Jack Pierce

"Did you bring the bed?" Lily asked as Abby led the German Shepherd inside the house.

"Yes, I did. It's still in the car. I have the food, her bowls, her treats and her toys. That should be all she needs for the long weekend." Abby was removing the lead from around Mort's neck. The dog immediately jumped up to greet Lily, rising almost eye-to-eye with her. She nuzzled and licked her once and then jumped over to the sofa to settle in.

"Abs, I have bowls."

"What was I thinking? I barely finished packing this morning and now I've got to go as soon as we unload the car. I can't wait to see Jeremy."

Lily followed behind Abby to gather the remainder of the dog's supplies. *Geez, the dog had more packed than Abby did.*

As they set up the items in the kitchen, Abby kept

looking down at her own engagement ring. "How do you do it? All this time apart is insane."

"Well, I've been alone a lot in my life, and I didn't think anyone would come along. I'm willing to have patience, just this once."

Abby laughed. "You're never patient, but you have been learning." She looked down at her watch. "I have to go or I'm going to be late."

"You sure you don't want me to drive you?"

"No, I get in so late it'll be great to just jump in the car and go home to bed. I'll get the dog at the shop the next day."

"Alright," Lily said as she gave her a last hug. "Tell him hello and have a wonderful time. D.C. on the Fourth of July is magical. My sister and her family took me down on the mall a few years back. There's nothing like it."

Abby was almost to her car. "Jeremy says he can see the mall from his apartment. I'll check in. Have a quiet holiday, and don't do any work."

"Yes, ma'am," Lily said as she offered her own form of a salute.

She turned to look at the already sleeping canine who took up the entire sofa. "Well, girl, it's just you and me now." Her computer pinged. Dev was calling in. She hit the button to connect and saw his wonderful, now very tanned face.

"Hello beautiful."

Mort heard his voice and joined her on the chair.

"Is that Mort?"

"I'm dog sitting while Abby visits Jeremy over the holiday. They're having separation anxiety."

Dev heard a somber tone. "And you're not?"

She offered a smile, but her facial cue was one of sadness. "Oh, I miss you, but I'm trying, really trying to hang in there. How do you do it?"

"I keep busy. I listen to music. I read. Was June good?"

Now she could talk about work and she could overcome how much she wanted to tell him she missed him desperately. "Actually, between the weddings, funerals and assorted deliveries, I had the best June ever. We were busy. Even I felt overwhelmed a couple of times."

There was some sort of movement behind him. Lily saw the back of another man who quickly moved out of the screenshot. "You are never overwhelmed. You are resting over the holiday, right?"

"I'll try," Lily sighed.

Dev appeared to be looking around. "Gretchen isn't there, is she?"

Lily laughed. "No, not today. I have to tell you that she and I have actually been talking. There might be a nice person under all that makeup."

"Impossible!"

"No, really. We've gone out a couple of times and she checks in on me. She is pushy though, always asking questions about us."

Dev looked straight at Lily. "About a wedding? How do you feel about planning something when I get done here?"

Lily's breath caught. She gulped. "That would be great, but seriously, I don't need to plan much. I just want to be your wife. Like you said, we can figure out everything after that."

Dev scratched the back of his head. "I did say that, didn't I? And you're very sure you don't care about planning anything? I mean, if you really mean it then we need to call the Guiness Book of World Records people because you are the only woman on the face of the earth who doesn't care about a wedding."

"I just want one," Lily murmured.

"So, as soon as I'm out of here and can carve out some time, you and I have a date, a date to get a date to get married."

She smiled. "That sounds about right for us and this relationship."

Lily heard some sort of siren going off. Dev looked around quickly.

"Lily, I've got to go. We've got something going on. I love you. I'm out." The screen went blank. He was gone.

Mort cocked her head and looked at Lily questioning what had happened. "I know girl, I don't understand either. I just have to have faith."

She hugged her companion. Faith, such a powerful word of future quality intentions. The term "if only" should be replaced with "when it will", questions needed to be answered with trust, and disappointment would be replaced by love. Sunday, she and God would be talking a lot, again.

Chapter Eleven

*B*ernard Notte's hotel was on the Promenade des Anglais, allowing him just a short walk into the old town of Nice, France. The sun seemed warmer than usual. Even the breeze off the water did not provide relief. Europe was having a very hot summer; tourists were expiring as they stood in line for the Eiffel Tower, and here in Nice everyone was seeking refuge in the sea or in air conditioning.

He wore a white straw hat with a wide brim, very colonial looking. His white linen shirt was over loose linen pants. He'd just come from Mykonos and had blended in very nicely. That's what he always wanted to do. He passed a few market stalls. Fresh fruit, vegetables and flowers were brought in daily, but it seemed the vendors had closed early in this heat. Artisans were beginning to display their wares of watercolors, oils and painted tiles. There was some good art but most were of poor quality, at least in his eyes. The tourists were swarming around them like great works of art. They reminded him of starving citizens during the French revolution, fighting over one piece of bread. They were sad little people.

He was relaxed, but in control. Everything was going very well since the beginning of this year. As soon as he had departed the country of his birth, and his son had been arrested, his life had truly begun. His mother wasn't running his life financially with all her little trust fund rules; the government had stepped in and "rescued" her from her grandson and only son. Apparently, he had an illegitimate granddaughter. The old woman would be happy with that little news. He shook his head as he thought of how many times Garrett had made mistakes. Well, that one was a whopper. But he was happy. He was his own boss. He liked his life now for the first time in many years.

He was reaching the café, searching for just the right table. A man sat under one of the covered tables, a large umbrella masking his appearance. His features were shielded by his very expensive looking sunglasses. His shirtsleeves were rolled to expose tan skin and a Rolex on his right arm, a gold bracelet on the left one. The man's light blue buttoned shirt was open enough for Bernard to notice a large gold cross around his neck. The jewelry looked like a piece he had seen in Turkey.

His glass of wine sat in reach of his relaxed hand. He was left handed. That didn't matter, but lefties had their challenges in a right handed world. Bernard understood that; they had one thing in common besides greed.

The man stood as Bernard came to the edge of his table. He removed his glasses. His tanned face contrasted with light grey eyes and dark brown hair. "Mr. Notte?"

"*Oui*, Mr. Pierce?"

The man extended his hand to the chair opposite him and motioned for the waiter. "Please, what will you be drinking?"

"A glass of champagne."

Pierce's eyes narrowed. A man who knew what he wanted and always got it. "*Champagne pour mon ami, s'il vous plaît.*"

"It is hot this year."

"Paris may set a record." The uncomfortable, unnecessary conversation needed to cease. "So." He stopped as the champagne was served. "We have some business, perhaps?"

"Perhaps. Our mutual friend informed me that you have some connections, perhaps of the tulip variety, a very specific bowl."

Pierce nodded. "Yes. I have made my name in acquiring such things."

"I'm looking for a very rare tulip. I hear it is available if you know the right people. I'm hoping you are that person."

The man smiled thinly. "For a price. Always for a price. It's dangerous to go to that specific location, but if you can get as far as Turkey, once you acquire the bowl, we can get you out. If we consolidate our efforts, I'm sure you have enough to bankroll your part."

It was a statement and a requirement, not a question. "I do. I have ventures in Antwerp, Brussels and Zurich, different commodities, of course."

Pierce took a drink slowly and watched his soon-to-be new partner.

"Such as?"

"Diamonds in Antwerp, drugs in Brussels and accounts in the best banks in Zurich, a few in Geneva too."

"I could use that cool breeze off the lake in Geneva."

Bernard nodded now. "Yes. My bank is just across the street from there."

"And any art or antiquities, Mr. Notte?"

"Our contact has most of my pieces that I've acquired,

but I've kept a few. I acquired a Matisse the other day. The Musée d'Orsay has been looking for it for years. Antiquities are more difficult for a man like me, but that market is open with the right contacts, and I have them for a price."

Pierce said nothing, studying the American instead. Wealthy, over privileged, a culturally astute gentleman who was not so gentlemanly. It would be interesting to work with this man.

"And, what do you bring to the table, Mr. Pierce?"

"I bring the intelligence, logistics, money, and security. I have those contacts to open certain markets. You have no protection at the moment, isn't that true?"

Bernard downed the remainder of his champagne. He twisted in his seat. Damn, what had he gotten himself into? This man was different than the rest. He was sophisticated but rough, clean but dirty. He was dangerous.

"I get by." He lied.

Pierce chuckled, absentmindedly swirling the wine in his glass as if he was totally bored or unimpressed.

"You will have to do better. I know you have no gun on you or in your hotel room. I know that you have been followed from Geneva to Nice. Two men are following you and they appear to be of Syrian descent perhaps Iranian. There's also a CIA agent dogging you here in France. He knows where you live in Paris; he sat at the table across from you when you had coffee near Notre-Dame Tuesday morning. You took several risks, including the passport you used at Charles de Gaulle Airport last month. It was very sloppy, Mr. Notte. The good news for you is that it doesn't seem that any government entity is none the wiser of your ventures." He emphasized the last word as if Bernard's ventures were inferior.

"If I've done such a poor job, how am I still here?" Bernard snapped back at the off-handed insults.

Pierce's low laughter sent a chill down Bernard's spine despite the trickling of sweat down his back. "By the grace of God and because of me. You see, Mr. Notte, I believe we can work together and do it very well. That's why your contact brought us together. The end game, if we are successful, could have a result beyond your wildest dreams. But I can't stress enough the dangers involved in this undertaking. Have you heard of a man named Khalid? If not, you will. He has been after the same artifact. He is persistent. Even after we have it, he may attempt a move in Paris. After all of this, are you still in?" He finished his wine in one large swallow and then stood up from the table. He threw several euros on the marble table top.

"It does intrigue me, and I suppose if I'm in so much danger, our partnership is necessary. Yes, I'm in." Bernard said not one more word. Yes, he had heard of Khalid. The man was a scourge, a terrorist, a killer. Yet, he was after an ancient bowl. He'd realized he was being followed by a couple of men, but the CIA?

"*Bien.* We will meet again, of course. Our contact will make the arrangements." Pierce noticed some movement near the tight alleys of the oldest part of Nice. "Ah, look, it's a wedding party. The bride is lovely and she's carrying such beautiful lilies."

Bernard Notte wondered what kind of a man could deal in danger and deception one minute and then enjoy a wedding the next, perhaps someone exactly like him.

Chapter Twelve

*I*t was over one hundred degrees when Lily returned with lunch for Abby and herself. Actually, she'd also brought a small hamburger for Mort as a treat. That dog was such a slug, but she was a great security asset. She heard someone at the front door of the shop before they even opened the door. Because of the danger in Lily's life over the last two years, she certainly appreciated any canine clairvoyance.

After their early lunch and all the work done for the day, Lily sent Abby and Mort home. She began to take apart the Fourth of July decorations in the shop's front window. As she was removing the last of it there was a tapping at the window. Of course, it was Gretchen Malloy. Did the woman ever wave? She was always making some sort of noise, tapping with her hands and feet, and clucking with her mouth. She was a real life mother hen.

"Hello, my dear girl," she yelled as she came into the

shop as Lily climbed out of the window. "It is too darn hot out there. I should have sang that." Her outrageous laughter filled the room.

"What's up? To what do I owe this honor?"

"I have news." Gretchen pulled up the nearest chair and dropped. "I was just at the club. Merritt Saunders has just returned from Europe. They had a lovely time. You know the Saunders family, don't you? Maybe you don't, well, she was in a Paris salon and you won't believe who she saw."

Lily plopped down in the other chair with no regard for what she looked like. She looked like a limp green bean with curly hair. She really needed a haircut. Her shoulders were hunched and her legs sprawled out in front of her. She really didn't need to say anything. Gretchen would just keep talking.

"She saw Bernard Notte, infamous Bernard Notte. Shouldn't he be in jail or something?"

Lily suddenly sat straight up to attention. "What?"

"Yes, him. He was in Paris. Do you believe the gall of that man to show his face in one of my favorite cities? We need to call your man and have the braggart arrested immediately." Gretchen pointed at Lily's phone on the table. "Do it now."

"I can't just call him. Actually, he did text last night. He's on his way home, well to Virginia for debriefing. But Dev can't just arrest Mr. Notte. I'm not sure who you would call." Lily thought about it briefly. Really, had he done anything? Garrett had implicated him. At any rate, he'd escaped America before anyone could do anything, whatever that might be.

"So, Dev is on his way home?" Gretchen questioned.

Gretchen gave Lily whiplash the way she changed from one subject to another. It was enough to make a person dizzy. "Yes." She would offer no more information to the biggest gossip in Kansas City.

Gretchen began babbling about some debacle at one of the reception sites. The DJ had been inappropriate about something, but Lily wasn't really listening. Her focus was on the sidewalk and the man, woman and small child walking toward her shop. She jumped up and greeted them at the door, ignoring Gretchen's beratements of how rude she was.

"Carlos! What are you doing here? And Alise? Angelica? This is fantastic." She hugged Carlos and turned to Alise for a quick greeting. The little girl looking up at her was swept up into her arms. "You've grown so much. Before you know it, I'll be doing your wedding."

"No, not mine," she answered. "But maybe--"

Alise silenced her daughter quickly. "Yes, she's a handful."

All four of them could hear Gretchen's cell phone ringing--*Yankee Doodle Dandy*. Lily would have to ask about that later. The reunited group continued to talk until Gretchen came over to them.

"My, my." Her eyes were roving over Carlos' physique, of course. "I have to go. A crisis has occurred and I must scoot. The bride isn't happy with the bodice of the dress. I will talk to you later." She pointed at Lily.

As she left, she turned around to look Lily's visitors over one more time, especially the male one. "Lily, you are always surrounded by the best looking men. This one is so, so *caliente. Adios.*" She patted Carlos' shoulder as she exited.

Lily heaved a sigh of relief and stifled a giggle. Was Carlos blushing? "Now that she's gone, come on in."

Carlos shook his head. "Do we need to know who that is?"

"Nope. She thinks we are best friends but actually she is an annoying wedding coordinator who inserts herself into my business, well my personal business."

Alise giggled. "Sounds like what a friend does."

"I'll ignore that. Well, she has her moments, but you can't stay too long in her world. You'll hurt yourself with virtual whiplash."

Lily sat down with Angelica on her lap. "So what are you doing here?"

"Look." The young girl pointed out the window at a very large black limousine. "She wanted to say hello."

Lily peered over Angelica's head to see the elderly Mrs. Notte walking slowly toward the shop with the assistance of her devoted butler. "Oh my gosh."

The small girl slid off Lily's lap and headed to the door, now held open by Carlos. "Come on Grandma. Lily can't wait to see you."

Lily couldn't see her through her river of tears. Dev had told her of his suspicions, that Angelica could be Garrett's daughter. The little angel didn't need to know how or why, but the outcome was offering her a life of her dreams.

Lily greeted the woman with a full hug, holding on way too long. Mrs. Notte didn't seem to mind. "Lily, I've missed you and this shop so much."

"And we've missed you," Lily whispered as she kissed her cheek. She stepped away and surveyed her guest. "You look wonderful."

"I had my hair done and I'm just so happy. I hear you had something to do with all of this." Mrs. Notte swept her hand out to include Alise and Angelica. "I have a new family, a much better one."

"And we care about you too," Alise added quickly.

"No," Angelica said as she stood in the middle of the adults, "we love her."

"And I love you, my little angel."

"We just wanted to stop in and say hello," Carlos interjected. "We're on our way to lunch. Have you heard from Dev?"

"Just last night. He's home. Hopefully, he'll be here in a couple of weeks."

Angelica ran to Lily and hugged her legs. "And then will you two get married and have babies?"

Lily gulped and looked toward Alise for an answer, or how to answer.

"She just thinks the two things go together. She loves both of you so much."

"And I want some wedding cake," Angelica added.

"Well, we can get you some cake in the meantime," Carlos answered quickly. "Enough with the questions for Lily. We better get going. We'll see her another day."

"Besides, if we don't go to lunch now, there won't be time for the pool," Mrs. Notte said.

Angelica looked up toward Lily. "Do you know Grandma, well she is actually my great grandmother, has a pool in her backyard?"

"Yes, on both counts. You are one very lucky little girl."

Angelica nodded and went to grab her new grandmother's hand. Barrett, Mrs. Notte and the little girl waved their goodbyes and headed to the limo.

"When did the two of you have time to get together?"

Alise slid her arm around Carlos' waist. "It's a long story, but we are very happy. Dev can fill you in on all the details."

"He better," Lily answered. She'd never seen so many smiles. As they drove away, Lily was still smiling. "Devlin Pierce, you better get here soon. I'm tired of being alone."

Chapter Thirteen

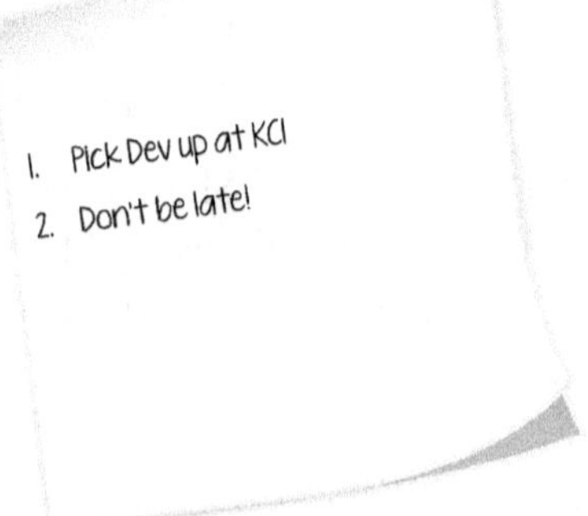

The car's text message voice said one word "landed".

"Crap," Lily muttered out loud. She was only passing the car dealership on her way to the airport. With her luck he wouldn't have any checked luggage and would be outside waiting on her. Dev was a master packer with the ability to travel out of a carry-on. She wished she had his skills, but she loved her shoes. She'd never taken any trip, even just a weekend one, without at least three pairs of shoes. A shoe fettish was embedded in her family's DNA.

She really didn't want him waiting on her and she was certainly tired of waiting on him. She wanted to see her fiancé. Lily giggled as she thought of the very word. As agreed, when they happened to be in the same place at the same time, he'd become her husband, and she'd become his wife. That pact kept her going all those days and nights when she was alone, trying to remember his voice, the smell of his cologne, his lips touching hers. She knew there would be more goodbyes, but she needed this hello today desperately. She needed to know and be assured that what they had wasn't fiction but reality.

Lily finally exited toward the airport and slowed her car down as she entered the terminal area. He'd probably be waiting outside in this weather. Even though it was the beginning of August, there was a low humidity breeze cooling down hot Kansas City to a mild evening temperature of eighty degrees.

She looked ahead, seeing other passengers spilling out, crossing to the parking lot or their waiting rides. She saw his tall figure, the top of his dark almost black hair. He saw her car and gave a little wave. He was talking to someone, maybe he'd met them on the plane. At least he hadn't brought her another dog. *Please, no surprises of the canine variety.*

Lily pulled up slowly and placed the car in park, popping the back for his luggage. She was focused on the oncoming traffic as she exited and came around the car. Her mouth gaped open.

"Dan, Father Dan?" Dev's friend the priest was greeting her with a rather large smile. He was attired in tan walking shorts, sandals and a black polo shirt.

"What are you doing here?" Lily passed the open arms of Dev to hug the clergyman.

"I came for the barbecue or a good steak. Isn't that what Kansas City is known for?" Dan wrapped his arms around Lily. "Besides, I needed a vacation."

"And you picked this town?" Lily questioned. "I would've picked some island."

Dan pulled back to look at Lily seriously. "Dev said he would take me out to eat and maybe to a baseball game. He said he would buy. I got on the plane." Lily smiled. Apparently, she wasn't the only one who appreciated Devlin Pierce paying for a good meal and a night out.

Dev loaded their bags and shook his head as he dropped the car's lid.

"I guess I'm just chopped liver now?"

"Looks like someone is jealous," Lily whispered to Dan.

Dan kissed her on the forehead. "He's in a mood. I think he misses someone." He winked as he looked over at his friend. Dev's arms were crossed in front of him; he was handsomely pouting.

Lily turned slowly, walking into his now open arms, her head burrowed into his chest.

"It's about time," he murmured as he leaned down for a welcome kiss. "Missed you so much. I wish the priest wasn't here."

"Well, you are the one who keeps bringing surprises. Come on, let's get the priest some food."

"About time you two thought of me," Dan said. "I want barbecue, a specific kind of food."

Dev pointed at the car as Lily went to the driver's side. "You, get in."

"Yes, sir. Thank you, sir," Dan kidded. "Bless you, sir."

Dev shook his head as Lily and Dan were already laughing about something, probably at his expense. "It's going to be a long week."

Monday morning came quickly for Lily. After the airport pickup, no sooner had the threesome finished dinner, it was time to drop Dev and Dan off at the hotel. She headed back to her house to bed. Alone. *Why had he decided to stay at a hotel? Was it because the priest was with him?*

The alarm the next morning woke her too soon. By the time she arrived at the shop, Abby was already there and working. She was processing flowers that had just been delivered out on an early morning run. Abby explained it was for her out-of-town client.

"Abby, what are you doing?" Lily asked as she saw the boxes filling the backroom. She appreciated Abby's interest in taking on more responsibility, and an August wedding, but she wondered if her assistant was in over her head.

"You said I should take on more so I did," Abby said defiantly, standing her ground. Inside she was shaking, but she couldn't allow Lily to see her fear.

"I know. I did, but for what kind of a client? These are some high budget items sitting around." Lily looked over at the white and lavender lilacs in the bucket near the cooler. Lilacs were her favorite flower, but to bring them in August was expensive. "Did you charge enough?"

"I've got it covered. Believe me." Abby smiled widely. She had it more than covered, and her boss didn't suspect a thing.

Lily threw her hands up when she saw strands of white orchids filling one of the boxes. She decided to relinquish control for once in her life. *Let the girl fail or succeed on her own. She had to learn.*

"Fine, you win. This will give me more time with Dev

today." She looked over to the lilacs one more time. "You are going to get these in the cooler, right? It's early in the week for all these flowers for a Saturday wedding."

Abby took her by the hand and stood her near her desk. "Please trust me. I know what I'm doing. It's going to be a long week."

Lily shook her head. "Are you crazy? It's the slowest week we've had in months. That's why Dev planned his trip here."

Abby could feel the phone in her pocket vibrate with a text. She knew immediately what it meant. She placed her hands on Lily's shoulders and faced her near the door. "I want you to keep looking at that door. Don't move."

Lily turned to face her commanding and now demented assistant, but Abby moved her straight again. "What the heck, Abby?"

All the insanity became sane reality, sort of, when she saw her sister waving through the large glass window and entering the shop.

Lily and Elizabeth ran toward each other into a head-long embrace. Both were pushing back tears. "What are you doing here? You look great and tanned. How was your trip to the Bahamas? Did the girls enjoy it? Wait, what are you doing here? Dev is here too."

Elizabeth nodded to Abby who presented Lily with her purse and phone. "Boss, you have the week off."

"Abs, I can't. We have that wedding Saturday."

The assistant pushed her boss closer to the door, a smile as wide as the Missouri river at flood stage crossed her face.

Lily was becoming increasingly concerned with Abby's

behavior. Was Abby dying? Wait, maybe they were all here to tell her she was dying? No, she was fine, but she was wondering about Abby's claim on sanity.

"No, boss, I have the wedding Saturday." Abby smiled at Elizabeth. "Do you want to tell her?"

"Nope, Dev said you have the pleasure." Lily now knew her own sister was part of some sort of scheme, apparently orchestrated by an ex-Special Forces officer. A chill went up her spine. What had he done?

"Ms. Schmidt," Abby said proudly, "I have the honor of doing your wedding flowers this Saturday at your church. The service begins at one. Your sis can fill in the rest, so scoot. I have work to do."

In shock, Lily couldn't move. She couldn't talk. *What had Abby just said? Her wedding?* Her ears heard the word; her brain wasn't functioning.

"Um, I don't understand."

Elizabeth patted her hand. "You will. Let it sink in."

Lily shook her head. "Nope, not sinking in. I don't get to plan my own wedding?"

Elizabeth planted her hands boldly on her hips. "Have you ever planned what your wedding would be like, look like? The answer is no. You never thought you'd get married, even when you thought you would to that jerk."

"He was a minister, and we were going to have a small ceremony."

"Fine, he was a jerk minister. You loved dating and being around men, but you've always been so busy doing other people's weddings. You told Dev you didn't care. So, we have. It has been a team effort for several months."

Lily stood in brief silence, her head tilted in contemplation. "I am marrying Dev, right?"

Abby laughed out loud. "You better after all of this. We've all been playing and planning nicely, even Gretchen."

Lily closed her eyes in prayer. *Lord, all those questions from Gretchen was for this?*

Her heart was beating faster but soon a smile crossed her lips. She was well loved. "Apparently, I have flowers and a church. Do I have a dress, guests, and a reception?"

Her sister and assistant nodded then Elizabeth answered. "No, yes and yes so we need to go shopping." She looked outside to see her daughters holding iced coffees in each hand. Lily saw them too, brushing the tears out of her eyes.

Lily began to jump up and down. "I'm getting married. We're going to get a dress, my dress." Suddenly, she stopped her happy dance. "I can't get a dress for this Saturday."

Elizabeth pushed her toward the door. "Yes you can and you will."

"But, I need to lose twenty pounds, yes that would be good. We need to wait."

Elizabeth shoved her out, nearly careening into one of the girls. "The only one waiting right now is Gretchen. Dev talked to her, and she has some dresses picked out."

Lily looked at her with concern. "No! Of all that is holy, I can't."

Chapter Fourteen

*L*ily and her small entourage were ushered into a private bridal salon, given glasses of champagne and sparkling cider, seated on a fluffy sofa and encouraged to eat the fruit and cheese set on the table near them.

She almost spat out her drink when Gretchen entered the room in true Gretchen fashion. She was dressed in a cobalt blue silk jumpsuit with numerous gold necklaces layered down her ample chest. Her strappy high-heeled sandals and long gold drop earrings completed the look which Lily figured was between gypsy dancer and harem girl. If she was going for that look, she'd nailed it.

"Bestie," she said loudly as she glided into the room with arms outstretched in model fashion. "I'm so happy for you. I'm sorry I couldn't tell you anything, but you must know by now that Devlin, yes Mr. Delicious, is the most magnificent man ever. I have never seen anything more romantic. How did you get him? You've never told me. There was this one man I knew--"

"Does she want you to answer?" Elizabeth whispered.

"Nah, she's just talking. She may never stop. Wait, she's getting to the part where they go to the zoo. No, just a brief interlude. Now she's onto the time she dated this much younger Marine in San Diego. She'll be done soon." What had Devlin Pierce been drinking when he concocted this entire production, including Gretchen Malloy? Maybe she wouldn't marry him now. *Really, Lily? Are you crazy?*

"And then we had crabs." Wait, what did she just say? Oh, they had dinner on the pier!

The epic stories were over as Gretchen grabbed her own glass of champagne. "Your sister and Abby told me a few things and of course, I wrangled some bits of info from you. As an older bride, we need to be selective."

Lily rolled her eyes. *Seriously, Dev?* Gretchen was making her sound like she was ancient, she hadn't had time to lose weight and her tan was reserved for only her neck and arm areas. Desperately, she wanted to call and tell him it was all off. Before she could, Gretchen was pulling her up and over to a rack of fluffy gowns.

"I've pulled some dresses in sizes ten, twelve, and fourteen. We don't have time for too many alterations." Gretchen looked Lily up and down. "It looks like you've lost a little weight. We can work with that."

In true hostess fashion, Gretchen waved her hand over the dresses. "Lily, select the ones you want to try on. Your sister and I will pick out a few and then you are trying on until you find your dress. No pressure, but you have no time to leave here without making a choice."

Lily gulped. No pressure. Find a dress that will fit you.

Find a dress that doesn't make you look like a cartoon hippo in a tutu. Find a dress so you can walk down the aisle and marry the man you love on Saturday. No pressure at all.

She touched the lace on one dress. It was too scratchy. She pushed right past the strapless number. *Who put that on the rack?* She laughed at the next one's plunging neckline. Obviously, Gretchen had selected that dress. Dev wouldn't be able to say his vows.

"Lily, what about this one?" Elizabeth held up an ivory and champagne gown. *Were angels singing?* Lily saw an A-line satin dress with a narrow waist. The bodice was straight across with nothing showing, but in the middle was a slightly plunging open v-cut. Lovely lace was under that part of the dress with long sleeves. The lace continued up to the neck buttoning at the back, but there was an open back which would probably hit her mid-back. The lace wasn't too scratchy and the satin wasn't too stiff. It was just right. *Were those pesky angels singing again?*

Her eyes widened. Could this be the perfect dress? It looked like something Grace Kelly or Audrey Hepburn would wear as they floated down the aisle to their prince or leading man.

"Yes, I want to try that one on." The words came out before her brain engaged. Calmness expelled her nervousness. Her heartbeat lowered; reality was setting in, a reality she was living in nicely.

Gretchen picked up another gown. "We can take this in too."

Lily casually looked in her direction. "No, I want to try this one."

Her nieces were clapping. Elizabeth went charging into the dressing room before Gretchen could pull another strapless gown off the rack. Elizabeth knew her sister. If they made Lily happy and she decided quickly, she'd be happy with everything and not worry about anything. The worrying and indecision would set in later but by that time Dev would be there to push all the fears away. Hopefully. Little Miss Over-Organized needed to be handled very carefully in the next few overwhelming days or she'd bolt. Elizabeth was there to insure that would not happen.

Elizabeth and Lily stood in the dressing room gazing at the hanging wedding gown. "I don't even have the right underwear on. Is this really happening to me?"

Her sister touched her arm softly. "This is. When Dev suggested all this, I thought he was crazy. Our brother wanted to have him checked out for severe PTSD. I mean, every girl wants to plan her wedding, except you. His plans were perfect. The bonus was you wouldn't have the opportunity to say no."

Lily mocked her sister with a put-on shocked face. "Have you seen him? No way I would say no to that man."

"Let's try on this dress. Let me see how it's constructed." Elizabeth unwrapped the dress and began to unloop the small buttons down the back. "Good news. There's support built in, oh and it has pockets!"

"I do love pockets," Lily whispered. She stood closer to the dress as though it was a priceless antique. She touched the lace and satin. They were soft. The coloring was rich and non-white. She looked terrible in plain white. It was romantic, yet is was modern.

Eventually, after much debate on what size it was and

whether or not it would fit, Lily took a deep breath and stepped into the gown. The skirt fit over her hips. So far, so good.

"How is it going in there? Usually I help the bride." Gretchen was tapping at the door. *Why did she always tap?*

"We're fine," the sisters yelled in unison.

Slowly, Lily removed her bra and pushed the sleeves over her arms and the dress toward her body. Her hands were shaking; her throat dry; her stomach churning. What was she going to look like? An old blimp, was the answer.

She chose not to look at herself as her sister buttoned the dress.

The door knob turned. "I'm coming in. I can't take the suspense any longer," Gretchen announced. "Lily, how are you doing?"

"I'm praying."

"Lily," Gretchen said softly, "please look at yourself in the mirror. Please. You're beautiful."

Lily's eyes opened and slowly she raised her head. Her sister and Gretchen were crying. Her reflection was of a bride. She was that bride. Her sister fussed with something on the back and asked Gretchen to look at it. They fumbled a little more, pinching here or tugging there. Some discussion was happening about letting this out and adding--

"It doesn't fit, does it? This isn't going to work. I need to call Dev." Lily was panicking propelling her into reality.

"Hush," Gretchen reprimanded. "You march out there and get in front of the large mirrors. We need to find something for your hair."

Lily grabbed her head. "My hair is awful. I can't do this." Her breaths were fast and uneven.

Gretchen pulled her by the arm, turned her body and pushed. "Stop it, right now. Go out there. Your hair will be fine. Go."

"It's too long," Lily complained as she pushed the dress forward with her feet. "I'm too short, and I look like one of the M&M's, the new one, champagne."

Gretchen shook her head. "We can fix the length. Get up on that pedestal, young lady."

Lily was mumbling something about murdering a certain wedding planner with a stiletto as she became surrounded by mirrors. This was not good for an uneven psyche, and it was sheer hell for someone with no self-confidence. But the dress was everything she never knew she wanted. *Hmm, just like Dev.*

Gretchen returned with a pearl laden lace band with a veil attached. Lily had pearl earrings somewhere in her bedroom that would be perfect. The wedding coordinator fluffed the back of the dress and stood back. There was no need to try on any more dresses on this nervous bride. She was perfect. Lily's nieces were clapping and cheering. Her sister was crying. This just might work.

Gretchen Malloy backed away and stood near the corner of the room away from their celebration. This was a first for her in a long time. Oh, not the surprise wedding. She'd planned many surprise celebrations and events, but never had a groom planned it alone without the help of the bride. Of course, Dev had the help of one of the best wedding coordinators in the business. She patted herself on the back.

For once in a very long time, Gretchen Malloy cried in public. It had been a long time since she'd been this happy. She had friends, friends who tolerated her outrageous behavior. She was happy for the bride who stood in front of her. This bride wasn't her client; she was her friend. This wedding might just come off without a hitch, but only with her guidance.

All of the women went out for a late lunch, including Gretchen. It was almost dinner time when the sisters and nieces reached the flower shop. They went on to meet up with Lily's brother-in-law at the hotel and Lily wanted to check on Abby, especially now since those flowers were for her.

"Abs, I wanted to check on you," she yelled as she entered through the door.

Dev was sitting at the table, looking up at her and smiling. His eyes were twinkling. Of course they were. "Hello Ms. Schmidt. I'm Devlin Pierce. I'm here for a consultation. I'm planning a wedding."

She looked him over, seemingly unnerving him a bit by her examination. He looked very uncomfortable for a man who was almost always in control. "Planning a wedding all by yourself? Mr. Pierce, you look very familiar. There was this federal agent who walked in here a couple of years ago. He was an interesting man, but he had his problems with commitments."

He stopped smiling. "Get over here."

"Where?" He opened his arms and her willpower left the shop through the closing door.

She fell into his lap and kissed him, ferociously, all over his face. "I really, really missed you."

"I can really, really tell. How was the dress shopping?" She sat on his lap, surrounded by his arms.

"It was hell," Lily paused, "and it was heaven. I have a dress. But you and I need to have a serious talk."

Dev touched her forehead with his. "If we have a serious talk you'll think of hundreds of excuses why this isn't going to work and then I'll start to think you might be right because you always think everything through and then we will lose all our deposits and money on this party on Saturday night. I want to marry you. I love you. How about this Saturday?"

"I do have the day off," Lily joked.

"Woman, is that a yes?"

"Yes." She gulped and sighed. "You really think that we can make this work?"

Dev's face was void of any doubt. "I know it. I want you, believe it or not, and I'm going to spend every day making you believe it."

She nodded her head. "Got it. You may have to hold my hand. So, what's next for the week?"

He fumbled with something in his pocket and pulled out a yellow post-it note. "I've made a list."

She grabbed his face in her hands and kissed him softly on the lips. "I love you!"

Chapter Fifteen

1. Be at the hair salon by nine
2. Limo at house by noon
3. Go to church
4. Get married
5. Live happily ever after

The week flew by with appointments, meetings, and checking over list after list. Between Dev, family, friends and Abby the guest list was perfect, including everyone Lily would really want in attendance at her wedding. It seemed like the only one missing was the groom's brother. His job prevented him from coming. The rehearsal had gone well. Between Dan and Father Mac, laughter filled the church most of the hour. There was some talk of the two priests forming their own comedy team and taking it on the road. The songs and readings were perfect. There was also a plan for Judge Stanley to join the priests as the couple said their vows.

The vows would be the tricky part. Lily had never made such a solemn pledge to anyone in her life. Now she'd be saying them in front of an audience. Of course, that group contained those who loved her, but still she knew her voice would quiver or she'd break down in tears, collapsing at Dev's feet.

But when he held her hand, she felt stronger. She felt like she did belong by his side; they did fit as Gretchen had told her. She fit right under his shoulder. She'd be a little taller for the ceremony. Her shoes were AMAZING!

Lily looked down at her nails. All of the ladies, including Dev's two aunts, had their nails done yesterday and then off to a bridal luncheon hosted by her sister. Obviously, she wasn't working. Her hands looked too good. Putting together flowers always gave you the occupational hazards of thorn-pricked fingers and green nails.

But usually she didn't wear makeup at all. She was complaining as she stepped out of her jeans in her bedroom. "I feel like I have two layers of paint on my face, like I couldn't decide what shade to paint the wall."

"You do not," Abby yelled. "It's very natural looking. You're just not used to it. My strap won't stay up."

Lily looked up to see Abby wrangling her shoulder strap. Abby had certainly stepped up to the plate this week. She was still silly and goofy, but she had become a woman who could be relied upon. Elizabeth went over to help her. Apparently there was a button involved. Once the crisis was averted, Abby was out the door and back to the shop to pick up the flowers for the church and all of their bouquets.

The front door opened again and Gretchen stood in her full glory.

"I'm here dearies and I brought the bubbly."

Lily peered around the doorway to see a woman with a champagne bottle in one hand and a small brightly wrapped package in the other.

She walked by the bride on her way to the kitchen.

"I need to open this bottle. Don't worry, I know where everything is."

Lily's sister looked confused. "She's been here?"

"Don't ask. It involved vodka and wine. It wasn't pretty."

"Did you see what she was wearing?" Elizabeth whispered.

"Everyone, even the space station, will be able to see what she's wearing. I'm quite sure that NASA is entertained on a daily basis." Actually, Lily had seen her wear worse, but today she seemed determined to be special in her own special little Gretchen way.

Gretchen came in with the champagne and poured three glasses for a toast. Lily and Elizabeth examined her ensemble. Her signature leopard print stilettos were on her feet, bold necklaces of gold and diamonds hung around her neck, a Rolex watch with two diamond bracelets were on one arm and on the other was a gold bangle adorned with more diamonds. Her lipstick was red, her smoky shadow and eyeliner were cat-like. Her hair was large, but not too large. Her not-as-tight-as-usual dress was black, probably a vintage designer, with one panel that displayed a matching leopard print.

"To the bride. I didn't know when this day would come, but I knew it would. To you, Lily, and the amazing adventures ahead of you." The toast was lovely, but wait. "And of course, to Mr. Delicious. I expect details."

Lily gulped down her champagne before the woman could add to the toast. Elizabeth and Gretchen were laughing, but all Lily suddenly heard were muffled voices. She was standing in the middle of her bedroom in her underwear, staring at a wedding dress hanging over her door. What was she doing?

"Everybody out," she ordered as she motioned them out of the room. "I need a few minutes. Please, get out." As she pushed them out, she shut the door and locked it. She grabbed her cell phone. She needed to talk to one person immediately.

"Yes, future wife."

"Devlin Pierce, what the hell were you thinking only giving me a week to get ready?" She heard a lot of noise on the connection.

"Why are you whispering, Lily?"

"I don't want my sister or Gretchen to hear me. Where are you? A bar?"

"No, I'm sitting at the pool with Dad and the guys having a drink. Oh, there's your brother."

Lily took another deep breath and resumed. "I'm sitting in my bedroom, staring at this dress that is probably a size, oh hell, I don't even know what size it is. What size is it?" She began to look for a tag. They'd probably removed it. Everything was a conspiracy. She heard Dev tell someone he'd won.

"Won what? Are you playing poker?"

Dev was laughing. "No."

"So, spill."

"It was a bet."

"Don't make me keep asking inane questions."

Dev cleared his throat in an attempt to be serious. He would just calmly explain. "Honey, you've been wonderful this week, but we knew at some point all of this would make you crazy, that you had no control and well--"

"Who won?" She wanted the joker's name and she'd get even later.

"My Dad." The laughter on his line was louder than before.

Lily bit her lip. "Your Dad? He thought I would freak out today?"

"Actually, he was a little more precise, thinking that when you were quiet this morning before the limo came, you'd start to think about everything and become overwhelmed."

"It's not about the wedding. It's about us."

The tone had changed. The back and forth conversation was replaced by silence. Dev became deadly serious. He motioned to his companions that he was going to step away to continue the conversation. He found a chair in a quiet corner of the hotel's hallway.

"Lily, honey, what is it?"

"Us, our future, our plans, where are we going to live, do we have enough money, will we have kids, can we have kids, and then we have sex."

Dev didn't answer.

"It's about us."

A wrong answer could sink the day. "That we are great together?"

"Stop joking." Lily's raised voice drew muffled voices outside her door. "Do you know that Gretchen calls you Mr. Delicious?"

"Yes, I've heard. What do you want or need me to say?"

"What are our plans?"

Oh boy, there was no right answer, and he wasn't sure what question was really being asked. "I was planning on getting married today."

"I thought so. You didn't consider me at all."

"Lily, what in the heck is this really about?"

"If I had time, I could have planned some things. I could have designed the invitations, lost twenty pounds, packed up a few things, dusted the house. Is this how it is going to be, not telling me, not considering me? You should have given me more time." Her right hand waved at her eyes. The tears would ruin her clown makeup and then she'd look like a demented circus performer.

"Listen to me. We don't need more time. I don't care about the invitations, the dusty house, or if you ever lose any weight. I am sure we will talk to death all the other things you mentioned, but right now we just need each other. Now, get it together or Mr. Delicious is going to come over there. If you won't have me then I'll just have to go grab Gretchen and find an elevator or maybe even an old fashioned phone booth and have my wedding night with her. I wonder if there are any of those around anymore?"

Her crying turned to laughter. "Maybe England has them for the tourists. Don't you dare do anything with Gretchen. I'm not sure where she's been."

"I'll meet you at one. I'll be the one at the end of the aisle so come get me."

"Don't play too hard to get, Dev."

"Are you ready for the best life I can offer you?"

"I will be. I promise."

"Do you trust me?"

"Lately, I usually do with my life," she answered sarcastically.

"Good enough for me. Just trust and breathe. I better go. Dan just asked me if there's still a wedding. I love you. Just remember that."

"I love you too." You can do this Lily Schmidt. No notes today, just do. Just trust.

Just a couple of hours later, Dev was straightening his tie. Dan was quiet as he dressed in his vestments. He studied his friend now and then. Devlin Pierce looked like he was getting ready for a full formal inspection by the West Point commandant. The groom was actually nervous. "Are you ready for this?"

"I've never been more ready." Dev's stomach wasn't. His nerves were getting the best of him and any technique he had acquired over the years was failing. He needed the rush of adrenaline from a mission. He needed the calm brought on by meditation to steady his nerves. As he looked at himself in the small mirror, a bead of sweat had formed on his forehead.

Dan came over and adjusted the tie one more time. "What's wrong?"

"Nothing. I just need to go for a run to clear my head."

"Come on buddy. I know better. It's me you're lying to."

Dev sighed and turned toward his friend. "Danny, what if I'm lousy at being a husband? She's trusting me, again, with her life for the rest of our lives."

Dan let out a laugh. "My friend, you have never been

lousy at anything in your life. You do know that many of us hated you before we liked you, don't you?"

Dev growled. "I'm serious. I don't want to fail her. What if I've gotten her hopes up of this life with me, and I'm crap? What if I'm all wrong for her?"

Dan grabbed his friend by his shoulders. "You two always do the right thing. That's what makes you weirdly perfect for each other. It's also infuriating to the rest of us. You two are a team, partners in this. You'll do fine, but you better keep her in the loop. Don't ever lie or omit anything from that woman. I'm not sure how pretty it would be if she ever turned on you. Not to mention, we all like her very much. She's part of our team. Don't make us choose, especially JT. I believe he is crushing on her."

Dev attempted a smile. "I think I'm going to be sick."

"Seriously, Pierce?" Dan reached for a nearby trash can. "Here."

Dev looked inside the bucket and saw nothing but a future with Lily. She didn't need him. When he was away, she was fine. They'd work out the logistics, they'd work out anything that came their way. He'd have to repeat that mantra.

He lifted his head. "I'm good. No one needs to know about this," he added as he pointed to the can.

"Really? Do you know me? Everyone is going to know about this before the end of the night."

"Just don't tell Lily, please."

Dan smoothed out his vestments and checked his watch. "Oh come on. She needs to realize you are less than perfect, my friend. She will find out on her own what a goofball you really are, but this is too good to keep to myself. However, I can be bought. We can discuss terms later. It's almost time."

Dev hugged his friend. "It is way past time. Let's roll."

At the other end of the church, Lily looked down the aisle as she took her brother's arm. Dev was standing there at the end of the very long aisle. It really wasn't that long of a walk, but it was one she thought she'd never take. The two priests were smiling from ear to ear. The church was full. How many people were here? Gretchen was behind her, fussing with the dress and Abby was standing next to her placing her bouquet to her body. "It's beautiful, Abs. Thank you. I love you."

"Don't make me cry." Abby gazed down the aisle. Lily's two nieces and her sister had already made their way. She crouched down in front of the bride. "Angel, baby, you need to go now. Carry your bouquet just like that."

"I'm not sure why I can't throw petals, but I do like being a princess." The little girl smiled up at Lily. "I'll tell Dev you said hello." She started on her way.

Lily shut her eyes. *Lord, thank you for getting me here. There were times I doubted, but I don't right now.*

As the music changed, her brother began walking, almost pulling her to begin. He looked down at her.

"Lily, it's time to go."

She knew her church was filled with family and friends, but if she dared look at anyone, she would fall to pieces, crying all the way down the aisle. Instead, she locked eyes with Dev and felt completely safe and content. But, she did see him wipe away a tear. *The big bad federal agent is crying?* She smiled. Good. He really wasn't always in control; he wasn't perfect. His eyes were twinkling; he was popping his watch band nervously. It was an unexpected surprise to see him so out of sorts and yet, she was calm and confident. It was a very good day for her.

Once they arrived next to her groom, her brother shook Dev's hand and kissed her cheek. She couldn't hear what they had to say to each other, but both men shared a laugh. She'd find out later. Dev reached for her hand and held it solidly in his.

"You are absolutely beautiful," he whispered.

"With as much makeup, hair gel and spanx that I have on my body, we'll be lucky if I don't pass out."

Father Dan cleared his throat. "You two ready? Is it okay if I begin?"

"Oh sure, go ahead, you're the one in charge," Lily answered out loud. She had forgotten that this Saturday she was the one standing at the altar in the bridal gown. The sanctuary erupted into laughter.

Dan leaned down. "Are you sure I'm the one in charge?"

Lily nodded her head and bent in prayer-like fashion.

"Let us begin," the priest said. Lily Schmidt was actually getting married to Devlin Pierce. During the vows, Dan and Father Mac were joined by Judge Stanley. The Judge stood proudly and added in his part.

"Do you Devlin Anthony…"

"I do."

"Do you Lily Catherine…"

"I do."

As Mass continued, Dev held her hand tightly. She thought she saw a grimace of pain on his face as the priests continued the service.

"You can sit down if your knee is hurting you," she whispered.

"I'm fine. I have a cramp. I just need to stand."

Lily made a note to herself, not only were Pierce men avoiders and deflectors they were stubborn beyond reason. This would be a true adventure. She would have to have patience. *Was there a course she could take?*

In all those weddings over the years, nothing had prepared her for what she was feeling right now standing next to this proud man, now her husband. She knew today would fly by, but she was determined to remember every second, every smile, every hug. On the other hand, the reality was that Lily was starving, and she really had to go to the bathroom. In this dress, the second would be a real adventure. Wedding cake! She suddenly remembered that there would be cake and there would be passed appetizers, a cheese bar with assorted breads, and there would be a magnificent dinner! The dress might burst. If it did, she was sure Gretchen probably had double-sided tape, maybe glue to keep her all together.

At the time for Communion, Dev and she finally sat down. Angelica decided all on her own to visit them as the guests made it up the aisle to participate. The little girl passed behind both priests and crawled onto Dev's lap.

"You happy now?"

She fingered his boutonniere.

"Very, how about you?" Dev asked softly.

She pulled on his lapel to whisper into his ear. "What about the babies? Have you talked to Lily about them?"

Dev smiled, looking at Lily and then back at his small fan. "I think we'll talk about it tonight, if that's alright with you."

"Perfect. I better go before mom gets mad."

"Good idea." She scooted off his lap and ran toward the pews.

"What was that all about?" Lily asked.

"Oh, we'll talk about it later." He kissed his wife on the cheek. "Much later tonight." Lily suspected something was up. Maybe there was a surprise for her, or maybe a special gift? But why would Angel be part of it?

It was time for Dev and Lily to stand in the middle once more. Both priests came down in front of them for a special blessing and then the end of the ceremony.

"And now, it truly is my pleasure to present for the first time, Mr. and Mrs. Pierce. It has a good ring to it. And my dear friend," Dan stopped to look over at Dev, "you may now kiss your bride, finally."

Dev winked at Lily. "Now, you're sure?" he asked his friend.

"Yes, and do it right, soldier."

The guests were filling the church with laughter once more, but Dev took it as a challenge of epic proportions. He raised his left brow as a warning to his new wife.

"Dev, remember we are in church."

"This is where we had our first kiss in the parking lot.

Let's make this one to remember." In one swift movement his right arm cupped her back and his left one wrapped around her. He began the kiss and finished it as he dipped her. She heard clapping, and she thought she actually heard bells ringing. *Wait, the church bells were ringing. The man was good, but he couldn't make bells ring, or could he?*

When he finally brought her up for air, releasing her, Lily took a step back and drew in a deep breath. He had his arm out for her, and she gladly took it to march back down the aisle together. Lily Schmidt was finally married. She was a bride and a wife, and she really had to go to the bathroom!

After a short bathroom break--well not exactly that short when you were in a handicap stall with two other women helping you--they waited for the church to clear before going back into the sanctuary to take photos. Gretchen and her sister knew how to let a bride have some privacy in the bathroom and now her "bestie" had become a saint. She slipped Lily a small fun size candy bar.

"How did you know?"

"I just knew you'd be hungry, and I'm very good at what I do."

Lily hugged the unsuspecting coordinator.

"Thank you, Gretchen for all you do and for everything you've done. You are a good friend."

"Your best?"

Lily's brow arched. "Don't push it."

"I'll take good," Gretchen whispered. She kissed her on the cheek. "You deserve every happiness. One thing though, who are all these delicious men? I mean even the priest is to die for."

"Gretchen, not today and do not, do not hit on the priest. God will get you," Lily reprimanded. She waved over to Dev who was visiting with JT, Paul and his wife. Gretchen gazed that way.

"I'll take my chances with God, but who is that gorgeous body?" Gretchen's glance was laser-focused on JT.

"Down, girl. I'll introduce you later, but for now, please don't and no touching."

"You have no idea what I want to do."

Lily chuckled as Dev came to her side. "Oh, I have a fairly good idea what you are thinking."

"But, Lily."

"No. Don't you have something you need to be doing for the bride?"

Gretchen looked at her pensively. She was debating her attack, but it would have to wait. "Oh yah, her. I need to clean up a few things and get the license for you, etc. My work is never done."

"And we do appreciate that, Gretchen," Dev added.

She sauntered away, but touched JT's shoulder, a glancing shot of her beginning volleys. She preferred the defensive position, but for that man she might just take an offensive maneuver. A shot over his bow might be the excitement she needed.

After the photos and a few on the Country Club Plaza, Lily and Dev were in the limo alone for the first time. They'd just finished in front of one of the many beautiful Kansas City fountains.

"My hair is starting to curl up in all the wrong places," Lily complained as she cooled off, reaching for a bottle of water.

"It's hot, it's humid, it's Kansas City in August. You taught me about all of that." Dev slipped his arm around her back. "Now where to? We have some time."

Lily looked across the street. She saw one of her favorite reception venues and one of Kansas City's landmark restaurants. She pointed at Winstead's. In high school, that was the place where they all walked to on beautiful fall and spring days.

Dev laughed out loud. "Drive thru or dine in?"

"Booth. In this dress, we're going in."

"Jerry," Dev directed the driver, "we will be going to Winstead's for a burger."

"And a milkshake," Lily added.

Dev leaned his head back against the limo's seat. "Somehow I knew this was coming."

Of course, all eyes were on the bride and groom as they entered the famous restaurant. Many patrons clapped.

Dev looked over the menu, but Lily knew what she wanted, she just didn't know how much she could have before the Spanx went splat.

"What time does the cocktail party begin?"

Dev flipped his menu down on the table. "Six. We should be there a little before."

The server stood by, staring at Lily and ready to take her order.

"I'd like a single burger with no onions. I'd also like a chocolate soda."

Dev shook his head. At least she hadn't ordered onions. "I'll have the same."

"Oh, and an order of onion rings," Lily added.

"Really?"

"What? They are wonderful."

Dev came closer across the table. "Onions?"

"It's not like we'll be kissing later," Lily joked, laughing so hard she snorted. "I'll get a mint, or two?"

Dev shook his head. "What have I gotten myself into?"

"Sheer bliss," she answered quickly as she held his hands across the table.

"Nice ring, lady."

"Dev, you really have outdone yourself."

"Are you thinking about Abby working on the flowers at the reception?"

She looked out the window and looked over at the building where normally she'd be working on a reception. She looked down at her ring. "I'm not thinking about anything but," she looked up at her husband, "those onion rings."

"Keep it up, and I'll eat them all."

"Didn't you listen to those vows? You have to share everything with me."

"And you have to obey me."

Lily winked at him. "You keep telling yourself that, buddy."

"Where has my sweet, unsure Lily gone?" He smiled as he tore the last onion ring in half and offered it to her.

"She's still here, but when it comes to onion rings, well it is every man and woman for themselves."

"So that's how it is going to be?"

Lily ate the deep fried wonder and stretched across the table for his hand. He freely gave it. "Sometimes, well you know how I am. I know I should be more confident, more patient, more of a lot of things, but it's hard work. You've seen me every which way. You know I'm confident with my work, and I'm unsure on the inside. But with you, I'm better. Since I know you are out there in the world, even if you aren't with me, I am a better person."

"Well, that was very thoughtful and serious. I really just wanted the onion ring to myself."

Lily smiled. "So this is how it is going to be." She slowly dipped two fingers into her water glass and flicked in her husband's direction. "And don't you dare retaliate. This dress is too expensive."

After lunch, they made a couple of stops for photos and so Lily could give a quick hug to a couple of vendors she knew that couldn't be part of the day because they were working. They headed on to the hotel, the same one Abby, Jeremy, and she fled to for safety two years ago.

"This is even nicer than the suite we had when Tom brought us here. Same concierge level. That's right, you weren't here then." She was quiet for a second and then began her examination of the room. This time there was a panoramic view of the Plaza below them. The living room featured a well accommodated wet bar, fully stocked. There was a bottle of champagne chilling in a bucket and a bouquet of white hydrangeas placed on the cherry dining table. *Cute, Abby, very cute.*

Lily was examining every little touch, the lovely Waterford crystal flutes beside the bucket, chocolate covered strawberries, hydrangeas, and the long-stemmed Amnesia antique lavender roses. She was touching the sofa and turned, to strike directly into her husband's chest.

"You have to make some noise so a girl knows you're there." He'd already locked her in an arm hold. He sensed Lily was thinking way too much, maybe memories, bad ones, he needed to erase.

"Oh, I'm here." He brought his face down for a long kiss that made her melt into his chest. She reached inside his coat to hold him closer as his lips trailed down her ear to her neck.

"Um, you need to slow down, soldier. Besides, I'm very hot and sweaty."

Dev continued his soft assault to the top of her shoulder. "Then let's get this dress off. I love this open back." He turned her around. His lips left a trail of heat everywhere he touched. Lily was beginning to regret the keyhole opening on her beautiful dress.

She laughed nervously. Her responsibility gene was actually yelling at her. *You are never going to make it to your own reception! You let him take it off, you'll never get it back on!* But now, her non-responsible gene was yelling. It never did that, well there was that time when she'd gone drinking with that softball team many, many years ago, but that gene had been muted for years. It was screaming at her to let him continue. *Who cared if they were late? Wouldn't they have to wait for them?*

"Guys, I'm here." The weak voice was coming from behind the bedroom door.

Dev and Lily looked up, suddenly questioning what they were hearing and their sanity. "Abby, is that you?" Lily yelled out.

The bedroom door opened slowly and there stood a very uncomfortable florist, a bag of rose petals in her hand. "I was decorating the bed, floor, and around the tub with petals." Her voice was cracking as she held up the bag. "I didn't mean to interrupt your--I'm just going to stop talking now."

The couple continued to stare as she shuffled slowly over to her shoes, purse, and supply bag behind the counter of the bar. "I'm so sorry. I didn't mean to still be here when you two, oh, I'm going to just leave now."

Dev moved over to her and removed the items from her hands. "Stop, Abby. Have you had anything to eat today?"

Abby shook her head negatively. She hadn't had time. She'd been working since five this morning and had just finished setting up the reception with Jeremy and the hotel staff's assistance. The general manager had allowed her into the suite to "romanticize" the bedroom, forming a huge heart on the bed with the petals.

"I'm going down the hall to get you some food, and when I get back, the three of us are going to have a champagne toast." Dev removed his jacket, leaving it on a chair as he grabbed his key card. "I'll be right back."

Lily waved goodbye and Abby and she collapsed on the sofa. Within seconds, both women had their naked feet propped up on the table.

"I am not wearing those heels down to the reception," Lily announced. "I think I should have those strappy sandals in my bag. Is it in the bedroom?"

"Yes, the hotel staff brought up your bags while I was here. Dev's is there too."

Lily looked over at Abby's pale face. She really did need some food. "How are you doing? Everything is absolutely beautiful. Thank you so much again." She patted her assistant's hand.

Abby rolled her eyes. "This is a lot of pressure."

"Yep, every weekend." Lily played with the satin on the skirt of her dress. "It's much easier to play dress up. I once told one of the wholesale flower distributors that they had to get the flowers right, well as much as they could, but they didn't understand that I just couldn't be one hundred percent right, I had to be one hundred percent right for every bride, every weekend. It doesn't become just a job, it's a life."

Abby understood completely, especially after today, being totally responsible for making this very special bride happy. "Are you having a good time?"

"The best, Abs. I never ever thought I could have a day like today, and I get the guy. I can't believe he did all of this, well with help, for me."

Dev returned in a few minutes with plates of fruit, cheeses and a couple of small tea sandwiches. He opened the champagne, the loud pop emoting cheers from the couch. He handed the women the glass flutes and poured into another glass. Abby switched with him.

"I'm not using your special bride and groom glasses."

"Fine. So, to the ladies," he toasted. "When I was assigned to Kansas City I never thought I would meet my wife or gain a friend like you Abby. Here's to Lily's and all the weddings over the years. None have been as beautiful as today's, nor as wonderful as the ones to come in the future."

Once Abby finished her food and the bottle was drained she headed off to make sure everything was perfect in the rooftop lounge and reception area. Dev took her place next to his wife.

"I wonder if she made a list." Dev took Lily's hand and brought it up for a kiss.

Lily leaned her head on his shoulder, careful not to lean her made-up face on his shirt. "Are you ever going to tell me how you pulled all of this off? I asked the other night."

"And I said later."

"When?"

Dev looked down at the top of her head. "Our tenth anniversary or a long plane ride, whichever comes first."

"I love you for it, for it all."

He looked at his watch to check the time, examining his hand and the new wedding band. He fingered it with his thumb as Lily rested against him. The ring was platinum and it had been partially purchased with some gift certificate Gretchen had given Lily. There was a story!

"We probably need to get going or we'll miss our own cocktail hour."

"What?" she murmured. "Sorry, I was falling asleep, but before we go I have to go to the bathroom, and this time you're going to have to help me." She stood up and began to pull him up. "Come on. I have to go. I know there's a few buttons at the top of the neck, and I'll just need you to lift the skirt up for me."

"Don't pull. I'm getting up. Geez, latrine duty. I have fallen so far so quickly."

Lily walked through the bedroom door. "My dress fits through the door. It's bigger than my living room in here."

"Mama Mia," he murmured and then laughed out loud. *Abba? Really, Dev?* "I'll be right there, honey."

Chapter Sixteen

Abby stood in admiration of her hard work. Every table was perfectly set with glass stemware, china, and elegant champagne colored tablecloths. Each centerpiece, and she knew each one of them intimately, was stunning featuring whites, creams and touches of antique lavender roses. Vines and greeneries with hydrangeas surrounded orchids, roses, ranunculus, and touches of lilies. She'd splurged on gardenias, tulips, peonies, lilacs, and lily of the valley from Holland. Those flowers were so out of season, but Dev had approved of the expense. "Whatever you need to do, Abby. Just make it amazing," he'd said. The fragrance was of heaven but not overpowering. She didn't need her boss collapsing from some allergic reaction to a flower. No one knew it, but Lily was allergic to some of her favorite blooms.

She felt Gretchen pat her on her back. "Abby, this looks amazing. She'll be so proud of you."

"I hope so."

"You know I told Lily that she and Dev were perfect for each other, but I did doubt. They were perfect in a weird way, like they knew each other in a past life and were rushing head long to discover each other again."

Abby was shocked. "I've been thinking the same thing!" *Crud, she was agreeing with Gretchen Malloy. The world was coming to an end.*

"Gretchen, thanks for everything you've done."

"I owed them. Dev really rescued me on a wedding. I'm sure you heard about the dog that ate the license, well he found that judge with a new license. The client fired me that day. I'd never had that happen on a wedding day, but I heard from them later. Dev had told them it was all my idea to get the new license and the judge. He saved my career when I acted very unprofessionally. And Lily, well, you girls have never judged me or treated me badly. She's been through so much over the years I just wanted to do something special."

Abby chose silence. If Gretchen ever knew what they used to say!

"You know, Abby, I'll probably be sending a lot more business to the little shop."

Abby placed the perfect fake smile on her face. "Oh joy." She couldn't wait to tell Lily that good news, or threat depending on your frame of reference. But Gretchen could be tolerated, not for long periods of time, but at least throughout the planning of this wedding and promises of liquor at the end of the day.

The couple had finally made it to their own reception.

Dev was talking to Gretchen and Abby in the cocktail lounge complete with darkened windows and candlelight as Lily wandered into the main dining and dancing area.

The flowers were breath-taking. She could only imagine the cost of this elaborate setup. Actually, she could imagine. Dev said he paid all the wholesale bills and had handed an envelope to Abby with a generous amount for all her hard work. Lilacs, Lily's favorite flowers, were completely out of season, but Abby had worked white and lavender stems in through the assortment of flowers. The tall centerpieces featured sprays of orchids spilling onto the table with calla lilies stretching to the ceiling. The lower arrangements were fluffy with hydrangeas and all the other flowers. There were candles everywhere that would offer ambience once the sun set. Across the head table there was a row of blooms from one end to the other.

Abby's work proved she was no longer just an assistant. She could do it all on her own. Her eyes tracked to the center of the room. Cake, finally, cake. Lily clapped at the sight. She could smell the icing, no doubt buttercream. She knew her friend had made it just by the look of each delicate layer. Each tier featured a different design with clusters of blooms here and there. There was a simple monogram on top with sprigs of lily of the valley caressing the letters.

Lily turned her head to spy on Dev. He was laughing about something with Abby and Gretchen. She surveyed the room. No one was there. She slowly removed a peony and swiped her finger across the icing, placing the flower to hide the hole she had just made.

The bride placed the icing inside her mouth and relished every buttery, sugar-filled calorie that was flowing into her body, well actually to her left hip. She even licked her finger. She twirled around in the room taking it all in. Her wedding was perfect.

"Everything to your approval?"

She stopped in full turn, embarrassed at her actions. "You really are going to have to stop sneaking up on me." Lily pulled him by the lapels into a warm kiss.

"The quietness is an occupational hazard from my training," Dev murmured. "I'm thinking from that kiss that all of this makes you happy. Do you feel like a bride now?"

She waved him away as she moved over to the head table. "I felt like a bride the minute I tried this dress on the other day."

"I'm warning you, I'm behind you." He embraced her, holding her against his chest. "And I do love the back of this dress. You are so beautiful."

"You won't say that tomorrow. It's going to take me hours to get this makeup off.'

Dev nuzzled her neck. "You seem to forget I've seen you in Elmo slippers and sweats, and I thought you were beautiful then."

"Liar," she joked. Her eyes focused on a small box at her seat. Abby had placed her bouquet beside it.

"There's many forms of beauty, darling. There's model beauty, a child's beauty, and a muppet's beauty."

She escaped his hold and reached for the box. "What's this?"

"A gift for my wife. I hadn't given her anything yet."

"You've given me these pearls, a wedding band--"

"Those I gave to my bride." Dev touched the top of the velvet box. "This is for my wife. Open it."

Her eyes widened as she lifted the necklace out of the box. The simple gold chain held a cluster of diamonds with gold leaves surrounding it.

"It's supposed to look like a hydrangea, you remember that flower, well actually the drugs that brought us together. I hope to make all your dreams come true."

"Wow, you are going to have your work cut out for you. I've been making a very long list over the years."

They were both laughing. He silenced her with another kiss. They both looked up as they heard voices in the hallway. Dev could hear his father with his friend Paul and his wife.

"I guess we need to greet our guests." Dev took her by the hand as another elevator door opened.

"Wait, do you think the necklace will be safe if I just keep it in the box on the table?"

Dev stared at his new wife. "Really, Lily? I hope to heaven it will be. We have former Army and Navy, a Marine, a judge, FBI and DEA agents, even the CIA, and a couple of police officers."

"Wait, one more thing," she added as she ignored his litany of law enforcers. As she placed the box near her bouquet, she leaned over and smelled the lilacs and lily of the valley. It was a new sensation to literally stop and smell the flowers.

As with any reception, Lily felt like the hours were going by in warp speed. The day would be over so quickly. The cocktail hour was a good time to hug those friends and family who had travelled so far. Dev's aunt in Virginia had already planned another reception at her vineyard for those who couldn't make it to Kansas City. Lily was reeling from the Pierce family surprises. It would be an opportunity to meet more family and to see her own brother and sister again. Maybe she'd finally meet Dev's wayward brother. Dinner followed with numerous toasts. Father Dan gave a blessing and a few others brought their own speeches forward, some serious others not so much, like JT's.

"I just want to say that on behalf of the guys, we really like you Lily. You are the only woman ever invited to our game day festivities. Just remember," he said solemnly as he raised his glass, "Go Navy, Beat Army."

There were numerous catcalls, Lily taking note of who was one side or another. The elegant reception had turned into a war of two arms of service. Then someone yelled something about the Air Force. Dev stood and tapped his glass.

"I want to thank all of you for coming to this surprise party, I mean our wedding." He looked down at Lily and smiled. "I wasn't sure this would really work out, but I'm so happy it has. I've travelled to many places and none felt like home until I came here and found you, Lily." He lifted his glass to his wife. "I've been many miles and no place has felt so far away as when I'm away from you. I've been to war and in dangerous situations, and yet you offer me the peace and that soft place in your embrace. I've lost my heart to many, well a few, but only one woman has found mine and protected it in her hand. We read from St. Paul today at the wedding and his beautiful words about love, but I want my new wife to believe these words I found from Solomon. Lily, you are altogether beautiful; there is no flaw in you. To my wife, I love you." He raised his glass as did everyone else in the room. He thought he saw Gretchen crying. *Really, cracks in the dragon lady's demeanor?*

As he sat down, Lily tenderly touched his face for a kiss. "That was quite lovely. Not sure I can live up to it."

"You will and you do," Dev whispered.

After a wonderful meal and Lily's favorite part, the cutting and eating of the cake, Dev brought her to the floor for their first dance. *Crud, we've never even danced together.*

"This is really our first dance, Dev. We should've practiced or something."

"Follow my lead," he said as he placed her in position.

She was completely comfortable in his arms, listening to the words and swaying to the music, so comfortable she didn't notice that the music had stopped.

She looked up and laughed. "Whoops. Music stopped."

There were some hints of laughter as she bowed to everyone.

"I don't do this every day, but I do know what a great reception is like, so everybody, let's party," she said loudly. Her proclamation was met with cheering. People drifted in around them for the next song, and the next. All night long the dance floor was filled with happy guests, delighted family and supportive friends.

It was nearing eleven when most headed to the elevators. Lily was kissing her nieces in front of the elevator as Judge Stanley and his wife Maureen waited for her.

She hugged Maureen intensely and then gave the Judge a quick kiss on the cheek. "I am so happy you both were here."

"I'm so happy you're here," Maureen joked. "Didn't I tell you about him?" She pointed in Dev's direction. He'd caught her eye and was headed toward them.

"You were right, and I was wrong," Lily lamented happily.

"You're going home?" Dev asked with concern. "Do you have someone to drive you?"

"Oh no, we are staying the night. We have a room. We'll leave tomorrow," the Judge answered. He placed his arm around his wife as the elevator door opened. "We're celebrating. It's our anniversary today."

"I didn't know." Dev was completely surprised. "We'll share the same anniversary."

"For many years to come, I hope, my dears." Maureen kissed the couple and then entered the elevator. They were holding hands and shared a kiss as the doors were closing.

"I want us to be them," Lily whispered.

"We can do that."

"Dev, you really think we can?"

He pulled his wife into his arms. "I'm counting on it. How long do we need to stay?"

"We can leave at anytime, says the wedding professional!"

Dev looked over Lily's head and saw someone he needed to talk to as he reviewed the almost empty room. The candles were lower, the glasses were everywhere on the tables and place settings had long been removed.

At one table, her brother and Jack Pierce were in a serious conversation with Father Dan. Gretchen was leaning on a bar in the corner talking to Abby and Jeremy. *Yikes, what were they so intense about?* She spied Angelica asleep on three chairs as Carlos and Alise huddled together in an embrace.

"Hey kiddo, we're going to go." Tom, the FBI agent and friend who had been so supportive, had his two hands on the back of her shoulders.

She turned to embrace Tom and his wife. "It was a great time, wasn't it? I will have to congratulate the man who planned it all."

"He did a great job. We are so happy for both of you."

Another round of hugs sent them on their way. Lily plodded her way over to the young bartender nearest her. "I'd like a glass of champagne, please. I'm not driving." She'd never drank this much champagne in her life. She was pleasantly drunk, tipsy would be the word. She snorted at the very word. "Tipsy, tipsy, kind of like amuck. I like it," she said out loud and snorted again. Oh boy, the champagne hit her like a brick falling from a decaying three story building. She couldn't feel her shoes. She snorted again. She wasn't wearing any shoes.

Lily knew she was tired even though she hadn't worked a bit on this wedding. She smiled as she finished her glass of champagne.

She set the glass on the bar. "That was very tasty. Thank you so much." She sat down in the nearest chair, touching one of the orchid sprays. "How much were these flowers?" She wished they were getting paid for this wedding. Her eyelids closed. She was so tired, that was it. She knew everything going on around her. She heard the soft music playing and she smelled the lovely fragrances of blooms mingled with buttercream icing. *Mmm, cake.*

Gosh she was tired. It had been a very long, beautiful day and now it was ending. She was married. She grinned. Was there any leftover cake?

She turned back to the young bartender. "Do you know if there's any cake left? I'd really like a piece, and a glass of milk, please."

"I'll check for you, ma'am." *Ma'am, yuk.* She hated that word, but she really was one now. She'd forgive him if he brought back cake and milk.

And suddenly it appeared in front of her. "Mrs. Pierce, here you go. We boxed up the top layer and the rest of the cake, and we will keep that safe for you." The catering manager had supplied her magical request.

Lily looked around for Dev's mother. *That can't be right. Oh, I'm Mrs. Pierce. Keep it together, Lily, you're losing it.* "Thank you very much. We're staying here tonight. May we pick it up later?"

"Your husband has arranged for that already, and we will be working with the florist on the flowers, all the gifts, and anything else like the guestbook, etc." The catering manager smiled at her like she was a client. *Wait, she was the florist! No, she was the client.* Ah, yes she gave those same looks on days that were particularly long with particularly difficult clients.

"Thank you and your staff for everything. It was absolutely wonderful, and you didn't have to deal with a difficult bride this time."

"No, just your coordinator." They both turned in Gretchen's direction. Gretchen waved. Lily grabbed the woman's hand empathetically.

"I am so sorry about that, really. I had no idea she was involved."

"She was fine, most of the time, but I did have to call your husband when she suggested fireworks and doves in the ballroom. I just called him with all the updates, and he vetoed the particularly unusual ones."

Lord, what else had she thought of? Lily grinned. She could see Gretchen recommending an Army mule, or perhaps a marching band spelling out THEY FINALLY DID IT in formation.

"Well, we certainly appreciate everything you've been through and everything you have done. I think we are about to call it a night, but could you get me just a little more champagne?" Soon, it appeared, right next to her milk. Heaven. She took a bite of cake, following it with a chaser of milk. Yes, heaven.

She remembered something the catering manager had said, gifts. *We have gifts? This was way better than Christmas, and she went home with the guy in the tux. Pierce, Devlin Pierce.* Lily snorted out loud at her James Bond humor.

She finished her milk and cake and sipped slowly on her champagne. She'd propped her elbows on the table and was mesmerized by her husband. She laughed out loud. *Husband.* The tux suited him, but once he removed the jacket, she marveled at how nicely a fitted white shirt looked on one man. *Damn, he was good looking.* She had to admit for once in her life she'd looked pretty good today. She didn't dare look in a mirror now. Dev caught her gaze and winked. He hugged his Dad, grabbed a few things from the head table including her necklace, and headed in her direction, waving to everyone remaining in the room.

Dev could tell Lily was done in. She was still smiling, but her eyes were glassy. Her hair had retreated to full humidity frizz, and she had her head propped up in her hands, well one hand. The other had an almost drained champagne glass in it.

He held his hand down to her in true gentlemanly fashion and drew her up in one move. "Time to go, little girl."

He winced when he realized what he had just said. John, one of her best friends in the world, who had been shot in front of her, always used that endearment.

Lily attempted a smile. She realized in that moment she was tired from all the emotion of today and also of who wasn't here to share in the celebration. John, Dev's mom she'd never met, her parents, Dev's friends Tom and Mike, and so many others. "John," she whispered. "Yes, let's go. It's been lovely."

"No, one more thing." Dev emptied the items on the table. "I need one more dance with my wife."

As they swayed to whatever song was being played, Dev smoothed one errant curl from Lily's face. "This was a good day," he whispered.

"It was the best, but it is time to say goodnight." She pulled back from his hold and grasped his hand. As she began to lead him away, he quickly gathered up the few items on the table, including her shoes and necklace.

"Thank you, everyone," she yelled as they walked out hand in hand, heading to the elevators.

Once inside, she leaned against the back glass. She saw herself in the mirror. Lord, she was tired, maybe drunk? No, she was relaxed with not one care in the world, well maybe just a couple. Those worries could wait. Years of doubt and anxiousness were off her shoulders and would be replaced by gentle arms around her.

The door shut right after Dan entered. "How the heck did I end up with the newlyweds? I mean this is some bad joke--a priest, a florist and a secret agent were on an elevator."

"Dan, you just got lucky," Lily said and was suddenly frantic as she looked down at her feet. "I don't have my shoes!" A large hiccup followed.

"Got them," Dev announced as he lifted the pair in the air.

She leaned against him and frowned. "And I forgot my champagne."

"We can get you more in the suite." The two men shared a smile. Lily wasn't drunk-drunk, but she certainly was happy-tired drunk. There was a definite distinction in the two.

"Dan, are you coming back to our suite? It's beau-*hiccup*-tiful."

This time, Dan couldn't contain himself. He shook his head. "Oh no, Lily. Your husband wouldn't like that one bit." Dev's look across from him affirmed his statement.

They'd reached their floor. When the doors opened, Lily was thanking Dan as Dev grabbed her hand. She waved goodbye, blowing kisses in the cleric's direction. He headed in the opposite direction as Dev led his wife slowly in the other.

As soon as Lily entered the suite, she began the search for the champagne. Her bare feet shuffled through the thick pile of the rug. Dev watched the entertainment, setting items on the counter and removing his jacket one final time. His tie had been in his pocket for hours. He began to remove the cufflinks, then rolled up his sleeves. Finally, he unbuttoned his shirt and released it from his waistband.

Why was Lily searching under the pillows in the chairs, Dev wondered. She quickly moved onto the refrigerator and stuck her head inside. "Found it. Oh and there's food in here." Her clapping sounds united with Dev's chuckles. "I need food."

"Yes, you do," Dev answered as he joined her, pulling out a platter of cheese and fruit, and of course another bottle of champagne. "Come on, let's sit in the comfy chairs." He grabbed all the items and set them out. Then he went back for his wife and two glasses. She had a small gift in her hand.

"What's that?" He watched her plop down in the chair opposite him.

"It must be Gretchen's gift. She brought it to the house this morning and told me to open it later. Do you know we have more gifts? I love this getting-married thing."

Dev popped open the bubbly and poured as she painstakingly unwrapped the many scotch-taped sides. The box wasn't that large, but it was demanding all her attention until the champagne came.

Lily took a quick drink and opened the box. "What the heck? Is this a scarf? Can you tell what it is?"

Dev sat down and removed the sheer material. Two thin

straps were at the top of the sheer, black, lacy negligee. Lily was pulling out the very skimpy thong.

"She is kidding, isn't she?" Lily made sure there was nothing else in the box and found one of Gretchen's business cards with a note on the back. *Bestie, enjoy! Have a delicious night. Gretchen*

Dev sat back in the chair enjoying the crimson color on Lily. It looked good. He held the camisole, nightie, whatever it was, up to Lily. "Did she have some brilliance to convey in her note?"

"Dev, you do know that sex on your wedding night is highly overrated? In fact, most couples don't even make love."

Dev's one brow raised. "Really?"

"Yes, and if they do, well it's lousy. You're so exhausted. It's quantity vs quality is what I think."

"I promise to give it a collegiate try," Dev interrupted.

"And that's the difference between men and women. Women want special, and men just want, well, they just want."

"I promise, Lily, I'll make your life special every day."

Lily snorted out some of her champagne. "That was so nice, but so cheesy. Sometimes I think you're from central casting from some Bond film."

Dev leaned his head on his hand. *What had he gotten himself into? He was going to have his hands full just keeping up with the ups and downs of Lily Schmidt, wait Pierce. She was so cute when she was nervous and drunk.*

Lily stood up quickly. "I need out of this dress. It took three women to get me into it."

"I'm sure I can get you out of it. There's just that one button at the neck and then the ones below the waist."

"You're very confident, husband of mine."

"Always." His low voice, sultry and dangerous required Lily's full attention. She gulped. Her mouth was suddenly dry as she examined the handsome man, the open stark white shirt, the loosened belt and his relaxed body. *Geez, he was her husband. How did this happen exactly? Was she going to wake up and realize that it was really two years ago and she'd just dreamed the story for a romance novel?*

She yawned. The day and night had hit her, again with that same brick. "I can barely keep my eyes open."

Dev stood up to hold her steady as she swayed. "My feet hurt too."

He turned with both hands toward the door. "Then let's get you to bed."

Dev only cussed a couple of times as he maneuvered the buttons on the back of Lily's dress. He had been overconfident. Over the years, he'd had no problem helping a woman out of her clothes. His record time had been thirty seconds. It was one of the few personal records he kept, and he kept it to himself. Of course, he'd never removed a wedding gown before. He'd never been a husband before. His nervous fingers fumbled, but soon the dress dropped in a pool around Lily's feet. She moved, almost ran into the bathroom. By the time she'd returned, Dev had swept away Abby's beautiful heart design of rose petals and was already in bed. She turned out all of the lights and she crept in. The

Plaza supplied the only filtered spotlight on the bed.

"I've had too much champagne, and I'm so tired," she whispered as she settled her head on his chest. One hand splayed protectively over him. "I know it's our wedding night."

The next sound Dev heard was a soft snore, then even breathing.

"Really, Lily?" he moaned. He stroked her hair for a few minutes. It wasn't difficult to fall asleep listening to Lily. He very much enjoyed it.

Chapter Seventeen

1. Now what?
2. Need a couple of ibuprofen
3. Need food
4. Do I wake him?
5. Make more lists in my head while I lay here

Lily woke as the sun was just coming up. Usually, she'd be rushing off to church on a Sunday. Today, she was laying on a man's chest, her makeup still heavy on her eyes. *Geez, I didn't even remove my makeup?* Good or bad, she wasn't going to get out of the bed and wake him.

She began to really study him as he slept. She fingered his chin, outlining his jawline, feeling the stubble on his face. His lashes were outrageously lush. Frankly, she'd always been a little jealous, especially when she had to add two layers of mascara onto her own. Her hand moved a bit on his chest, and she felt some sort of indentation. She saw a scar below his right shoulder. Had he been shot there too?

She remembered she'd fallen asleep. She remembered Gretchen's gift. *Holy Moly, did she even know me?* Lily was mortified. She wasn't even sure how to put the darn thing on. She couldn't wait any longer. She had to go to the bathroom. Slowly, she removed herself from Dev's body and slid out of the bed to the solitude of the massive bathroom. She saw her face. She looked like Gene Simmons in his first attempt at KISS makeup. Cold water and makeup remover might just save her, oh and aspirin, ibuprofen, anything to make the throbbing of her head go away. She brushed her teeth. She was a little better. Her stomach seemed fine. Well, she had eaten--all day long. It was amazing that the dress didn't blow open when she was dancing. She could almost hear what it would've been like. *Clean up on the dance floor. Bride has busted through her gown. Is there a seamstress in the ballroom?*

Lily turned to find a towel and saw her beautiful dress. *When had Dev done that? After she was asleep?* It held just as much magic this morning as it had the day she had first laid her eyes on it. She touched the fabric of the skirt. Soft to the touch, the satin was liquid in her fingers. She reached into one of the pockets and removed a clean tissue. Lily felt something else in there and removed a beautiful linen handkerchief. The blue embroidery featured a large *P* in the middle. She sighed. It was Dev's mother's something blue. She'd carried it on her wedding day. Someone had slipped it into Lily's pocket. She placed it into her bag. On the counter next to it was her something blue from her mother. Elizabeth had given it to her at the church; it was a blue miraculous medal that her mother used to wear on a chain around her neck. Lily had attached it to her bouquet. Abby had removed it before she took the flowers up to the ballroom. Lily secured it within the bag too.

She found the ibuprofen and the nightgown she had planned on wearing for her wedding night. It was black; black always made you look slimmer, with ivory lace around the edges. It was pretty, not sexy. Hopefully, it would do. As she exited, Dev remained asleep. She passed into the outer room and checked the refrigerator.

"What are you doing?" Dev was right behind her. She nearly hit her head on the door.

"You have to stop doing that!" She yelled. She grabbed her head quickly. "Sorry. Didn't mean to be that loud." She closed the refrigerator door to face him. "I was looking for food so I can take my ibuprofen. I know, that's no surprise."

He wasn't smiling, he wasn't frowning. He was just standing there looking at her. "Sorry about the stealth-like behavior. I never knew I did it until now."

"Dev? Everything fine?" He was very quiet; too quiet, even for him.

"More than fine. You look amazing."

She looked down at herself to discover what he was seeing, who he was seeing. *Yikes, the nightgown clung like pantyhose on a hot day.* That's probably why she didn't wear hose anymore. The material clung to every curve and every peak and hollow. She was feeling very much like an admired lamb, admired by a wolf!

He turned back into the bedroom and grabbed his shirt to top off his lounge pants. "I'll go get something down the hall. I'll bring coffee too. I'll be right back."

"I'm not going anywhere." He was already out the door. In a matter of minutes he returned with two hot coffees, two breakfast souffles and a couple of danishes.

The first few bites agreed with her stomach. She had been hungry. The danish melted in her mouth. "I love you so much right now."

"The danish or me?"

"Mm, let me think on that. And I do love a good concierge level of a hotel."

"I did order brunch for later, and they'll deliver it here to the suite."

"That was very thoughtful." She was sipping on the most glorious liquid in the world, caffeinated coffee. She'd finished her food before Dev. The headache had almost disappeared, and she was almost a human being again. He should be mad and hurt, but he seemed relaxed. Maybe he'd been too tired last night? *Yep, keep telling yourself that, Lily, you little idiot.*

"Dev, are you done?"

"I can be. What do you need?"

She stood up slowly, took his hand and drew him up to stand in front of her. She unbuttoned his shirt and tugged it off his shoulders. "I need you. You know, I hear that wedding mornings are trending and have replaced wedding nights."

He followed her naturally, slowly into the bedroom. "Well, that's because you're usually so tired and have had too much champagne. Quality versus quantity is much more important."

She led him to the bed. "But I've heard practice makes perfect."

"Over the years, I've been very good at practicing. In fact, I'm a very good instructor. If you need basic training, I'm your man."

She slid under the covers, and he was soon beside her,

in each other's arms. "And I've always been an A student."

"You aren't going to make lists, are you?"

She giggled. "Maybe, you'll never know." His laughter filled the room as his first passionate kiss nearly curled her toes. His hands slid up and down her satin covered form. Body to body, Lily couldn't think of anything but how long she had waited for this man. Her hands held his head; her fingers massaged through his full hair. His lips trailed down her neck and both straps of her gown were gently lowered to expose her skin. Gentle hands moved up to caress her.

She giggled again, and Dev's head shot up. "What? Did I do something?"

"You're doing a lot of something, but I was hearing that song in my head. I wasn't making lists, I promise."

He pulled back to glare at her. "What song?"

His wife laughed again. "Oh a few songs about becoming a woman." She snorted. She couldn't stop herself. She was nervous and now she was the one deflecting. "What if this, we, don't work very well together? I mean, we haven't had much time to practice."

He pulled her even closer to him. "Then we keep doing it until we get it right."

"Ah, good evil plan."

"Now, stop thinking."

"That's very hard for me to do."

"Try."

Dev slid her nightgown up to her waist, caressing her backside. Lily began to giggle again. "That tickles."

"Geez, Lily."

She tightened her lips and frowned. "I'll be serious, I promise. I'm sorry. Go for it."

Now Dev was laughing, but his irritation was rising as was another area of his body. "Go for it? First, you fall asleep on our wedding night, and now you're cheering me on as if I'm going for a first down or hitting a homerun?"

"I'm sorry. Just nervous and overwhelmed by everything this week. I didn't even get you a gift."

He pulled her close again. "You will, right now."

Lily aggressively sought out his mouth and kissed him with everything she had. His unshaven face didn't even bother her; its friction strangely spurred her on. They both pulled back breathless.

"That was some kiss."

"I am a fast learner."

She rubbed his back slowly as the tone of the morning changed, and they began to make love. Gretchen was right, he was delicious and frighteningly passionate. And he was a bit of a dork. After they made love for the first time, he was retelling some of the advice everyone had given him about her. And he explained how he did want the fireworks at the reception, but he knew she wouldn't and it probably wasn't the safest idea given the fondness for explosives that some of his guests had. He also wanted the Army fight song played, not the mule, but he knew she wouldn't. Playfully, he explained he had sacrificed a lot for her perfect wedding day, and she owed him.

Lily rested, playing with the light hair on Dev's chest. She found a grey one. "Dev, I have one bit of advice for you."

He was concerned. Her voice was like velvet, the murmur of it felt near his heart. "Honey, what? What can I do?"

"I need you to remember only one thing."

"Fine, whatever it is, I'll do it." Her soft face was looking up into his.

She kissed him and then softly said, "Go Navy, Beat Army."

He rolled her over in one swift move. "You are going to pay for that dearly, Mrs. Pierce." His playful tickling turned into another trending wedding morning practice session of lovemaking.

Chapter Eighteen

1. Finally, the fall weddings are over
2. Pack and remember passport
3. Need at least two evening outfits
4. Go over everything with Abby
5. Make sure all holiday items are ready
6. Talk to Dev about the holidays
7. I'm finally going on my honeymoon

The lights in the cabin of the plane had dimmed for the overnight trip to France. Despite a very long day of flying into Reagan National Airport, lunch and visiting with Dev's dad, and then heading to Dulles Airport for an international flight to Paris, Lily was wide awake.

She'd never flown in business class to fly overseas, and on this French airline, they served real food, not just a cheese tray that cost a fortune. The seats would actually lay down with their own pillows and blankets. She cradled a glass of wine in her left hand and leaned her head on her husband's shoulder. That was still so weird to say, but she was happily getting accustomed to it.

"Paris? I can't believe we are going to Paris for our honeymoon. I'm not sure I can sleep."

Dev's eyes were already closed. "You better get at least a few hours of sleep in. This is our honeymoon, but I do have to do a bit of work."

"Normally, I would care, but two to three weeks in Paris is unbelievable. After being away from you off and on these last few months, I'll take what I can get. Do you know how many hours you'll have to work?"

Dev smiled. "It doesn't really work that way. I'm meeting up with an old friend. Claude is currently working at the Louvre in antiquities."

"That sounds romantic."

"Old stuff in an old building is romantic?" Dev mumbled.

"The Louvre, antiquities, not old stuff," Lily mocked. "Are you asleep?"

"Huh?"

"Nevermind. Go to sleep. I'm way too excited. But one question, why Paris?"

He turned his head to steal a look at her bright eyes. "Where else would you take a foodie?"

Lily giggled. "That is true. Well, I'm very happy. You sleep, and I'm going to watch a movie or read, or something."

She finished her wine and placed the headphones on her head. She selected a movie and within a few minutes was dead to the world. When she woke, the sun was streaming in through the window, and her husband was gone.

"This better not be a bad airplane movie," she whispered as she removed her headphones and moved a bit in her seat. *You come on with your husband, and he suddenly vanishes on a perfectly good plane.* She raised her head over the row in front of her and saw Dev's form. He was talking to two of the flight attendants. As he finally turned, she saw he was carrying two coffee cups.

"I thought you'd wake up if you smelled coffee." He handed one cup to her. She gathered it up in both hands and took a sip.

"Oh, that's so good. I'm having a spiritual moment here. Are we almost there?"

Dev settled into his seat. "No, we have a little while. They'll serve breakfast in a few minutes. Next stop, Paris."

"Have you been awake very long?"

"No, not really, but I took a walk in the quiet plane. I thought I saw someone I knew as we were boarding so I was asking the flight attendants."

"Of course you were. A bad someone or a good someone?" she asked suspiciously.

"Nothing to worry about, but if it is him, you never know until it is too late."

She rolled her eyes. "Oh, that's comforting. Well as long as he isn't the T word." She could tell he didn't understand her reference. "Terrorist," she whispered.

Dev sat quietly and didn't answer her non-question question.

"Really, Dev? You think you saw a terrorist, on our airplane?" Her voice was barely audible. If there was a marshall on the plane, she didn't want to be the one taken away in handcuffs.

"Oh great, breakfast is coming."

That good old family trait of deflection was getting old rather quickly. But breakfast was coming, and she was famished. She'd let it slide, for now. She also wanted to know a little more about what kind of work he'd be doing on their honeymoon. But, for now, again, she'd just enjoy.

After a much needed bathroom break, she returned to her seat to see the distant suburbs of the city of light out the window. She understood enough French to know they were instructing everyone to return to their seats to prepare for landing.

"When do we meet Claude?" She tightened her seat belt.

"I thought we'd have a few days to ourselves. I made a list, organized it, and planned everything. I think you'll be happy with that. Sorry, no post-it notes." Lily wrinkled her nose at him and his attempt at humor. "Oh and there's this gala we'll be attending later. I think you'll enjoy it."

"I hope I brought an appropriate dress. I'm not sure I've ever been to a gala. Where's it at?"

"The Louvre."

Lily gulped. "You make that sound like we're headed to JT's for a game party. The Louvre and gala in the same sentence is much more. I'm not used to parties like that. I only provide the flowers for those sort of events, but I never stay."

"It's not a big thing."

"Who is it for, some charity?"

Dev was packing up their electronics into his carry-on. "For the President of France and the art patrons, I believe."

Lily's mouth dropped open. "Dev, I now know I don't have a dress for something like that."

"I have to get a tux; we'll get you a dress. Don't worry about it."

He said that so calmly. *Don't worry? Did he know her? Geez.*

Less than thirty minutes later, she could make out the dome of Sacré Coeur and the streets of Montmatre. She was landing in Paris with her husband. She grabbed his hand in hers and held on.

"My life has certainly changed with you in it." She kissed him on the cheek.

Dev smiled, but he had an odd feeling. The hairs on the back of his neck were at attention. Someone from behind was boring a hole into his head. He didn't want to alert whoever was doing it, but he'd have to be on guard sooner than he'd expected. The flight attendants had looked up the man's name after Dev showed them his credentials. *Omar Sands. What an idiot name to use. But they allowed him on the plane. I know who you are, I just don't understand how you are here, and have been in America.* The man was dead, yet here he was. Dev knew he couldn't tell Lily. He shut his eyes. *Damn, what was she going to do to him when she found out? Was he placing her in danger one more time?*

No amount of post-it notes, wine, food or lovemaking was going to protect him if Lily's honeymoon was destroyed by a mission. He had to lie to her again.

Chapter Nineteen

1. Must see Notre-Dame and light a candle
2. Musée D'Orsay
3. Boat Ride on the Seine
4. Eat a crêpe on the street
5. Buy a piece of art

Dev was with the gentleman who had brought them up to their room. He was one of the hotel managers. Lily looked out their window at the view of the Eiffel Tower in the distance and the Tuileries below her. Most of the trees had lost their leaves, but there were still a few who held onto the golden leaves of fall. They could literally walk to the Louvre and the Champs-Elysees. Heck, she could probably wear short heels and feel comfortable. The city of Paris was at her feet. This was much different than the school trip. She'd worked nearly a year in the flower shop during high school just to go to France. As students, they never had a view like this, nor stayed in any hotel with a star rating. This one had five stars for the view and the hotel.

"Madame." Lily turned to the two men. The manager was opening a bottle of champagne and pouring two glasses full. She hadn't had a drink of that stuff for over two months. "I also arranged for a petite respite after your long flight. Bottled water is provided."

Lily looked toward what seemed to be a small wet bar in the corner of the sitting room. There was plenty of seating too with a small sofa, chairs and even a window seat below each large window. Gold curtains accented this room. At the other end of the room was a separate bedroom and a very large spa bathroom. *Yep, much nicer than a school trip.*

"If you need my services, just ring. It is a little cool today, but that's November in Paris. Enjoy our lovely lady." His hand swept toward the window and its views.

After his departure, they toasted. "Lily, always remember I love you. Je t'aime."

They both smiled at each other as they took their drinks, but Lily's eyes quickly squinted.

"Why do I need to always remember that? What aren't you telling me?"

Dev ran his hand through his hair.

"Ah hah! There is something going on, already. Holy Moly, not even our honeymoon is immune from intrigue and danger?" She plopped down in the very cushioned lounge settee, and began examining one of the overstuffed brocade pillows. "Wow, these pillows are absolutely stunning. Now, spill."

Dev sat down beside her and removed the glass from her hand. "At least our wedding was immune from my job." His eyes were twinkling. Lily folded her arms over her chest defiantly.

"And that was a surprise attack on me, remember? Now, tell me. What's up?"

He popped his wristband. Lily smiled. He better never play poker with all his tells. She'd watched him at the airport. He was his usual cool self, but he was different, more cautious, even more stealth-like if possible. He had occasionally looked over his shoulder and around the corner. She'd known then, but just wondered when he would tell her.

"I think, I *know*, we were followed here to the hotel. I knew this man during the war, and he was on the plane. I was right."

"And," Lily prompted.

"He's very dangerous. He wasn't part of my work here, honestly."

"Can you tell me what you are doing?"

Dev looked calmly into her eyes. "I'm meeting up with Claude to look over some documents. There may be a drug ring of some kind. That's all."

"You couldn't have looked at those documents over the internet like real people do?"

"No, they're very sensitive and very fluid, and well, we were already coming here so I sort of volunteered. I thought you would like the special treatment at the Louvre."

Lily nodded. "You sort of volunteered. Right. Well, I should be angry, but I'm getting used to this agent stuff, besides, I'm not complaining about this hotel or this suite."

Dev touched her hand. "That was all me, not the government."

"Good to know, it is beautiful. So what's on your itinerary first?"

"How about a walk over to Notre-Dame?"

Lily smiled. "So I can light my candle?"

"It would be a good place to start, so get some walking shoes on, but first." He raised his glass and gave hers back to her. "To us and to Paris."

Their glasses clinked, the sound of an expensive clink. "And to our apparent adventures to come." Her addition to the toast was met with eyes that turned dark at her slight sarcasm. He'd have to check in with the United States Embassy. He needed a gun.

There was a sedan available to them for the ride. Lily waited in the lobby, surrounded by American flags, impressive artwork and Marines, several Marines. She'd never been in an embassy, and she'd never been this close to men in uniform, spit and polished, who carried guns. She had been near her brother when he was in the Army, but he'd never had a rifle or sidearm on him.

She examined every inch of where part of her taxpayer money went, specifically to the decorating. *Did they really need that painting? Could they really afford that lamp? Was it a Tiffany? The President's painting was obligatory, but did they have to use that expensive frame?* Her legs were crossed, one shaking from nerves. Checking in with the embassy upped her anxiety level. Of course, they didn't want or need to talk to her. She was just the wife. The little woman wasn't necessary. Well, this little woman helped take down a drug dealer!

Lily smiled at the receptionist. She smiled back.

"Ma'am, is there anything I can get for you? Coffee, hot tea?"

"No, thank you. I'm just waiting on my husband." *Gosh, Lily, can you sound more 1950's? I'm just the little woman behind the big bad man. Get it together.*

"Have you lived in Paris for awhile?" Non-committal conversation might bring her back to normal, whatever that was anymore.

"I've been here less than six months. It's a fantastic assignment. Let me know if you need anything." The young woman put her head down.

It was a tactful way of saying she was done with inane conversation with the federal agent's wife. Paris was lovely as long as a terrorist wasn't blowing up a food mart or café, or even a large event like a concert a few years ago. *Lily, can you get more jaded?* She preferred to think she was realistic and practical.

Lily stood up suddenly as Dev exited from behind a very large door, accompanied by a suited man.

"Remy, I'd like you to meet my wife, Lily."

The gentleman smiled broadly and extended his hand to her. "Lily, it is so wonderful to meet you. Dev and I go way back to a tour in Iraq. That's when I first met Dr. Barbin. I'm sorry about the government's invasion of your honeymoon, but I hope you'll have a lovely time all the same."

"Do you think I can write some of it off on my income taxes?" She smiled coyly.

He patted Dev on the back. "And she's funny? You really do need that. You were always so serious."

Dev shrugged his shoulders. "Well, we better get going.

Could the driver drop us off at Notre-Dame? We can walk back from there."

"Of course. Lily, again, it was a pleasure and I'll see you at the gala. *Au revoir.*" He bowed gallantly and then retreated behind the large door.

Lily had been to the Cathedral of Notre-Dame years ago, but as Dev and she walked hand-in-hand, the emotion was overwhelming. They both made the sign of the cross with the holy water from a very large font as they entered into the church. Her eyes set straight ahead at one of the Rose Windows. The colors were stunning as the sun was lowering for the day. The cathedral was just as she remembered it after all these years. She recalled the peace she had felt there the first time, the simplicity of the massive wood arching near the ceiling, and the beauty of the statues acquired throughout the ages. A simple gold cross at the altar was the focus of all those many people across generations just striving to understand a higher being. You didn't have to be Catholic to embrace the love Notre-Dame offered.

She motioned Dev over to the right aisle and walked midway down the side to a beautiful Blessed Virgin statue. She began to search in her purse for an offering. Dev dug in his pocket and pulled out a couple of coins. "I have no money," she whispered.

He placed the euros into her hand. "Now you do."

After she placed her money in the secure box, she picked up two matchsticks and handed one to Dev. "We need to light this one together."

Dev understood. She picked the candle, and they lit the wick. They stood in silence as the flame fired up.

Oh Lord, how did I get here? Obviously, only with your help. I shouldn't ask for more, but I will, you know me, I can be a little spoiled. Fine, a lot spoiled on occasion, but I was the baby. I didn't know any better. You know what I want next, oh and thank you again for this man beside me. That's all for now. I'll try not to bother you for awhile.

Lily leaned into Dev's shoulder and held his hand tighter than before.

"You alright?" Dev whispered. Maybe she was tired; it had been a long day already.

"Yes, more than alright. Can we come back here on another day? I'm sort of getting hungry."

Of course she was, but actually he was starving. "Of course. Let's go. I know a place."

He knew a place. Her husband knew restaurants in Paris. She could tell him where the nearest taco place was in Kansas City.

Just a short walk from the cathedral, they entered a brasserie. An hour later, the sun had long set, and Lily's stomach was full of confit de canard, baby potatoes, and carrots. She never knew she loved roasted duck until today, but she really did love it. They'd drank a bottle of wine and their desserts were placed in front of them. They shared bites of a fruit tart drizzled with caramel and rum sauce and drank café creme.

"How do you like the coffee with all that creamy milk?" Dev thought he could see her eyes roll back in her head with pleasure.

"Please, quiet. This is a spiritual moment."

He laughed. "You and your spiritual moments."

She held the cup up against her face. "I love this coffee. Oh, and I love you too."

"So, I'll be coming in second to coffee while we are here?"

She smiled. "Oh honey, I'm not sure. There's also chocolate here, isn't there?"

Dev had thought it was a good idea to bring her to Paris, but now, not so much.

The romantic dinner was only the beginning of the first few hours of honeymoon as they walked back to the hotel. They'd stopped on one of the bridges to watch the bateaux mouches sailing down the Seine River.

"Can we do that? That's always been a dream of mine, heck it's a dream of just about every woman to sail down the Seine at night in the arms of some good looking man."

Dev was leaning on the bridge. He leaned over and kissed his bride.

"You have anyone in mind?"

She nudged him. "You'll do."

"You know what my dream is?"

"I didn't know you did that sort of thing."

"I do. I have dreams. Well, I'd like us to walk back to the hotel and get out of this cold weather. Then, maybe I provide you with another café creme to keep you awake, and we see where the night leads." He whispered what he had in mind once they returned to their suite.

"Dreams happen every day, especially if you bribe me with coffee."

Chapter Twenty

For the last four days, Paris was at Lily's feet. She had her romantic trip down the Seine with the man she loved, she'd eaten a luscious chocolate and banana crêpe from a street vendor, and she'd purchased a wonderful piece of art near her favorite bridge, Pont Alexandre III. They'd even managed to spend a sun-filled day in Montmartre, eating lunch at a sidewalk café. Their afternoon at the Musée d'Orsay was beyond words. Dev didn't hurry her as she sat down to view Edgar Degas' work *The Ballet Class*. When they travelled to the Musée de l'Orangerie, she was left speechless at the beauty of the large panels of the *Water Lilies* by Monet.

Her days were the magic that consumed a romance novel--clutching each other's hands as they walked through the Tuileries with the cool breezes and the warming sun on their faces, stopping for a kiss or embrace. Her nights were always in her husband's arms.

"Dev, could you move your arm please?" she asked as she used his bare chest as her pillow.

"I'm sorry, is it too heavy?"

"No, it obstructs my view of the Eiffel Tower if you have it there."

Dev's eyes were suddenly wide-open. "What? You're picking the tower over me?"

She giggled. "I am while I'm in Paris, big boy."

"You are in so much trouble." He rolled her quickly onto her back and began tickling certain areas of her body. He knew by now what would send her into uncontrollable laughter. Her laughter made his heart lighter. He'd known that for two years now.

"Stop, please. I can see the tower tomorrow," she gasped.

He stopped immediately and moved his attention to her lips, tenderly kissing, and then each cheek, the edge of her nose, her forehead, her hair until he returned to her mouth.

"You can't see the tower now while I'm right above you."

"I'll sacrifice it just this once," she murmured as she looped her hands around his neck and pulled him down to her. "Just this once."

"It'll be more than just once."

"Promises, promises."

"Lily," he whispered as he set fire to her neck with his lips, "just stop talking."

"You wanted to say shut up, didn't you?"

"Never. You are always extremely witty and intelligent."

His lips were trailing a path lower. *How could the man talk and do what he was doing?*

"And now you're just trying to placate me, trying to make me not think."

Her hands moved to brush through his hair.

"Is it working?" he murmured.

Her body was betraying her as he touched her in all the right places. Her legs went limp. She could barely answer. "Yes," she moaned.

One thing about her husband, he did keep his promises.

The next morning, the Paris sky was still dark as two figures met in the quiet gardens of the Tuileries. Paris was still sleeping. Their meeting was reminiscent of a bad spy movie. The only character missing was the bad guy behind the tree, hopefully.

"So, today you must meet your contact."

It wasn't a question, it was a factual statement. "Yes, I understand. I'm hoping all is set for the gala?"

"It will be. I'm not sure when we will meet again."

"Fine, Mr. Pierce. It is a pleasure, so far, doing business with you."

One man turned and headed into the B-movie fog from the early morning. He jogged away, the passing policeman thinking the man was on a morning run. The other figure, went in the opposite direction near the Musée du Louvre.

Lily's eyes opened slowly to the streams of sun bathing the suite. She rolled over to welcome her husband to another beautiful morning in the city of light but found an empty pillow. There was a note instead. Gone for a run. Good morning sunshine. Je t'aime

"A run? On your honeymoon? Healthy people are nuts," Lily complained to an empty room. Fine, she'd get in a long hot shower and decide what she was wearing for their private tour of the Louvre. She would also be meeting the famous, or infamous Claude Barbin. Actually, Dev really hadn't said much about the man except they'd met each other on one of Dev's first tours after Afghanistan. That's when he had met Remy from the embassy. Claude had been sent in to gain intelligence on the looting of antiquities at the National Museum of Iraq when Sadaam Hussein's regime fell. Apparently, Claude had also worked at the Museum in Cairo during the Arab Spring a few years later.

She was finishing dressing in her leggings and a sweater tunic with her black tall boots when Dev walked through the door with two coffees and a bag of something, probably delicious somethings.

"You better have a high caloric delight in that bag, mister. I missed you this morning."

He walked over and kissed the top of her head. "I didn't want to wake you, and you were so pretty sleeping. Yes, I do have some pastries in the bag. You look great."

"Thanks. I even put on makeup for your friend."

Dev was laying out drinks and the sack on the table near her. "I'm going to jump in the shower. Go ahead and eat." He quickly headed to the bathroom and shut the door.

When they emerged from the hotel for the short walk to the art museum, Lily thought they looked like the quintessential cosmopolitan couple. Her boots were comfortable and kept her legs warm on this cool morning. Dev wore his short leather jacket with black slacks and a grey button down shirt with black short dress boots.

Lily looked up above the reception area at the painted ceiling as she heard Dev check in.

"I'm here for Dr. Claude Barbin."

Dev had certainly gotten her out of her box with all these adventures, but the box she was exiting now was a freight container! Lily's stomach flipped. She remembered that a few days from now she'd be attending some big deal party at the Louvre for heaven's sake. Kansas City seemed miles away in the rearview mirror.

Dev came back with passes to attach to their clothing and a docent provided a short tour while directing them back to the doctor's office. They passed pieces of art from before the time of Christ--Egyptian, Persian--

"Syrian pottery, Lily." Dev pointed at the encased bowl. "ISIS has been destroying so much. So many UNESCO sites have been destroyed in their caliphate. So sad."

"UNESCO?"

"UN's educational, scientific and cultural organization. Our soldiers have worked with them on occasion to attempt to save historical sites, ruins, etc. In Syria, it's too late and some of the early churches are rubble."

Apparently, these hallowed halls made everything serious. Dev's face was stone cold, no twinkling eyes there. Lily stole a glance at her husband as they neared the door at the end of the hall. He had his DEA face on, the one she couldn't read. At least he had not been looking for terrorists around every corner. If he had been, she hadn't realized. The docent opened the large wood door, and waved them through.

There was a large desk with maps and small items cluttered all over it. Lily was shocked at the mess. *Wow, the doc needs some post-it notes, well at least a list or two or perhaps a housekeeper?*

"Dev, is it really you?" Lily heard a very beautiful lilting French accent, and then she saw Claude. She saw HER. The woman was tall and very French; slender, like most typical French women. She looked like a mix between Charlize Theron and Gwyneth Paltrow with long blonde hair, petite black rimmed glasses, steely blue eyes and a body to kill for. *Crud.*

The woman quickly rushed to Dev and kissed him the European way, kiss one side, kiss the other side and then do a return run back to the other side for one more kiss. The kissing was excessive, especially since she was kissing Lily's new husband.

He'd worked with Claude on one of his tours. Claude would show them around the Louvre, the greatest collection of art in the world. A private tour would be wonderful. We'd be going to a magnificent party. Lily was boiling inside. She remained quiet, but took her fist and projected it stiffly onto his left arm.

"Claude," he exclaimed, part shock from the greeting, part from the belt he'd just received from the sweet woman he called his wife. "Claude, this is my wife Lily. We're here on our honeymoon."

The doctor extended her hand. "Welcome to our museum. So sorry that your honeymoon will be a little interrupted."

Lily smiled and shook her hand, saying nothing. *No, you are not sorry. You don't care about my honeymoon.* Lily was fuming, still maintaining her plastic "on" smile. *Where were her little kissy, kisses? Hmm, none for me?*

"Dev never mentioned you were a woman. And you're a doctor, I'm assuming in art?" Lily could talk through clenched teeth. It was an artform too, and she had majored in it over the years. Abby and she could converse in complete paragraphs while never moving their lips.

"*Oui*, and in various civilization antiquities, primarily the time of the Ottoman Empire, some Samarian through Roman rule. I met your lovely husband on one of my missions to rescue certain pieces from Ur and to protect the artifacts. The soldiers were very understanding." She winked at Dev.

Lily protectively looped her arm through Dev's. She felt like she was at prom again, and a cheerleading interloper was after her man. Wait, she'd never gone to prom. She was still feeling very uncomfortable. Had they been more than just comrades during a war? "Amazing. That was a very worthwhile undertaking. And the danger? Do you get used to that?" *Shut up, Lily. She's probably a secret agent of some kind too.*

"Ah, well it is very exciting. I know Dev understands that rush of adrenaline." She sent a knowing smile his way.

Dev coughed. "Do you have time for a tour? I'm sure Lily would really enjoy it."

"Actually," Claude admitted, "I have someone to take her on the tour while we go over some papers together." The woman removed her eyeglasses and Lily could've swore she flipped her hair seductively. *Was there a wind machine in this room?* Lily looked around.

"Well, I was hoping to go with her."

Claude hit a button on some sort of phone system and a small man popped into the room. "I've arranged for Albert to escort Lily. His English is very good." She looked down at her watch. "*Albert, une heure, s'il vous plaît?*"

"*Oui.* Madame Pierce, this way." He extended his hand to show her the way out. Lily felt like she was being rushed out, away from her husband.

"*Claude, je ne comprends pas,*" Dev said as he held onto Lily's hand, preventing her from departing.

Claude whispered something to Dev in French, and he nodded affirmatively. "Lily, go with him and I'll join you by the *Mona Lisa*. I'll text Albert. Please." His eyes were pleading with her.

"I'm counting on that, this time." She pulled her hand away. "My French is a little rusty, but if you don't understand why she's doing this, then there's something very wrong. *Á tout á l'heure*, and it better not be too late. Meet you at the lady."

She smiled at Albert, introduced herself, and they retreated down the hallway. She never looked back. They were having their first real fight and neither one of them had uttered one mean word.

Albert was actually a delight. He had three daughters and one of them was marrying in a few weeks. Of course, they talked about the wedding plans, but in France it was much different than in the US. The couple would go to the magistrate's office and marry in a civil ceremony that dated back to the French revolution. Then, perhaps, there was breakfast or a lovely celebration dinner. Some had flowers, some had a very simple meal with family and a few friends while others had large dances and receptions.

"I'd go out of business," Lily remarked as they passed by several Renoirs. "These are so dark."

"They are all dark in this wing. I much prefer Monet, Manet, Degas. They are so beautiful and the light, the colors amuse me." He was whispering. "Don't tell. It is our secret."

"I understand completely. Albert, I was here at the Louvre many years ago. I can't remember the gift shop. I'd like to pick up a few gifts."

He looked at his watch. There was no text yet. "We have time. Wait until you see the shops on the lower level below the pyramid."

"Shops in the basement? Now you're talking. Lead on, Albert."

The escalators revealed a commercial cavern. There were a variety of shops featuring the usual tourist fare with *Mona Lisa* tiles and plates, but there were also perfume and soap shops, scarves, brightly colored macarons, and other French delicacies.

"This will do." Lily smiled. It was time to use her new credit card with the name Lily C. Pierce. "Albert, let's go shopping."

Claude Barbin had a doctorate, but so did Lily Schmidt Pierce--in shopping! Four shopping bags later, she had gifts for just about everyone including a lovely gift set of assorted soaps for Albert's daughter and a small painted pill box for his wife. It was the least she could do. Albert had an employee discount and allowed her to use it. They left their packages at the check-in desk and took the elevator up to the *Mona Lisa*. Dev was standing there. His smile comforted any fears she had. Besides, as tired as he looked, she had enjoyed the better end of the visit.

"*Merci*, Lily." Now she was the recipient of the kiss festival. She returned the favor and slipped her card into his hand.

"You'll email me photos of the wedding, yes?" She was hugging her new friend. Shopping was indeed a bonding experience all over the world.

"*Oui*." He looked down at the card. "I will email you, I see it here on the card. My day was *magnifique* because of you. We will be friends."

"Yes. *Au revoir*."

"I will see you at the gala. You will meet my wife that night."

Lily's face lit up like a Christmas tree. "Wonderful. I will be so happy to know someone. Thank you so much for today." They kissed again, and her little elfin friend walked away.

"Someone had a good time." Dev's arms were crossed in front of his chest as he leaned against a corner wall away from the most famous woman's portrait in the world. "People just fall in love with you, have you ever noticed that?"

Lily could feel her face warming. Her blush outwardly showed the depth of her lack of confidence at times. "Stop being sweet. I missed you, but I'm not happy with you, well with the situation. She dismissed me."

He unlocked his arms. "Yes, and I'm so sorry. That was inexcusable, and she knows it. She's going to make it up to you tomorrow afternoon. I have some work to do, and she's taking you shopping. She's picking up the tab, and you will let her, especially if she takes you to some designer place. The government and I can't afford that."

"So she's attempting to buy me off?" She stood close to his body, and his arms took her in.

"Nope, just apologizing for rude behavior."

"And you, sir, didn't tell me Claude was a woman."

"Did that matter?"

"Did that matter?" Lily mimicked her husband. "War zone, you, and a beautiful French woman? You bet it mattered."

"That was before you."

She looked up at his face and couldn't read him. *Dog gone. Did they teach them the unreadable face look at agent school?*

"So, there was something between the two of you?" She saw him flinch. *Really? There really was?*

"Friendship. That's all. She had a boyfriend. She may still have that same boyfriend. I don't know. We didn't keep in touch, besides, she was one of the guys back then."

Lily laughed a little too loud and had several tourists look in her direction. "Sorry. I want to see the painting and then can we go and get some lunch?"

"I know just the place. We can have lunch, fantastic desserts and the best hot chocolate in the world. Besides, you're going to love the look of the place, belle epoque, just like the set of that musical *Gigi*. It was good enough for Coco Chanel and Audrey Hepburn. Apparently, they used to go there."

She pulled Dev down to kiss him on the cheek.

"You always know the best places."

They said their hellos and goodbyes to "Lisa" and headed toward the exit. "Oh, wait, I have to pick up my bags."

Dev eyed her suspiciously as she went to the desk and retrieved four large shopping bags.

"You convinced the man to take you shopping?"

She raised the bags proudly in the air. "Shopping is an international sport, and I play it very well. Used my new credit card too."

Dev followed behind as she walked proudly out the private museum exit. "Would that be my credit card?'

"Ours, honey. Is this place close? I'd like to drop the bags off at the hotel."

He caught up to her and grabbed two of the items. "Yes, hotel first and then Angelina's is just down off the Champs Élysées." He glanced at her face. She was glowing; shopping was a good look on her.

"Oh, can we ride the carousel? Not now, but maybe tomorrow?" Lily's smile was as wide as her frown had been when she had encountered Claude.

"Yes, honey. We can do everything and anything you want."

"No on the ferris wheel. Those make me lose my food." She kept walking quickly toward the hotel's large ornate doors.

"Yes, dear. No on the ferris wheel, yes on the carousel. Got it."

Chapter Twenty-One

*T*he sun was rising when Lily felt cold. Dev's usual body heat was enough to warm her. She reached over and felt cool sheets; she turned over and saw an empty pillow. She sat straight up and saw his figure sitting by the window.

"Dev? Everything alright?"

He turned and flashed his trademark smile. "Honestly, I don't know. My mom used to say some weird feelings were like someone walking over your grave. I'm finding that feeling resonates here in Paris. The shadows bother me."

Lily reached out to entice him back to bed. He slowly walked over and sat on the side of the bed, holding her hand. "Is that why you were acting so unusual last night when we walked back from dinner?"

She could tell he was surprised she'd noticed. "Yes. Some intel Claude showed me yesterday bothered me and, honestly, well I should come clean, we are being followed."

Lily should be concerned, but as Abby had said a few times, danger was becoming her constant companion. At least he'd finally told her the truth. "So what do we need to do?"

Dev grinned. "We don't need to do anything. I need to make some calls. You're still going with Claude today and I can get some things straightened out. She's going to make sure you have security so I don't have to worry. I need to reach out to an agent I know. Tonight, we're having dinner with her. She's bringing one of her benefactors."

"A double date in Paris? I never thought of that one," she quipped. "Do I have to go with her today? I don't think she likes me."

"What's not to like? You charm everyone you meet, well at least the little guy yesterday, and what about the bartender downstairs? What was his name?"

"You know perfectly well it was Louis. He said I was cute."

"Right, cute. I remember Louis. He said he was originally from Chartres."

"He is very nice, but I'm not so sure about Claude."

"She's just guarded."

Lily frowned. "She's French, I mean she is the definition of a French woman. You go to the dictionary and her photo is there. She's skinny, wears heels Gretchen would kill for, she dresses like she took the outfit off a Chanel model, and she has that Bardot pout down to a science."

Dev could see all his wife's insecurities rising to the top

of her discomfort meter. "The pout is overrated. Give me cute and frizzy anyday." He brushed his hand through her soft curls.

"You are a dork. No one knows it do they?"

He laughed. "A few people, and now you do. Have fun with Claude today. She will pay for any outfit that works so have a good time. It will be your Cinderella day."

"I already had that day a few months ago." She kissed him lightly on the cheek. "Are you coming back to bed?"

"Nope. I'm going for a run." He pulled away from her and headed off to change.

"You're a dork and a crazy person. I will never understand going for a run in Paris, on your honeymoon." Her muttering continued as she returned to her pillow. She fell quickly back to sleep to dream of freshly baked croissants, not skinny French women.

While his wife slept, Dev ran to the small garden of the Grand Palais. Claude was waiting. She looked every bit the spy with a black trench coat cinched tightly around her slender waist. She was wearing a headscarf and high heeled black leather boots. Lily was right, she did look like the definition of a French woman. She was only missing a long cigarette holder.

"Well, are we still on for tonight?" He sat beside her on the bench.

"Yes. It should be interesting. You are sure they have never met?"

"As far as I know. She's not certain about today with you. Lily is very secure when it comes to her business, but her self confidence could use a bolster. Please."

Claude was suspicious as she eyed him closely. "You really love her beyond reason, don't you? I never thought that you would be felled by a normal girl."

Dev shot a cold glance at his friend. "Don't underestimate her. The day I did I realized I'd made a huge mistake. And there's nothing normal about her."

Claude giggled.

"I didn't mean it that way. She's special; she's amazing. Please play nice. I know you can."

Her pout appeared. "I always play nice."

"That depends on your definition of nice. Your skills in hand-to-hand combat are nice to watch, not so nice to receive."

She nodded. That had been a few years now. She was older, slower, but she could still hold her own. "I will play nice with your little wifey. Oh, and you have complete access to my office today. Henri, my assistant, will meet you there as will Remy."

"You'll drop Lily off at the hotel when you both are finished?"

"*Mais oui.*"

Dev stood up. "You know I told you I thought I saw him the other day on the plane? Last night, I was sure I saw him following us. We had dinner at that restaurant you recommended, and as we were walking back to the hotel, I saw him. My eyes were not deceiving me. I thought he was dead."

"No terrorist is ever dead unless you do the job yourself. Look at all the rumors about Bin Laden."

"Then I need to add a job to my bucket list. I won't live my life looking over my shoulder. I'll talk to Remy about Khalid, and I need to get in touch with an FBI agent over here."

Claude joined him and patted his arm. "My dear, the past is always behind us. You have now said Khalid's name, and so he is real and most definitely alive. I have a feeling the agent you need is seeking you. He will be at the museum around noon. He and I have been in contact. I will pick up Lily after breakfast. *Au revoir*. Oh, you will be able to see the tulip. It has just arrived. If Khalid is following you, then he knows about the tulip. I hope he takes the bait. If not all of this will have been for nothing."

"But, at the very least, you'll have a beloved artifact on display for all to see, and you will have saved it from destruction."

Claude shrugged. "To save an artifact, I tire from whom I must work with and what I must do. I can not do it alone anymore."

Dev grimaced. Claude's admission was surprising. Who else was working in this endeavor? He didn't like being out of the loop, but this wasn't his operation. So the FBI agent was here. That figured. Maybe he was working with her. "By the way, have you arranged the security for Lily?"

"*Oui*. She will meet him today. He is very good."

"I'm trusting you with the woman I love," Dev stated plainly.

Claude shook her head. "Oh my, you are besotted. I would never have believed it would ever happen to you, my friend."

Dev swore Claude walked into a fabricated fog, the mist of a 1960's spy flick with all it's dark danger and uttered cryptic messages. Though he did know what she was talking about. She disappeared across the gardens. *Where was that fog machine?*

Lily was on her second cup of coffee in the lobby of the hotel by the time Claude arrived. Her heels were high, her clothes were chic and her face was void of any emotion. On the other hand, the simple girl from the Midwest was hyped on caffeine with a side of nervous energy.

"You just missed Dev. He's working in your office today? Wow, it's lovely outside. How do you walk in those heels? They are amazing, but I'd fall over in them. Do you ever get stuck in street grates? My mother did once. Did you grow up in Paris? It is so amazing."

Claude lowered her sunglasses to the tip of her nose to peer at Lily. "Yes, yes, very well, sorry, no, really, yes, and I suppose so. You say amazing quite a bit."

Lily tried to stand up a little straighter. *Shoulders back, Lily. Pretend you are Gretchen, the irritating Gretchen. You can do this, Lily. Take this one for the team and for Dev.* "Yes, when I'm on my honeymoon in Paris I suppose I do say amazing quite a bit, because it is."

"The taxi is waiting." Claude turned and walked right back out the door. Lily followed quickly looking more like Quasimodo behind Esmeralda. Dev was going to owe her, but it was an opportunity to drive through the city with a Parisian.

But the Parisian didn't talk. Claude looked down at her phone the entire time, texting a little now and then, but Lily enjoyed the ride. Eventually the taxi stopped, and the women retreated into their first shopping venue. They proceeded up one floor.

"I love the clothing here. They use the best fabrics. We should be able to find you something." Claude looked her up and down. Then she frowned. *Crud. Could she be more disdainful? She was Dev's friend? How could he? Of course, war did things to people. It must've made him lose all perspective.*

Claude began to search through the racks of dresses. Lily was right behind her, touching this fabric and amazed at the dazzle on some of the gowns.

"I usually only wear black. I'm a florist, so it's great to wear something that won't show the dirt."

"Hmm." Claude continued to search through the dresses. She was listening to Lily, but concentrating on her mission. As soon as she completed this task, she could return to her office and meet up with the men. She was worried about Devlin Pierce. She knew he was suspicious, way too suspicious. He never was one for just believing what he was told. She understood his professional persona, but she was having a hard time understanding his personal preferences, such as what did Devlin see in his wife? Lily was nothing spectacular; she was a normal American woman complete with self-doubts, plain hair, and ample hips. *What did Lily just say?*

"I have a nice dress with me that I'm sure would work," she suggested. Claude hadn't acknowledged anything she was saying. The woman wasn't exactly rude, but there was no way they were going to be besties. Lily smiled. She could use Gretchen right now; she might devour Claude in one bite!

Claude pulled one deep green dress off the rack, lifting

it to Lily's body. She shook her head negatively. "No, this will not work. The color is good, but the cut on your body will not do."

Lily was already finished with this girlfriends-go-shopping episode, and it had been less than an hour into the adventure. "I said I had a dress."

Claude made a noise similar to a Gretchen cluck. "It won't be good enough," she answered blandly. "This is a benefactor's gala and we are introducing a piece of pottery from the Ottoman Empire. Your American clothing will not do."

"Wow, you don't sugarcoat it, do you?" Lily's exasperation sounded like annoyance, and she was fine with that. "Next, you'll be telling me you can't find my size."

The French woman was feeling a fabric. "It will be difficult."

Lily threw up her hands. She'd dealt with difficult women in her life, but this one was the abject epitome of a stereotypical European snob.

"That's it. I'm done. I won't stay here and be treated like the ugly stepsister. I can do nicely on my own. Goodbye." Lily turned to the chair where she'd placed her purse. She grabbed it and turned to leave.

Claude grimaced. Dev would not be pleased if his little wife dissolved into tears. "No, no *cherie*. I meant no disrespect. Please sit. I don't want you to cry."

Lily turned and sat down. She crossed her arms, a barrier against this snob. "I'm not crying. No tears here."

Lily knew enough French to hail a taxi and get back to the hotel, at least she hoped she did. Wait, there was the man at the door downstairs. He could get her a ride. She had a plan of escape. She'd explain to Dev that Mata Hari would never be her friend. He'd understand, afterall, he was the one working on their honeymoon. The cards were all stacked in her favor.

"Lily, Americans are larger," Claude said as she sat across from her in the other chair. "Your lifestyle is different. Please, take no offense. We walk every day, you go to the gym. We purchase our food daily, you stock up at the grocery or, oh yes, Walmart. We have slender builds, you are perhaps from Germanic heritage so you have hips, curves. Our designers are being pushed to produce fashions for plus sizes. They've been ridiculed and shamed for their adolescent starving models who are less than a size zero. An American size ten is a large woman here in Paris."

Lily's head dropped in shame. She looked up to see a softening of the French face. *Was there a faint smile or did she just have something in her mouth? Probably not. The woman didn't look like she ever ate.*

"Are you kidding me? I'm doomed. Just when I'm beginning to feel pretty good about myself, you tell me I can be a plus size model. I can't do this. Dev can go to the gala, and I'll stay at the hotel and stare at the Eiffel Tower. I'm very fond of doing that." She suddenly rose from the chair.

Claude stood too, but reached out for Lily's hands to hold in her own. She could hear the pain in the woman's voice, not knowing if it truly was about weight or the uncomfortable predicament Dev and she had placed her in by default. "You are going with your husband. We are leaving, and we will find a little café with plenty of wine, maybe a bottle of champagne. Shopping is always better after I've had champagne."

She laced her arm within Lily's and steered them in the direction of the door. Lily heard names muttered--Michael Kors, Christian Siriano, Lagerfeld, vintage Chanel--as Claude hailed a taxi.

In less than thirty minutes, Lily was living another dream. She was sitting at a café on a stone street within yards of the Cathedral of Notre-Dame, staring at the fountain of Saint Michael. She sipped from her glass of champagne as tourists walked by. Claude looked over her menu to study Mrs. Pierce.

Lily was cute, unassuming, but dear. She wasn't who she suspected Devlin would bring around, but she did look like a wife. Lily could never be a mistress! Claude laughed slightly at that thought. The new Mrs. Pierce was an individual with common sense and a sense of morality, integrity and intelligence. Lily could possibly be your best friend or your worst enemy if she felt threatened. Dev had recounted the apprehension of Garrett Notte. His wife was a brave woman and very determined when she had to be. Besides, Claude needed to keep Dev happy. As long as he was happy and occupied, he wouldn't ask questions or get involved. She couldn't afford him to get too close if she were to succeed in her project.

Claude placed her menu down and waved to the server. "Lily, I'll order us a little cheese and bread. Tonight's dinner will be magnificent so we just need a little before we find you that dress."

The server placed fresh baked bread, butter, and olives in front of them. The women were face to face again, but this time there was bread. The aroma just made Lily's heart a little lighter. As she took her first bite, the world changed. The colors were brighter, Notre-Dame was larger, the sky was bluer, and Claude no longer appeared as a foe to her. She could hear the water in the fountain, and she could hear angels were singing. There was hot bread, and then there was hot bread in Paris with its crust with just enough butter, flaky, with dough that was as soft as feathers.

"Lily, what was the first thing you liked about Devlin?" Claude picked through the olives to find the perfect one.

Lily was relishing her bread, slowly chewing and not answering. Finally, she swallowed.

"His eyes. They twinkle."

Claude's brow furrowed. "Really? I never noticed that."

Lily took a drink of courage. *How could champagne be life changing?* It was here in Paris at a café on a stone street.

"I have to ask, did you and Dev ever, well you know."

Claude literally spit out her champagne in a very unladylike, un-French like manner. "*Mon Dieu*, no. We were not like that, and we never made love."

Lily choked on her next bite of bread. She just wanted to know, well she did want to know that, but she hadn't expected such bluntness.

"Oh, you weren't asking about being lovers? Sorry. No, nothing like that, nothing ever romantic. We were both doing our jobs, and I was perhaps the annoying little sister who kept bothering the Americans. They weren't concerned about my items. They were, but they weren't. They protected what they could, but it was war. There was a famous photo of a tank outside the museum in Baghdad. So much was taken, looted, and still is."

Her thoughts were carrying her away to many years

ago. "Look at what ISIS has done to Palmyra. The Mosul Museum was pilfered, and those bad agents have been selling iniquities on the black market for many years. That's how they fund their operations. So many artifacts from Apamea, especially Roman mosaics have been removed. I could go on for days, perhaps years explaining my disgust. Actually, I've been yelling for years. It's sad, but to save many things that are priceless, you must deal with unsavory people and pay the price."

Lily could hear her passion. "I understand. I can't imagine what that's like to see history leveled into rubble. I would cry."

Claude nodded. "Lily, I have. When you see a site and it is just sand and dirt and you know that Romans walked in that city, I become physically ill. I also wonder if I'm doing the right thing when sometimes I have to do the wrong thing."

Lily set her glass on the table and reached for a piece of cheese. Claude had completely relaxed and sat back in her chair. There was more to Claude, Lily speculated. She'd have to ask Dev a few questions, but there was so much more than her French stone facade. She did have a heart, just like Paris.

Claude returned her attention to the plate in front of them. "Lily, this is your blue cheese, and this is epoisses de Bourgogne, comte, reblochon." She pointed at each delectable item. Her hand halted. "I didn't think. You aren't pregnant, are you? If you are, I'm not sure you can eat any of these. We would have to ask if they are pasteurized."

Lily gulped. "I'm on my honeymoon."

Claude laughed. "It only takes once, Lily."

"Well, let's say I'm not, so hand over the cheese, woman."

Claude laughed again, this time full throated and genuine. "I now see why he loves you."

"Good for you. I'm still trying to figure that one out. How about you, Claude? Anyone special?"

Her smile faded instantly. "Once. He was a very nice boy. An American."

"Details."

"Well, he was part of Dev's group. He was smart and knew art even though he was from a very small town somewhere in your middle America. He died."

Lily reached over and touched the top of Claude's outstretched hand.

"I'm so sorry."

Claude placed her other hand over Lily's. "I am too. His death affected all of us. I know the guys were changed and I, well, I left to go home soon after that. They never knew how close we were. His death was an accident, a very bad one. If the boys had known all the details it would've resulted in many more deaths than just his. By the time I heard how the Army had determined how he had died, there was no point in resurrecting the tragedy."

"I don't understand." Lily was searching Claude's eyes for an answer to the confusing information. "What had the Army done?"

One small tear floated down Claude's cheek. "The officer in charge knew that something awful had happened, but if his men had known the truth, they would've gone off and tracked down the murderer. He and I decided that would not be in the best interest of my mission, nor theirs."

"So, you both made up a lie?"

She pulled her hands away and took a quick drink. "For the better good. It seems like I'm always playing somewhere between devil and angel. It's an impossible role to play out. *Oui*, we did it to protect the rest."

Lily shut her eyes and silently prayed. *My God, how did she live everyday like this--this agony of deception?*

"Lily, we had to protect them. If we hadn't, Dev would be dead, Dan, JT, Paul, and all the others. They would've gone up in those caves after the terrorist and never returned. We had to, don't you understand?"

The woman had desperately needed someone to talk to, and Lily was it. "I do understand, but what story did you two concoct?"

Claude wiped away more tears and then threw her hair back to gain some sort of control. "We said he committed suicide."

Lily's stomach was churning. "Tom?"

The shock threw Claude back into the chair once more. "*Oui*. So, you know about him? Dev told you about him? Of course, he did. You see, you can't tell Dev."

"I can't promise that," Lily pleaded. "Besides, you need to tell him."

Claude laughed nervously. "I think I know another reason why he loves you. You are so damn honest to a fault, aren't you? And people want to talk to you; spill their guts out, even if it isn't wise. It was not wise for me to tell you."

"So, you know who killed Tom?"

"Yes, and I fear that man is somewhere in this city right now."

Before Lily could say another word, the server brought the check and Claude paid it. She took one final drink from her glass. "We need to find you a dress."

"Really? You want to shop now? You are almost as good at deflection as my husband."

Claude rubbed her face and planted a simple smile on her lips. "And you good lady, need a dress. Now, let's go."

The second salon they entered, Lily found three dresses to try on. She wasn't sure if the shopping was actually getting easier or if Claude and she had drank too much champagne. After the café, the first salon had insisted they treat the ladies, and now at this one the bubbly was flowing freely. The first dress was fairly low cut.

"I'm not sure I want you to see this one," Lily yelled from the changing room.

"Get out here," Claude insisted.

The low cut, pale blue gown swept over Lily's hips. The bodice of the dress was sequined with crystals and pearls, down to the waist of the dress where it formed a belt. The full soft fabric of the skirt, swirled around when Lily turned. She was holding the middle of the dress.

"Lily, remove your hand. I need to see. It is a beautiful color on you."

Lily sucked in a breath and did as she was told. She wasn't able to wear a bra under the dress. The dress was v-cut in the front and in the back. Her exposed skin formed a look Lily had never worn.

"Oh my," Claude exclaimed. "You have cleavage. Amazing."

"Very funny." Lily turned to look in the mirror. It was beautiful, but she needed way more fabric for coverage.

Claude joined her and looked at her in the mirror. "And I now know another reason why my friend loves you." Lily blushed immediately.

"Not this one. One more to go."

As Lily returned to change, Claude was agreeing to her decision. Soon she heard muffled noises. It sounded like her companion was talking to a man. Perhaps Dev had decided to track them down?

Privately, Lily was still reeling from the information Claude had shared. It would be difficult to even glance at Dev without telling him. She certainly couldn't keep it from the rest of the guys when she saw them in just a few weeks at the Army-Navy football party. That one incident had changed their lives forever. Claude needed to tell Dev, and he needed to tell the others. That was the only answer. It was the right thing to do.

She checked herself in the mirror and smiled. It was a beautiful dress, something she would never have selected, but Claude did know best. It was almost as perfect as her wedding gown. Deep green in color, the dress floated away from her hips. The front was slightly low cut; something she would feel comfortable wearing. "This may be the one, Claude."

She marched out, still smiling at her success. A man had joined Claude on the small settee. Obviously, he wasn't from around here, his features reminding Lily of a younger version of the actor Omar Sharif. He was extremely tan, clothed in a perfectly tailored shirt and suit. Lily wasn't that versed on clothiers, but she suspected he was wearing an expensive suit from Armani or Versace. He was extremely good looking, dangerous and obviously made of money or pretending he was.

His smile reminded her of a cat plotting the demise of a baby mouse. Lily gulped. *Squeak, squeak.* Claude was relaxed next to him; Lily felt uncomfortable. *What was that phrase, someone was walking on your grave?*

"That's very nice," Claude said as she applauded. "This is Lily, Dev's wife, and this is Ari."

Lily nodded and then turned to face the mirror to examine the dress. It was stunning and probably cost more money than her last month's worth of weddings. She saw the man rise from his seat and stand behind her.

"She'll need drop earrings that will fall right here on her neck." He touched her. Lily tried not to jump, but her insides were yelling, *Danger, Danger* from an old television show. *What would Jessica Fletcher do now?* Lily moved over two steps; he followed, smiling.

"And, she'll need a lovely necklace, perhaps a choker." He moved to touch her back. Lily turned quickly.

"If you don't mind, keep your hands to yourself." His eyes bore a hole through to her soul. There was no twinkling there. Dev could make her melt; this man made her smoulder. Fire was in those eyes, the destruction of your very soul. If you let him. If Gretchen sounded like the devil at times, this man was his human form.

"I'm so sorry, I didn't mean to intrude. I was just trying to help." His speech pattern was deliberate and in perfect English.

"And I want your help, why?" Lily in control had returned.

"Because, I'm here to protect you."

"I'm sure you could do that, but does my husband know?"

His smile became genuine. "Not yet, dear lady." He turned to Claude. "You're right. I would never have picked her for Devlin, but she's absolutely perfect. I'm sure he'll have his hands full with this one."

Lily curved her body to look around him at her companion. "Claude, this dress?"

"I think it is lovely, Lily. It's perfect. That color of green is quite beautiful with your perfect complexion. We just need some shoes, and jewelry would be a good idea. Ari is right."

"I usually am," he muttered. He straightened his shirt from beneath the sleeves of his jacket.

Lily moved a little closer. "Really? I do find that difficult to believe."

He looked up, throwing his head back in laughter. "Lily, I think we will become good friends."

"Must we?" She didn't wait for his answer as she left to remove the dress. Once in the changing room, she slowly assessed the entire day. Rude French woman, nice French woman. Massive secret and regret, trying on dresses depressing, finding a beautiful one and being excited. Need protection from what and why is he doing it? I'm supposed to be on my honeymoon! Keep breathing, Lily, that's all you can do right now.

By the time she returned to the salon, Claude had arranged for the dress to be delivered to the hotel, along with a matching wrap and three pairs of shoes Lily could try on. She'd also selected a cocktail dress for this evening. The salon would pick up everything the day after the gala, but not this dress. Lily might not want to wear it, it's cleavage not as low as the gown she had tried on, but just low enough to make her husband very happy. Claude hoped her new friend would wear it, and she could take it home as a souvenir from Paris. The dress had sheer sleeves with the low cut in the back as well. It was a perfect shade of blue. She remembered it was Dev's favorite color. It was ironic what you remembered about a person, Claude thought. She still had memories of watching her friends play volleyball in their compound. Dev always wore this one light blue tee when he played.

"Now, where?" Lily asked as they came out onto the street.

"This way, ladies." Ari was directing them to a very impressive limousine. Lily followed Claude, but she didn't feel good about doing it. As they rode along, Lily was searching for landmarks just in case she needed to make a run for it and dive out of the moving vehicle. If she was going to be living in a movie set she might as well do all her own stunts.

They stopped in front of a very well known jewelry store. Ari and Claude left the car, but Lily remained.

"Come on, Lily. We're going to get you some jewelry to borrow."

Ari extended a hand to help her out. "I won't bite."

"I'm not sure about that."

"Trust me. I won't let anything happen to you."

She looked into those piercing eyes and didn't miss a beat. "Really? The last man that said that to me, lied and then I married him."

He tucked her arm into his. Claude was on his left side. "Well, you will just have to trust me. Besides, apparently that worked very well for you? *Oui?*"

"*Oui.*"

In a matter of minutes, Ari was selecting the perfect necklace and earrings and Claude was agreeing. Lily was content to look around the store at all the beauties. There were no price tags, but every one of the pieces were out of her budget, for the rest of her life.

Ari was talking to the manager as Lily pulled Claude to a far corner of the store. "He's here to protect me? Is Dev fine with this? And why should I trust him, or you?"

Claude smiled. *Lily isn't just normal. She is a force of nature! How did she get me to open up, to tell a secret I've held for so long? Was it her smile? Was it the way she looked softly on me without judging my confession?*

Claude could tell Lily was frightened, but the new Mrs. Pierce seemed to be planning her escape if necessary. She'd noticed Lily counting blocks as they drove to the store. "This all may be a bit overwhelming, but we mean you no harm. Dev will be fine with this, eventually."

"Eventually?" This wasn't going to end well. Lily's whispers were becoming audible to another customer. "He doesn't know about Ari? What else doesn't he know?"

"Ladies, we are ready to go," Ari said as he handed a small bag to Lily. "Make sure you place this in your hotel safe, please. I've signed for the items, and I don't mind paying for them if I have to, but why should I when another man receives your attention?"

He winked as he asked the question. Lily gulped. *Was Ari beginning to sound like a British super agent?* Maybe she was dreaming. If she'd eaten too late at night, she'd have dreams like this. Usually they involved a secret agent, a motorcycle, and a wild ride through the streets of Paris with Tom Cruise. No more champagne for lunch.

After a short drive back to the Louvre, Claude announced that Ari would return her to the hotel, and she would see her again at dinner later that night. Lily protested as Claude waved goodbye. Ari smiled like a cat sated from a bowl of milk and not the skim kind.

"So you are a little flower girl?"

Lily's eyes narrowed. "If you mean I own my own flower shop, then yes, *une fleuriste*." He might be attractive, drop-dead gorgeous, but he was rude.

"*Pardon moi*, Lily. Does Devlin Pierce really know what he has gotten himself into with you?" He laughed out loud. Lily did not.

"I hope he knows. By the way, how do you know him? If you are going to protect me, I'd like to know a little more about you."

"I knew him in Iraq, Saudi Arabia, Afghanistan and a few other 'Stans', Jordan, Egypt, Syria, oh and I can't forget Israel. He and I had a good night in Cairo once." He paused as though he was recalling the excitement. "There was also a night in Tel Aviv that was quite memorable."

"I'm doubting you were in our Army or Navy."

"What gave it away? My looks, my charm, or my accent?"

Lily searched his eyes. *Lord, they twinkled too.* "Your lack of boundaries, especially personal space. Your condescending nature, even though you may not be trying to be rude. Oh, and I think you act quite a bit. A soldier wouldn't be so glib about the danger he has been in, well at least the soldiers I know."

Why was she taunting him? What was she thinking? She was thinking she could walk to the hotel from here very easily.

"Touché," Ari said softly. "I wasn't trying to be rude, or to invade your personal space. I do pretend quite a bit in my line of work, and I'm glib because I have given all my tears to God for safe-keeping for all the men and women who have been destroyed in the years of hate."

Lily saw a spark of humanity. "You were a soldier."

"Everyone in Israel serves. It is our duty and our honor."

"You're an Israeli?"

His head bobbed back and forth. "Yes and no. I have a diverse pedigree that allows me to move freely between many worlds. I met your husband on one such occasion. He arrested me, after he tried to kill me."

Lily gulped. "That's not like Dev to miss."

He laughed loudly once more. "No, you are right. I didn't say I wasn't injured. He doesn't miss. He wanted intel so he just shot me in the shoulder. He is a good shot."

Lily was dreading the day Dev took her to the shooting range, but that day would come. He had guaranteed it. She had to at least know how to shoot a gun for her own safety.

But she had her own bodyguard sitting across from her in the limousine. *Oh thank God. They had arrived at the hotel.*

She tried to dismiss him, but he insisted he would go up to the room with her. Apparently, he wanted to wait for Dev. "I really don't think this is a good idea," Lily explained as they stepped onto the elevator.

As Lily hit the button for her floor, Ari watched her carefully. He knew what she was thinking. "I'm not going to hurt or ravage you. I promise. I am only here with you to protect you, to keep you safe. I just need to explain to your husband why I was chosen to do the job."

"Good luck with that," Lily muttered.

"You don't believe I can soothe his beastly heart?"

Lily turned to face him. Even though he was distant, he was softer than Claude, much easier to read. Surprisingly, she did trust him.

"Perhaps you can convince him with all your fancy words," Lily admitted as they departed the lift.

Ari followed behind her to the suite. "Words have never really worked on your husband. Actions, perhaps, but he isn't very patient or understanding."

As they entered the sitting room, Lily headed toward her favorite window seat. She kicked off her shoes, removed her coat, and laid her bag on the side table.

"I've found Dev to be one of the most patient and understanding men I have ever met." *He had to be. The poor man had understood her even when she didn't understand herself. As far as patience, God bless Dev Pierce. He waited for her.*

Lily sat in her window seat; Ari sat on the small sofa with his arms extended on the back. His body filled the entire space. He'd unbuttoned his jacket and seemed more casual. He didn't look like a wolf now. A few minutes later someone was at the door. Ari opened it, retrieving the dress for tonight.

"Claude wanted you to have this dress for tonight. You are to keep it. It doesn't go back to the salon."

"What?"

Ari handed it to her. "Yes, she was quite taken with you today."

Lily removed the outer wrap and saw the gift. "Oh my. I can't take this kind of a gift. It's too much."

"Nothing is too much in the city of light, Lily, nothing."

Lily tried to keep herself busy. She hung up the dress. She found shoes that would go with it. She moved her purse, until finally, Ari requested, almost demanded her to sit down across from him.

"Now, how did you and Devlin Pierce meet?"

"He just walked into my life one day," Lily answered blandly without emotion. She was back on guard. She wanted to like him; supposedly he was safe, but she knew he oozed danger. He'd be the double-agent in her Tom Cruise movie!

"No doubt he was doing something dangerous or looking for someone nefarious." His words were again precise with a distinct English tone. She'd noticed his French spoken earlier was that of a native.

"Something like that," Lily answered evasively, "and what about that arrest with you?"

"He had me, and I was the wrong guy. He actually wanted one of my relatives, Khalid. We look similar, but my nose is more French, more German."

"My, you really do have an unusual pedigree. In America, we call someone a mongrel, or a mutt. I don't mean any disrespect." *Maybe I can get a rise out of him with that rude comment.*

Ari smiled. "None is taken. No you are right. I am not pure. My maternal grandparents lived right here in Paris. In fact, I purchased their home a few years ago. My mother was born here. I'm French and German. Then on the other side, my father's family is mostly from Saudi Arabia with a long pedigree with alliances and marriages to the royal family. I grew up in France, Israel, and Jordan. There were a few visits to Saudi Arabia, but they were very few."

He had been smiling, but now his face was drawn. Lily saw a softening. She saw the little boy, and the man who was attempting with all his might to forget some awful days.

"Would you like a glass of something? I know we have water or wine, or we could order something?"

The smile returned to his face. "Water, wine, anything would be fine."

Lily walked to the wet bar area of the suite and found a chilled bottle of white wine. "We have wine. Woo hoo."

She heard his chuckle. She poured two glasses and walked back to the man. As she handed him his glass, their hands touched slightly. He pulled back quickly, probably out of habit? But he had touched her neck, her shoulder.

"You know, everyone has a bad relative or two," Lily commented as she took a drink. His laughter filled the room.

"We had Nazis years ago, and now I have an entire tribe! And they're terrorists."

"Bummer, and I bet you don't even celebrate the holidays together." She was laughing before she finished the sentence, and then she snorted. Her hand went quickly to cover her mouth.

"Did you just snort?" Ari was bent over in laughter as Lily tried to compose herself. And that's when Devlin Pierce entered the hotel suite, with gun in hand. He had it pointed at Lily's guest.

"Hi honey." Lily saluted her husband with her glass held high.

He shut the door slowly, the gun still had Ari as its target. "Claude said she was sending someone, but you? I just knew you were in Paris. I was trying to find you today."

Ari nodded and took a slow drink of wine. "And so I am here. You have found me. We've been having such a good time. Your wife is delightful. Now put that gun down, and let's talk about the good times."

"I don't remember too many of those, but I do remember we always had our hands full whenever you were involved. Here you are in Paris, and I have a feeling you have partnered up with another agent. I haven't figured it out yet, but so help me, I will. You better be working with the good guys this time." Dev holstered his gun under his jacket. He walked slowly to the table to pour himself a drink. He found the bourbon. Claude picked Ari, of all people, to protect Lily. *Really, Claude? Had the woman been hit by an old piece of pottery and damaged her brain?*

"You'll have your hands full with this one," Ari said as he pointed toward Lily. He ignored Dev's rant completely.

"She is very surprising. I'm not sure you understand yet what a rare jewel you have."

"I understand that Claude chose you to look after my wife," Dev began as he sat in the other chair near Lily, "but you have to understand, I didn't sign off on it. My wife, and anything about her is out of bounds, got it?" Ari hadn't acknowledged his suspicions, nor denied his concerns.

Ari saluted him. "Yes, Major, I understand. *Oui, je comprends, ja.*"

"Show off," Lily muttered. She had her glass held up to her mouth. Ari winked at her. He'd heard. Strangely, she thought she might be some volleyball in-between two of the best players in the world. She knew for sure she was in the middle of two very strong men, and it seemed like her husband had issued an ultimatum to the other to keep his hands off of her. She giggled at that thought. *Wow, if her high school classmates could see her now, what would they say?* At least she would've had a date for the prom.

Ari drank the rest of his wine and placed it on the small table in front of them. "It was so nice to meet you, Lily. So nice to see you again, Devlin. It was wonderful catching up. I'll be seeing you." He headed quickly to the door and then looked back. "And Lily, if you need me, all you have to do is whistle. You do know how to whistle, don't you?"

Dev rolled his eyes. "Really? That old line from *Casablanca?*"

But his wife was enjoying every word of it. She pursed her lips and let out a small noise. Dev turned his head to offer a displeased look, almost a reprimanding gaze.

"Ah, but it still works, my friend. *Au revoir*, Lily." He swept out like a wave.

"I like him."

"Honey, we don't like men like him." He gathered her hands in his. "We stay away from men like that."

Her brow rose. "If that were the case, we wouldn't be married."

Dev hung his head down in defeat. "*Touché.*"

Chapter Twenty-Two

1. Stand up straight, sit up straight
2. If you don't, the dress will gape open
3. Calm down, it's only a dinner
4. Wear this dress, only on special occasions

"Lily, you can do this." If she kept saying it out loud, wouldn't it come true? Lily was still looking at herself in the mirror. The woman before her was much different than the one she knew six months ago. But she was still faking the confidence. She took a deep breath before she walked into the suite's seating area where Dev was waiting.

"We should be on time if we leave now," he commented as he looked up from his watch. Time stopped suddenly, without one word spoken.

"Wow." He was literally staring at her with his mouth open.

"Wow good or wow bad?" Lily tugged at the left side of her dress. One breast showed more than the other. *I never knew I was lopsided.*

Dev stood up slowly as he examined her from bottom to top. He wasn't sure what he was seeing. There was a metamorphosis of the woman he loved into another woman he loved. *Did that make sense?* Lily was Lily, but this Lily was--he had no words.

"Wow, just wow, good, very good," he stammered. He was speechless. On her wedding day, his wife had transformed into a beautiful bride; the Lily before him was sophisticated, ready for a night out in Paris.

Lily's eyes narrowed. His eyes were roaming every curve on her body, and he began to remind her of Ari. *That's scary.*

"You are still just a guy under all that, oh Lily, it doesn't matter what you weigh or what you look like, aren't you? We need to go." She grabbed her purse and coat and headed for the door.

He caught her wrist gently and pulled her toward him. "You're wearing my favorite color."

She looked up into twinkling eyes. "I know, well actually, Claude knew. I'm not sure how she knew, but I'm sure that's some secret between the two of you."

Dev wrapped his arms around his wife. "It's not really a secret. My friends all know. I had a couple awful light blue tee shirts that had different Virginia phrases on them. Ask Dan. He'd tell you. I guess I never expressed to my wife what my favorite color is. I know right now, I would very much like to express my love to my wife and forget about going to dinner."

Lily gently tapped him with her purse. "Wake up. We need to go. It's just some makeup, nice shoes and a dress, well it is an amazing dress that I would never wear. But it is still me under all of this stuff. It's all just window dressing."

"Then let's stay here and get that all off." He reached for

the back of her dress. "And I don't know what fragrance that is, but I love it."

"It is called soap. Now stop it." He began to nuzzle her neck. "Stop it for now, Dev. We need to go."

His head pulled up quickly. "Ah, for now?"

"Come on, we're on our honeymoon. I told you I was a sure thing. Let's go." Lily literally shoved him out into the hallway.

He smiled down at her in the elevator. His view of her made him forget any intrigue, any secrets.

Lily could feel him admiring her bustline. "Dev, if you don't stop it, there will not be a later."

"Yes, ma'am. Wow, you just sounded like a wife."

She smiled. She tugged at the bodice of her dress again and buttoned her coat before they left in the taxi. It was certainly satisfying to surprise her husband. She'd have to make a note to continue to do that in the future. Her surprises were much easier to take than his. At least they were enjoying themselves, and he wasn't using her as bait to catch the bad guy.

They arrived at the restaurant before Claude and her benefactor. Dev continued to nuzzle her neck romantically while she was looking over the very large menu in her hands. She playfully slapped him with it.

"Honey, I love it when you do that, but not right now, not here. Now, help me with the menu. My French is a little rusty and I don't want to end up eating swordfish."

Lily looked up briefly toward the door and saw Claude. The skinny French woman was actually smiling and waving at her. That was an improvement, Lily thought. She smiled back until she saw the man standing next to her new friend.

She didn't have to worry about her gaping bodice or her lovestruck husband; Lily was stiff as a board. Dev noticed the change and placed his arm around her. "Honey, what's wrong?"

"Claude is with Bernard Notte."

"Shit," Dev muttered. "You two haven't met, have you?"

"Yes," she faintly answered. "We met last Christmas. Abs and I took over a plant to Mrs. Notte. I told Tom. I told Tom. The FBI knew." Her eyes told Dev everything he needed to know. He'd placed his wife in danger, again, unwittingly, but again. She was petrified.

"We didn't know. Just play this out tonight. Follow his lead and ours. It'll be alright." His voice was soothing, bringing her back to this time and place and not one in the past. His arm was strongly around her shoulders now for support. Lily took in a deep breath and placed her shaking hands on her lap.

"You are in so much trouble, husband," she muttered through clenched teeth.

"Seems like I've been in trouble since we landed." Dev smiled at the couple coming toward them.

"*Bonsoir*, Lily and Dev." Claude was all smiles as she greeted Lily with the traditional kisses. "May I present a benefactor of the museum, Bernard Notte."

Lily and Dev nodded as the couple sat down across from them. *Just follow their lead, Lily. Don't do anything stupid. Where was Ari when she needed him? He was supposed to be her guardian angel. Maybe he was a dark angel instead?*

Bernard Notte shook Dev's hand and nodded briefly at Lily. She knew what he was thinking. It was similar to what she was thinking. *What the hell are you doing here?*

"And your last name, Dev?"

"Pierce, it is very nice to meet you."

Bernard's confusion quickly set in. He looked at Lily. She was that florist. She helped with the arrest of his son. Now, this man was saying his last name was Pierce. He wasn't the man Notte had met in the shadows, planning the acquisition of the tulip bowl. *What the hell was going on? Was this a trap? Had Claude double-crossed him or set him up for the fall on all this criminal activity?*

The rest of the evening was filled with tentative conversation and knowing glances. Thankfully, the wine and food was good and the foursome could win an award in small talk; very small talk. Lily kept drinking through it. She was following Dev's lead. She even tried cognac when he ordered one. Drinking numbed her fear. No amount of alcohol could make him disappear. If only he would. Bernard Notte sat passively on the other side of the table seemingly evaluating his next move. This was like some sick, lengthy chess game--and you already knew who the winner would be. Why bother at all?

Lily felt like that captured mouse again. *Squeak, squeak.* Of course, why shouldn't her honeymoon be like this? Since she had met Devlin Pierce, danger was her middle name. She was currently drinking a glass of champagne and a few of the bubbles made her snort. *Lily Catherine Danger Pierce*; she snorted once more, this time in amusement. Dev reached over and held her left hand.

Lily was finishing her last bite of dessert, a very chocolatey one, when Notte finally asked something of substance.

"Dev, you look somewhat familiar to me. I've been acquiring artifacts for various museums. Perhaps you have been involved in art, maybe that's when I met you?"

Dev swirled the cognac in his glass, his eyes watching the liquid's movement. *So, it was time to play.* "No, I'm actually involved in drugs."

Claude spit out the wine she had just placed in her mouth. She quickly brought her napkin up. "Pardon." Lily was feeling superior right now. She smiled across the table at her newly minted French friend. Squeak, squeak said the little mouse, and the sound was probably the same in French.

Notte laughed. "Drugs? Well, legal or illegal?"

Lily heard the tone. Dev was working; Dev was now dangerous. "Both."

"That must be interesting."

"It is. I meet all sorts of people, rich, poor."

"Then, if we've never had business together, I wonder who you look like."

"It is getting late," Claude announced.

Bernard patted her hand. "No my dear, this is bothering me. Dev reminds me of one of my contacts. I wonder how that can be?"

"I remind many people of someone they've run into," Dev stated softly. "Mainly I remind them of someone they'd rather not know."

Notte laughed. "Ah, that's it. The ones you meet in shadows all look the same. I try to protect myself so I keep records on all of them."

The former drug dealer allowed the sentence to linger in the air. Notte was attempting to threaten him, but Dev knew he was going down the wrong path. So, he reminded Notte of someone. There could be only one person. He'd been trying to get in touch with that same man. *Baby brother, what are you up to now?*

Bernard Notte rose from the table. "It has been a long night. Yes, we should go. It was very nice meeting both of you." Bernard Notte's eyes focused on Lily as he held his hand out to Dev. "Mr. Pierce, perhaps we will meet again."

"That is highly unlikely," Dev answered. "If we do meet again, I'm sure it will be my pleasure."

Lily watched one metaphorical glove thrown and then the other. She blinked; Notte was still there. She didn't realize she had been holding her breath until he turned with Claude and was placing the coat on her shoulders.

"Well that went well, Dev. I thought you two were going to start fighting right here in the middle of the restaurant."

"Too bad we couldn't. What an egotistical ass."

"I couldn't agree with you more, honey. We need to go home."

Dev was already standing. He pulled Lily up and placed her coat around her shoulders. "Let's go."

Claude and Bernard were already on the street waiting for their car. They had moved in front of the large windows of the eatery and were having a heated discussion. Dev and Lily had just exited the establishment.

"Let's head away from them," Dev suggested. In that moment, his eyes focused on a black sedan speeding in their direction. He caught a glimpse of a gun out of the window as it turned toward Claude and her companion.

"Claude, get down!" he yelled.

He saw a face, who was all too familiar. He pulled Lily quickly under his shoulder and threw her down on the brick pavement They hit the sidewalk at the same time he saw the flash and heard the gun.

Suddenly, Lily was pushed down onto the bricks. "Stay there." He pulled his gun and began shooting. Claude had done the same. It was too late. The car was speeding away.

Lily could feel a hand on her back. She glanced to her left to see sneakers and the frayed edges of jeans. "Lily, just stay down."

The air that she had sucked in, she finally let out. Ari was there, above her, comforting her. "Lily, just stay down."

From her viewpoint, she could see him run to Claude. Dev was standing too, thank God. Bernard Notte was on the sidewalk, gasping for breath.

Dev bent down. Notte grabbed the lapel of his jacket and pulled him down. "Pierce, Ari," he gasped. "Ari knows. He was the protection. He knows the men, both of them."

The sirens were blaring as they arrived on the scene. Lily finally sat up as Dev joined her on the sidewalk. He held her in silence. Ari and Claude stood behind them. Notte was loaded quickly into an ambulance. Lily wasn't in shock; she was in disbelief. She shook her head.

"This is a fine mess you've gotten me into, husband. You are going to owe me for a very, very long time."

"I know I will. I'm sorry about all of this."

Lily put her head on his shoulder. "No you're not. You're having the time of your life." She waved her hand around in the air. "Sadly, I'm sort of getting used to all this spy stuff." She wasn't even worried about a gaping bodice anymore.

A dark car pulled up next to them. Remy, the embassy official, stood before them. "I'll take you two back to the hotel. We can get your statement to the police tomorrow. What hospital did they take him to?"

"I called in a favor with INTERPOL," Dev answered. "He is being stabilized and then sent to a hospital in England, to an American base. He is an American citizen and is wanted for questioning."

"By whose authority, Pierce?" Remy shouted. Lily's body shook. Ari quickly gathered one of her hands in his.

"Mine, maybe not on this soil, but Ari called in some favors too. Of course, you don't have much power here either, do you Remy?"

Remy's eyes squinted while looking at Dev Pierce. "We're friends. Don't act like this."

"I'm not acting like anything. I'm doing my job." Dev's cool tone sent shivers up his own wife's back.

"Then, let's get those statements tomorrow. Are you going back to your hotel?"

Lily was watching the dynamics of the situation. Why was Remy so nervous? Why did he want them to do their statements in the morning? It sounded reasonable, but Dev didn't like the idea for some reason.

"I want to do our statements tonight, to those officers

right over there." Dev pointed to the officers near Claude. "Lily saw nothing. She can return to the hotel. Ari, you didn't see anything either, did you?"

"No, I was just walking by after this all happened, whatever all of this is. Lily, let me take you back." He took Lily's hand in his.

"Mr. Pierce, I'd really like to take the two of you with me tonight," Remy stammered nervously. "Those are my orders."

"I have my own ride. We will be fine." Ari began to steer Lily away from the scene. She looked back at Dev, and he winked. He knew his wife would be safe with Ari, but did Lily know it?

"Mr. Pierce, I must," the embassy official continued.

"I must have my wife safely home, and I must give my statement to the French police, now. Thank you for understanding." He completely disregarded the government man, a man he'd known briefly many years ago. It wouldn't be the first time. Dev Pierce was all about following the rules, but there were those times when you just didn't. This was one of those times when you didn't, and you lied to succeed in protecting your wife. He needed Lily safe. Ari would provide that safety even if it meant his own death.

Dev held Claude's hand as they introduced themselves to the police on the scene. It would be a long night, but right now he didn't trust anyone but the Paris police. They didn't know what was going on either. But Dev was beginning to put together all the pieces.

It was almost two in the morning by the time Ari had convinced Lily to go to sleep, without Dev. They had sat in the hotel's bar for over an hour waiting for Dev to call or text. They drank a little coffee. He watched her glance toward the main door over and over.

Ari studied Lily. She kept her coat buttoned, her arms tight around her bodice. She had told him a little about her life before Dev. He almost yawned. But she owned her business. That was an accomplishment for anyone in today's society. His own sister was an aspiring dress designer. She wanted her own shop someday, just a little one to call her own.

"You know, I once dated a giraffe."

Lily was captivated by the hotel's massive entry doors.

"Really. That's nice."

"But sadly, I fell in love with a turtle. We were married in the Bahamas last June."

"Was the wedding pretty? Did you have flowers?" Lily turned and smiled. "I can be concerned about my husband, watch for him, and listen to your idiot stories. I have a friend back home who does the same thing." *Lord, she had just referenced Gretchen as her friend. It was official.*

"You really are fascinating, Lily Pierce. I'm not sure I've ever met anyone quite like you."

"Should I say thank you to that? I'm really unsure if it is a compliment."

Ari finished his coffee. "Oh, it is. You are extremely honest. That's a fault and a virtue, at least in these times. Dev is a lucky man. I'm not joking now."

Lily lowered her eyes. "Thank you. I may have misjudged you."

"No, you didn't. I'm exactly who you thought I was, and I'm the man you think I am right now. But tonight, I have one task, to protect you, and that's what I will do."

Ari's eyes lasered onto the front door. He saw someone.

Lily noticed his attention. "Is it Dev?"

"No, it's someone we don't want to talk to. Please, please, follow my lead. We need to get upstairs."

Quickly, they headed for the elevator doors, but the man stood waiting for them. "I was told you would be here."

"And so you have found me," Ari answered cooly. Lily stood behind him, her head down as he had instructed her.

"I was wondering what the man without a country was doing in Paris? Are you playing with the Americans now?" He peered his head around to see Lily. "Hello, American."

Lily's head shot up. She said nothing. Ari's hand had found hers and she held on for dear life. This man was not a friend. Ari could smile and melt your heart, this one would probably poison you before you took your next breath. He would kill you and never give your life another thought. This man was a terrorist.

"So, you are taking on odd jobs, protecting a businessman's wife?"

"Well, with the depressed euro, I have to do something. I hear the dollar is making a comeback. So, I work for the dollars. This is an easy job."

The man lightly tugged on Ari's lapel. "Be careful, Ari. Do not stick your nose where it does not belong. I am here in Paris for one thing. Do not stop me."

"Does it involve blowing up young men and women

while they are enjoying music? If it does, then I will stop you."

"You couldn't before. It was a shame your sister was there. I better let you get back to your little job. Goodbye, American." The man turned and walked slowly out the door.

Ari said nothing to Lily until they entered the hotel suite. "I meant to tell you earlier how lovely this room is. Dev is doing quite well on his government salary, unless he is doing something on the side."

Lily kicked off her shoes and coat. She reached for a bottle of water and sat down in one of the chairs opposite the almost reclining bodyguard.

"You know as much as I do." She wasn't going to tell him anything until she got all of this straight in her head. "Ari, what was all that about? Who was he? Is he the man who has been following Dev and me?"

"Yes, and he is the one who probably just shot Bernard Notte. I'm not sure who he is working with this time, but he is here to steal a very old clay bowl, among other things."

Lily was staring him down now. He'd offered some information, but not enough. "What about your sister?"

"She was at a concert, and he blew the place up. He is a terrorist and all of us, including your dear husband, have been after him for many years."

Lily's brow furrowed. "Why can't you all capture him? He moves around like a normal person." Now was not the time to discover if his sister had survived.

"You think so? There were two guards who had casually

made it into the bar before he entered the hotel. If I had made a move, maybe, just maybe I would've killed him. He would never go back to Tel Aviv with me to stand trial. Those two guards, even if I had killed him, would have slit my throat and your throat and never thought anything about it. They might have thrown a grenade into the concierge area. Who knows with those people. They are fanatics. They are paid more if the man lives, but if he dies, they still get paid. So, my lovely lady, I did nothing."

"So, there's way more to you than just a handsome face?"

Ari smiled. He relaxed. "Aw, shucks, ma'am."

"Don't ever do that southern accent thing again."

He sat up to remove his jacket. "You didn't like it? I've been practicing for when I go to the United States."

Lily choked down a drink of water. "No, just no. Just be yourself, whoever that is."

"Now, that is the conundrum. Who am I? I've been someone else for so long I really don't remember. That is the hazard of my job."

"Now, I understand that." Lily yawned. She looked at the clock on the wall. It was almost two in the morning. *Where are you, husband of mine?*

"Lily, you need to go to sleep. With the French police, you never know how long it will take. They may send for croissants for everyone before they are done. Go in there and change, and go to sleep. I'll be on guard out here on this short little sofa, this short little uncomfortable sofa."

Lily was having a hard time keeping her eyes open. "Fine, but you men need to wake me up when Dev gets back here."

Ari nodded. His hand pointed to the bedroom. "Go."

After an appropriate amount of time, Ari tapped on the door of the bedroom. "May I come in?"

Lily had changed and was climbing into the large bed. "Sure, what do you want?"

"Just checking on you." Ari walked in slowly and began to laugh. "What the hell do you have on? You brought those pajamas on your honeymoon?" He looked suspiciously at some sort of comic strip character adorning Lily's nightwear as she lowered under the sheets.

"It's a joke, besides, I get cold."

Ari stood next to the bed. "A beautiful woman should never be cold. You have your husband to keep you warm."

"Not you, that's for sure."

He smiled and she saw his eyes twinkle. What was he thinking? "I wasn't offering. Now, let me tuck you in."

"And why exactly am I allowing you, a perfect stranger, to tuck me in?"

"Ah, you think I'm perfect." He was shoving a coverlet under her neck.

"I give up." She rolled her eyes. She hadn't done that in a few hours.

"You remind me of my little sister. You have a pinch of innocence, mostly steel resolve to accomplish a project, and a desperate need to know the truth in anything." He looked at her face and saw her concern. "Dev will be here, do not doubt that."

"So you two do trust each other?"

He stepped away from the bed into the darkness of the room. "When we need to do so. He is a good man, an honest man. I do believe he thinks something is very wrong with all of this or he wouldn't have done what he did tonight." Ari reached for the light beside her bed. "Now, go to sleep. I'll be in the other room cleaning my gun."

"I'm not sure that's so comforting."

She blinked back a couple of tears. *Where had those come from?* The man she had only met today, tenderly removed them with his finger before they could trail down her cheek.

"Never doubt Dev. He sees more than you think. He sees danger before we know it is there. He sees the good in a man even when they don't always deserve it. He sees the beauty in you even when you don't see it. Go to sleep." He kissed her on the forehead. She was asleep before he left the room.

Lily woke to whispers in the other room. Dev was finally there. The whispers were getting louder, and she could make out a word now and then.

"He said you knew the man. He said your name, Ari, and there's two men. I also suspect that there is another agent involved. What the hell is going on?" Dev grabbed another shot of bourbon as he paced the room.

"I have no idea, my friend. I only met Bernard through Claude." Ari stopped before he said something that might outrage Dev and there was plenty that would make the man mad. But Dev knew him too well.

"What?" Dev demanded. "What do you think? I know that little mind of yours. I know how Mossad work, spill it, Ari."

"I think Claude is in over her head this time."

Dev took the statement in and slowly walked to one of the chairs. "Go on."

"I know she's had Notte smuggling art. I've been following him, watching him, more for his protection than to know what he is doing. We already know that. I'm not sure if Claude knows he's been smuggling in more than just art or an antiquity."

"More, as in drugs?"

Ari nodded. "I think she's been played for the last few years. Everyone has been desperate to save the heritage sites and artifacts from the beginning of civilization. It is a race before it is all destroyed in Syria, and you saw yourself what happened in Baghdad and Cairo. I believe the powers that be, museums, UNESCO, others have averted their eyes. Notte was being paid in diamonds. I know that much for sure. I know that Claude was obtaining those diamonds from several sources in Zurich, Bruges, even Russia. The rich and privileged deal in the gutters sometimes."

"So, you think she is an unwitting pawn in all of this?"

"I didn't say that. We've all known that Claude will do anything for what she wants. Remember? I just believe she's working with others who may have their own agendas."

Dev thought about Remy and his insistence on questioning them in the morning. Did he want them all to have the same story, one he fed them? "I've been thinking about the past, and she was willing to do anything for an old piece of art." Dev swallowed the last little bit of liquid from his glass. The taste was bitter, not from the bourbon, but from his memories. Sometimes your friend was not your ally.

"But why did he insist you know the man? What man, and who else are you teamed up with?"

"Do you want me to say his name out loud and curse us?"

"No. I know who I saw tonight. I saw his face. I'm just surprised he got his own hands dirty."

Ari stood up and headed to the door. "Your wife is safe. Notte has been taken to a secure location where he can't be touched. We must have patience. Khalid is like a cockroach; he always survives." He had finally said the name. He bit his lip.

"Ari, you aren't answering my questions. You all are using that tulip bowl as bait, aren't you? Now, I just have to figure out who else is playing with you. And I will find out. You know I will."

Dev's companion nodded and headed to the door. He didn't turn around. He couldn't lie to the man, not tonight. There was no need to tell Dev about their visitors earlier in the lobby. Lily would do that. He knew she would.

Before Ari could answer him, he was gone. Yes, they'd have to deal with the man, and this time, if they were lucky, Khalid would die. Dev could feel Lily looking at him.

"Come to bed."

He looked up to see his wife, and her pajamas. He smiled. He did like how she looked like a walking muppet.

Chapter Twenty-Three

1. Try with all my might to enjoy tonight
2. Watch everyone
3. Find the exits at the Louvre
4. Take my time getting ready
5. Bad things happen when drinking champagne!

Lily looked over at the empty pillow. *The silly man is running again.* She raised herself up and saw her beloved Eiffel Tower, and the blue sky of a sunny fall day. After her morning bathroom visit, she walked slowly into the other room. Dev was standing at the window, looking out on her same view. She stood in silence, watching him.

Dev took a deep breath. The honeymoon was not going as planned. Last night was proof of that. He took a drink from the cup in his hand. He'd brought Lily coffee too, as his own form of sacrifice to a deity. He'd need all the help he could get. This morning's discussion would not be an easy one. He took another breath and looked down below him. No wonder Lily was captivated by this view. The golden statue of Jeanne d'Arc was glowing in the morning sun. *That's what I need, an avenging angel.*

Lily's smile faded as she saw her husband's face. He looked worried, then she became worried. Joy flew out of her psyche's door like a runaway balloon. If Mr. Cool was worried and out of sorts, how bad was it? Was it a terrorist attack bad or cartel drug shipment bad?

In just the last few days she'd met so many different characters. Her life had become an intricate soap opera, never knowing who was going to come through the stage door.

Enter Bernard Notte, the benefactor. Her evening of dinner and conversation became a surreal practice test of how to deal with your past to survive your future. Lily was due a very lengthy explanation from Claude Barbin. Dev had appeared shocked, but perhaps he was a better actor than the lovely French woman? And then he had deviled the man in a verbal volleyball match.

They'd lived through dinner, and then a drive-by shooting. Sidewalks in Lily's life were very dangerous places. But, she had lived through it. Ari had magically appeared like some genie out of an Arabian tale. Claude, Dev, and Ari had pulled guns from God knew where. *Geez, where did he hide that gun?*

Dev could feel his wife in the room. He finally turned in her direction to face her. "I didn't know you had ever met him."

Lily sat down on the sofa and pulled her hotel robe around her for warmth. "Did Claude? She knew who he was, didn't she?"

Dev slowly walked over to her and sat opposite his wife. "She didn't know you knew him."

Lily held up her hand. "Stop. Just stop. I've been involved in a shooting so I need some answers. You both knew we were meeting him. Did she or did she not know who he was? What he was? If you don't answer me I could continue in one of these long homilies you love so much."

Dev took a drink of coffee. He'd been discovering many things about his wife. Father Dan and she could match each other in a homily match-off, if there ever was such a contest. "Alright, I knew who was coming. If it is any consolation, it looked like he was more surprised by us. He kept thinking he knew me, and he definitely knew my last name."

"That's just peachy." Sarcasm oozed from her speech. "You probably can't tell me anything, again. You will keep me safe, or Ari will, whoever Ari really is, this is bigger than you and me, save the world, yadda, yadda, yadda. Is that pretty much it?"

Dev focused his eyes on hers. "Yes, except I just heard that Notte is in a secure location and is in critical condition."

"So, does Claude know who Bernard is? That he is--was a bad guy?"

Dev bowed his head. The silence embraced the room. He could hear Lily breathing. She was still looking at him. His thoughts were many, his answers should be few. "Ari and I believe she knew exactly who Bernard was, and that could be the bigger problem. She's playing a dangerous game. Ari is playing another one, and it all orbits around an old bowl that a terrorist wants to return to his family."

Lily stood up and removed the coffee from his hand, placing it on the table. She sat in his lap and turned his chin up. She kissed him lightly on the lips as she placed her arms around him. "Your friend may be an accomplice in all this going on?"

His eyes told the story. She saw embarrassment and disappointment, two feelings that were not standard practice for Devlin Pierce. "She may have deceived you all in some way?"

Dev pulled her closer in his arms and shifted her weight off his bad knee. "Some very big way, for many years. I am hoping, just hoping that she is doing it all because of her passion. She is desperate to retrieve so many artifacts. She sees the antiquities destroyed or sold on the black market on a daily basis. Sometimes good people do bad things, or work with the wrong people for the greater good."

"Has Claude talked to you about Tom when you all were deployed?"

"No. I don't understand."

Lily kissed him again, only deeper. "Then we need to talk. She's had time to tell you, well maybe not, but you know I can't keep a secret to save my soul."

"What is it?" Dev searched his wife's eyes. She really couldn't keep a secret. "What would she tell you that she wouldn't tell me?"

"A confession. Lunch and shopping in Paris can be a bonding experience. I need to figure out how I'm going to tell you this one. Besides, we always communicate better over food."

Dev shook his head. "The Mona Lisa is actually a fake? Claude sold the real one?" He smiled, his eyes twinkling.

Lily kissed him softly on the lips. "Stop. Trust me. I need to figure this out, and I probably need to tell you this in public so you can't throw things."

"I don't throw things when I get mad. That's you." Dev's one eyebrow arched with superiority. "Besides, now you are the one deflecting. You can't just drop a bombshell about some secret and then wait to tell me."

Lily popped up from her position. *He does have a point, but right now I can't look into his eyes and tell him. I need time to figure this out.* "Mister, you are taking me out for breakfast. Then, I want to stop and buy macarons from the most popular shop in Paris. I'm buying all the flavors, all those magnificent colors. I think Abby will love them, oh, and we should get some for your dad and his friend Arlene. I don't know if your aunts would want any. You know how your Aunt Maggie is going to the gym daily now." Mission deflection was a success.

Dev shook his head. His wife continued to talk as she stepped into the bedroom. She was babbling. She was nervous. *Perhaps there wasn't some dark secret or it was so bad she really was trying to figure out how to tell me. I'm confused. How will a revelation be better over food?*

"Honey, do you want to talk about the shooting last night? Do you need to?"

"No, I'm good," she yelled back. "I'm getting used to people being shot on sidewalks in front of me. I'm not getting used to all the characters and the intrigue. The intrigue is killing me only because I haven't figured out how this movie ends yet."

Dev walked slowly into the other room. He leaned against the door frame, watching her pace between the closet and the bed. She was grabbing clothing.

"I suppose before tonight's gala I should get you up to speed on all those characters." Apparently, the secret could wait. He'd wait, for now, until she was ready. If he pushed, his wife might pack her bags and leave him alone on their honeymoon. She was already dealing with Ari, Notte's shooting, Claude and the supposed secret, along with the uncertainty of tonight. Lily looked up from her activity as though she had heard his thoughts. Her eyes were wide.

"And the intrigue, and where the exits are. My plan of attack is to flee the building."

"Lily, what's your read on Albert, that man who took you shopping?"

"He is very nice. I'm supposed to meet his wife tonight."

"Would you trust him?"

Lily nodded. "I guess, but you're the one who said go with Claude, you'll be safe with Claude."

Dev grimaced. "That hurt a little. Well, I just want you to have someone you could go to other than Ari or me."

Lily slowly walked into her husband's arms. "Or Claude?" She looked up into his face and smiled.

"I can be wrong now and then."

Lily grabbed her chest in mock surprise. "You can be wrong? I would never have thought that."

"Enough. Let's get breakfast and then those cookies."

"Macarons."

"Macaroons."

"You are trying my patience, Devlin. Macarons, French ones. Ooh, and I want to stop by that chocolatiere down the block."

"Are you eating for the apocalypse?"

Lily placed her hands on her hips in exasperation. "Do you know me? Have you met me? I need to have food in storage just in case all you super sleuths fail. I'll exit the museum, run to the hotel, and be very happy with my food. You all can save the world."

"Well, get dressed so I can brief you on tonight's mission, Mata Hari."

"But we'll still get my macarons and the chocolate?"

His nod sent her back into his arms. Lily covered his face with small flutter kisses. "I love you, even if you aren't perfect."

"Don't push it, love."

"By the way, what is the purpose of this gala?"

Dev held her tighter in his arms. "It's a fundraiser for that piece of pottery. Imagine an entire party for a clay pot with tulips painted on its sides. Claude told me it was smuggled out of Iran and dates back to the Ottoman Empire. That's the piece I think the terrorist is after. Lily, I need to know about that secret."

"Let's go to breakfast. You need to eat before you hear this or you'll yell or growl or do both."

Lily left his arms, and he hung his head down. "And we're back to food."

Her voice echoed from the bathroom. "Besides, I also have to tell you about Ari's visitor last night. You won't believe this one! I'll tell you that one first, and you'll be mad. When I tell you the other story, you'll be livid."

Dev hung his head down. "Honey, please stop making all this sound normal. It really isn't."

Lily peeked her head around the corner. "If I don't make it sound normal, Dev, I'll be so afraid I can't go out that door. And I need chocolate."

What the hell was she going to tell him? What could revolve around Claude and Tom? And who was Ari's visitor. *Don't push Lily. She'll tell you when she's ready.* Dev would have to wait.

"Lots of chocolate!"

"Damn, it must be bad," Dev whispered to himself. He would soon find out.

Lily's husband sat across the table, his arms folded in front of him. He had promised to not yell in the restaurant, no matter what information she conveyed to him. At times, she thought he was dispassionate, but in fact, he was taking it all in. He said nothing after she finished. Her story about Tom confirmed suspicions he had already created in his mind. However, Claude's involvement with the Army, and their decision, made him sick to his stomach. As Lily recounted the meeting of Khalid and Ari, he couldn't wait to get his hands around the man's neck; Ari or Khalid, both or whoever came into his path first. He was unusually silent, but smiled at Lily's joy as they ate their meal and strolled to the shops. They held hands; he had her walk nearer the storefronts, away from the street.

By the time they arrived back at the hotel, Ari was waiting in the bar. Lily wanted no part of this meeting. *You are in so much trouble, Ari.* Lily went up to the room, leaving the two men alone to fight it out. In a few hours, she would be attending a party in one of the most famous museums in the world. She would be dressed in a designer gown and jewels. She'd be on the arm of a handsome, wonderful man who cared deeply about more things than she could imagine. She'd mingle with rich and powerful world leaders, and dangerous nefarious ones. *Lord, just get us through this one night.*

After a light early dinner, they dressed. Once downstairs, Lily and Dev entered a waiting car. Lily watched historic buildings and fountains pass by her in their short trip. Paris was beyond belief at night. Once they arrived at the Louvre, they didn't enter by the side or the "basement" entrance under the pyramid of glass. There was a red carpet set on the stone pavers, welcoming them to the massive front door. Kings and queens used to enter here, and now it was the little florist's turn. Other cars were lined up.

As Lily exited the sedan, Dev took her hand. "You look so beautiful tonight. You must know that."

Lily could see other women arriving and realized her nice dress from Kansas City wouldn't have been good enough for this group. "I believe it because I believe you. I do feel pretty good."

Dev placed her arm through his. "Geez, Lily, pretty good?" He leaned down so only she could hear. "You look damn good, honey. I have some ideas for later tonight."

"After you've saved the world?"

"That and improved the world economy, removed all dictators and despots, burned some bad movies, and brought back Scooby Doo."

"Wow, you are energetic."

"But first, let's just go and try to have a good time. Just be yourself and don't worry about anything. This is a once-in-a-lifetime opportunity."

Dev was completely correct. As Lily entered the grand hall, it was all overwhelming. It was after hours at the museum and here she was. There was something delightful in being somewhere when it was closed to others, something very special. It was a dream come true with lovely ladies dressed in amazing gowns, and men in their finest tuxedos. If she went up the main marble stairs, she could see the Mona Lisa again, but she much preferred staying with Dev.

Her husband didn't miss a beat when they saw Claude. He was playing himself. They laughed, they commented on how lovely the gowns were, Claude told them where the champagne and the food was located. But Lily noticed Claude was babbling. She knew what that babbling meant. Dev and Claude agreed they needed to talk about someone who was there--Khalid. Dev's posture became even straighter, if that was possible.

"You go with Claude. I'll be fine. I'm going to find the champagne," Lily said as she patted his arm for assurance. Dev looked at her suspiciously.

"You'll be fine?"

"Yes. I want to see that old clay bowl." She waved him away and walked through the crowd. She heard music and followed it to another room. She heard an Englishman remark that the Paris Philharmonic was entertaining. Lily took it all in, including the enormous urns with massive amounts of tulips within. They were all white tulips. They must have cost a fortune, and how big was the greenhouse they grew them in? Of course, they may have gotten them from South America?

"Dear Lily." She heard Albert's voice from the other side of the room.

Lily moved closer to the duo. "Albert, it is so nice to see a face I know." He kissed her on each cheek and turned to introduce his wife. "I was a little distracted by the tulips."

"My wife, Anne, and this is the lovely Lily."

My, no one ever has introduced me that way. "You are too kind and it is so nice to meet you." The petite woman hugged her without the traditional kissy face tradition.

"My dear Albert had such a wonderful time shopping with you and thank you for our gifts. It was so kind of you."

Lily was relaxed with these two kind people. *And Anne had hips! Finally, someone in Paris with hips who wasn't a tourist.*

After a brief tour of the room with her new friends, and Albert's assurance that she could always find them near the entrance, Lily headed on her way in search of the old bowl that had brought everyone together tonight.

She followed a group into a larger room. Under a spotlight of soft white sat the tulip bowl, under protective glass. Lily slowly made her way to the object. It was protected by four guards, one on each corner of the ropes. It was a simple bowl with blue tulips painted around the sides. Each tulip, which reminded her of Delft pottery from Holland, had a bloom, a small bud and two petite leaves. There was a rim of gold at the top and at the bottom.

"Do you know that tulips were worth more than gold at one time in civilization?" The low voice came from behind her, the breath blowing a few out of place curls.

"Yes, smarty, I did know that. Did you know that a tulip is like a turban? Did you know someone stole some bulbs and took them back to Holland, and the rest is *histoire, mon ami?*"

"*Touché*, Mrs. Pierce. I did know all that. I know things." Ari was now standing next to her. She looked up to see a super spy, well at least in her imagination. His tux was fitted, emphasizing his wide shoulders. His shirt was whiter than white, only matching his glowing teeth. Every hair was in place. He wore a black tie with a diamond pin. *Holy Moly. If Abby saw him she would faint.* She needed to get a photo. *Crud.* Dev had a phone. She'd have to wrangle a photo of the two of them later.

"I bet you do. How long do we look at this?"

Ari stifled a laugh with his hand. "You know, many have wondered, but very few have actually asked something like that out loud. You are delightful."

"So?" She tilted her head, waiting for an answer. "Mr. I--Know--Things, how long?"

He squinted his eyes intently. "Until we are thirsty. What about the buffet and a little libation? I hear they are serving caviar from Russia, and I saw some lovely crab claws."

"So the French like Russia?"

"They like their caviar. And did you not hear me that they have crab claws? Come on, little one. I know where the food is."

He extended his arm out and she took it. "I like a man who knows things like that."

Lily was carefully placing food on her plate as Ari piled his on. "You know, I half expected to see you tonight with a black eye, or two black eyes on that face of yours."

"Did you see these mushrooms? Beautiful. Well, your husband was a little understanding. Thank you for that. He said you told him to be nice. He was grateful that you were in perfect condition, thanks to me."

"I see. You haven't come clean with him yet, have you?"

Ari smiled. *My, in such a short time the woman knew him very well.* "There are some things that need to be left unsaid. There will be time enough for that, but for now I've spotted us a couple of seats."

Lily shook her head. *Deflection must be an artform in Europe too, heck all over the world.*

Ari had found them a small table where they could eat and drink, and watch everyone go by.

"I won't get into all the nasty details, but our dear tulip was at the base of a love story; lovers separated, never in the same place at the same time. Oh and there was intrigue, murder, and deception. We Arabs do have our stories."

Lily nodded nicely, but said nothing. *Geez, the story sounded like her relationship with Dev. The tulip could become her new favorite flower. No, she still loved lilacs.*

He pointed out the president of France, a prime minister of some European country, a countess, and a princess. An elderly gentleman made his way over to them.

"Hello, my dear. You are so beautiful tonight. Were we not married at one time?"

Lily almost choked on her food. The gentleman grabbed her empty hand to kiss it gently. "I'm sorry, sir, but sadly we were not."

"Then you must remind me of my dead wife. She was an actress." He smiled and leaned down to Lily. "Actually, I met her at the Moulin Rouge. She was a dancer. She was *magnifique.* A lively one she was. She so enjoyed being my duchess. That's when our dear Charles was president. He is such a wonderful man."

"And you, sir, are?" Ari questioned.

"I am the Duke of Burgundy, well one of them. I believe I'm actually the illegitimate duke, but I have a castle nonetheless. Charles and I are so close. I talked to him just the other day."

"You mean Charles de Gaulle, your grace?" Ari was standing now out of respect for the elderly man.

"Of course. Do you know him?"

"No, I'm sorry, I haven't had the pleasure."

"Shame. Good man. Enjoy your evening. Madame, you are a vision tonight." He turned and walked away to another group of people.

"Great, a man tells me I'm beautiful, and he thinks de Gaulle is still the French president."

Ari returned to his seat and his vodka. "Well, I have been remiss. Lily, you are absolutely breathtaking. I was right about that jewelry. I hate to admit it, but I'm slightly jealous of your husband tonight. Dev is a lucky man."

"How many of those vodkas have you had?" *Now who was the one deflecting?*

"Can't take a compliment, eh? Interesting. Who was he?"

Lily finished her last bite of a crab roll. "Who was who?"

"The idiot who left you behind? The idiot who made you feel less?"

She tried to stare into his deep eyes, but it was difficult.

She felt like he could see her soul, see everything about her. "Less than what?"

"Less than beautiful, less than smart, less than anything?"

"He was an idiot, well he was the last idiot. Then I just shut down, until one day."

"Until Dev walked in?"

Lily looked away. Ari had seen too much of her; she felt naked in front of him. *What a talent he had, and how did he acquire it?* "Yes."

He raised his glass. "Good for Dev. I'm proud of him for seeing the real, true you. Many men only see mirror images with the perfect filters of makeup, hair dye, perfect shoes, and clothing. A real man sees beyond the window dressing to the soul of the woman, her true texture, her lifeline. Your heart and soul are beautiful."

Usually, silence was not Lily's strong suit, especially when she was nervous or out of her element. She took a minute to take a deep breath. *Deflect, Lily.* "Now, I've had a crazy duke and a super agent tell me I'm beautiful. It's been the perfect night." She leaned her chair back slightly, and the tall column holding an urn of tulips began to move. "Oh no."

Ari quickly moved to save her from disaster. Lily was standing next to him in awe. "Great move." She touched the column. "We need to get it straight again." She touched the column again and realized it wasn't solid.

"I would've thought a party like this would have heavy columns. This is resin. We use these on weddings all the time."

"Is that unusual?"

Lily moved the pillar back in place and saw a white powder below. "No, but for a gala like this I would've expected something better, heavier. Could you pick up the urn?"

"I'll try." He brought his hands around the base and lifted it up easily. "This isn't heavy at all."

By now, Lily was crouching on the floor. She touched the white substance at the base. "What the heck is this?" Hopefully, it was from a packet of flower preservative, but as they moved the column in place, more was dropping out. *No, please.* Flower preservative packets had gotten her into trouble two years ago when the substance was actually drugs. She brought up her finger for Ari to examine. "Surely, they've dusted. It sort of looks like my house after a few weeks," she joked.

Ari crouched down beside her and brought some of the powder onto his finger. He tasted it. "*Mon Dieu.*"

"Oh, that can't be good. Do not tell me that it's what I think it is!" She reached for a napkin to wipe off her hand and the edge of her dress.

"Fine, I won't tell you that it's cocaine."

Their faces were only inches away from each other. "It is, isn't it?"

"Yes."

"*Merde.*"

Ari smiled. "Lily Pierce, you've gone from duchess to guttermouth in a matter of minutes."

"We need to tell Dev."

"Must we? He will get all DEAish and then the night will

be ruined. He'll insist we call the police or INTERPOL. He is such a boy scout. Worse yet, they'll shut down the open bar, and they'll remove the buffet. I wanted to go back for the lobster tails. And he'll blame me. Somehow it will be my fault."

"Is it your fault? Are you involved in this too, whatever this is?" She stood up suddenly and looked down on him. "If you are involved in this, you know he will not be happy."

His face looked up at her as though he was a small boy being reprimanded by his mother. "I swear to God, Allah, Buddah, anyone that I have nothing to do with this. Lily, don't ruin this night. There is nothing, nothing Dev can do about drugs in the Louvre in France." He finally stood up in defiance.

"I'm going to go find him." Lily stood up and gave Ari her napkin. "You do whatever you do, whatever that is."

"I do things and I know things. This can wait. Waiting is an attribute and is a skill you should acquire. I want nothing to do with this. It will only lead to trouble." Ari's voice became deadly low. Lily stared at him. Staring down at him was so much easier than seeing eye-to-eye.

"How do you exist with your vacant conscience?"

Ari smiled. "I learned very early to be very careful where I stick my nose. My mother was Jewish and my father Muslim. I have walked a delicate, dangerous line since the day I was born. I have learned patience and how to live in the darkness. You should sit down, and I'll get us dessert. Perhaps you have low sugar." He smiled charmingly. He was stalling, hoping his partner would finally arrive and take the heat off of him.

Lily smirked at him. "I'm not you. I have a funny feeling you are up to something, maybe this, maybe something else. Suddenly, I don't trust you."

She waved him off and headed in through the throng of people. Ari didn't follow, instead choosing to wait for his accomplice.

She'd have to be subtle. She couldn't just scream out that her new friend and she had just found cocaine. *Mon Dieu, indeed.*

Lily reached the main room and saw her husband by the bar. She wrapped her arms around his back. "Mr. Pierce, I am having such a good time. I feel like a princess. Come dance with me, and we can talk about something."

"It'll be my pleasure."

The man's voice was similar to Dev's. The stranger turned to face Lily.

"You're not my husband."

"No, but I am Mr. Pierce." He held two glasses of champagne and offered one to Lily. "We should toast."

Lily took the glass, but took a couple of steps back. She examined the man carefully. "It seems champagne gets me in trouble, besides, what are we toasting?"

"Who. We are toasting to you, princess." He lifted his glass. His eyes twinkled. His smile reminded Lily of her husband's when he woke in the morning and turned his head to say good morning. He needed a shave. His eyes weren't as bright as Dev's. Their light grey color was unusual with flecks of gold. He did have Dev's lashes. It seemed to be a family trait.

She lifted her glass to his, her eyes never leaving his as she took a sip. This man could be Dev's brother. *Great, he couldn't make it to the wedding, but he shows up on our honeymoon.*

He could tell what she was thinking. His smile slowly faded with the new frown that was born on her brow. "You know," he said as he pointed to her face, "if you do that too much you'll end up with wrinkles on that pretty face."

"Mr. Pierce, are we related?" Lily finally asked. "I'm not very fond of games right now, nor do I have the time to play them."

He nodded, soft hair falling into his eyes. When he looked into her eyes again, he brushed the errant strands away. "Actually--"

"He's my brother." Dev was standing next to her, his hand protectively placed around her waist. "Hello, Jackson. I've been wondering when you would finally pop up. I've been trying to contact you."

"Hello, Devlin. Your wife and I were just getting acquainted."

"Were we?" Lily asked, tilting her head suspiciously.

"Well, I thought we were. Congratulations, you two."

"You missed the wedding," Dev answered calmly. He tightened his hold around Lily's waist. She looked up to see his face, his very calm face, except for one pulsing vein in his neck.

"Dad was supposed to tell you I've been working here in Europe for months for the FBI."

"He did." Dev examined his brother. His little brother

was too calm. He doubted he was just working for the FBI. "Do you need to fill me in on something?"

Jackson Pierce smiled. "Perhaps. Maybe you already know about it."

"Maybe I do, and I don't approve, at all."

Lily watched the verbal ping-pong match and was becoming dizzy.

"Alright, you two, enough with the brotherly word-master contest. I need to talk to my husband, alone. Wonderful meeting you Jackson. See you at the next family gathering." She grabbed Dev's hand and pulled him to the dance floor. *When did she stop caring about rude behavior? Gretchen must be rubbing off on her.*

"Well that was a bit unusual for you." Dev smiled slightly as he held her in his arms.

"I needed to talk to you. I'm not sure what all that was with your brother, but I was in a hurry. Sorry." She looked up at him with a look that melted his heart.

"What is it?"

"You aren't going to believe this, but I found drugs in one of the columns. I almost dumped the urn of flowers off of it, and the column moved and surprise, I found drugs, again."

Dev laughed out loud. Stoic French couples glared at his impudence.

"That's funny."

"I'm not laughing. I'm serious. I'm not sure what is going on in the universe, but I'm like a dog-sniffing drug magnet. Ari said it was cocaine."

Dev's facial muscles straightened. "Ari? Where? Show me." The puzzle was coming together. His patience was vanishing.

Lily led her husband off the dance floor and to the table. Ari was still sipping a glass of champagne, and he had found the lobster tails.

"Oh wonderful," he sighed. "You brought the boy scout to ruin the night. Lily, the desserts will be out any minute, and you know the French and their desserts."

Dev ignored him, moved the column and knelt down to view the white residue. "Boy scout? Yippee."

In a matter of minutes, Devlin Pierce went to work. He removed the urn and tipped the column over to see bag after bag stuffed in the core of the structure. He tapped on the urn and suspected it was filled with drugs as well.

"Now, what, Mr. Agent Man?" Ari had turned to watch his friend's examination. "Who are you going to call? The Ghostbusters or Bruce Willis?"

"Neither for now." Dev removed his phone and began to take photos of the drugs and the column and urn. "I'm sure there is more than just this one. What are you and my brother up to?"

"Your brother is here? How nice. Why don't you go check the tulip bowl over there?" Ari pointed to the centuries-old clay artifact setting in the middle of laser sensors and armed guards. "Let Lily look and she might find the drugs for you."

Dev's look bored a hole through Ari. "So you are using the bowl as bait. I knew it." He stopped. "Are you two using me too? Am I bait for Khalid?"

Ari took a drink from his glass. "I never knew that was an option."

"What was last night all about then?"

Lily sat down in one of the chairs away from the two men. Although they were handsome men, she was becoming bored with the "save the world" thing they had going on and who was after whom. Her head was whirling as Ari and Dev continued to verbally attack each other. Only two years ago, this wasn't her world. Her world was work, flowers and repeat again the next Monday. She hadn't expected much more than that. Now, she was at a divine party with dignitaries, in Paris, at the Louvre, after hours, watching two drop-dead gorgeous men decide what they were going to do about the drugs SHE found. *Holy Moly.*

"Claude, and I'm not sure who else, are funneling drugs in and out of various countries. We talked about this. I wasn't sure the operation was this large. I just knew about the drugs in the frames and in some of the paint of forgeries. But Devlin, my boy, you need to tread carefully. You have no jurisdiction here, and I just saw one of our old friends pass by. Remember Agent Brad Keeting? He just took a look at the old bowl. As for Jackson's operation, it is none of your business."

"You made it my business when you placed my wife in jeopardy." *Keeting? The last time I saw the man was while I was working on the Notte drug case. This just keeps getting worse.*

Ari shook his head and smiled. "Dear boy, you said Khalid was on your plane coming over here. He was in your country flying into Paris. You were already on his radar, or you are one unlucky man."

Dev ran his hand through his hair. "I don't know who to trust in this mess. I'd talk to Remy, but there's something off with him."

"On that we can agree," Ari lamented. "Dev, please just take the night off." Ari looked over at the unusually quiet Lily. "I told you he would ruin our party. The lobster tails were amazing, by the way." He threw his napkin down on the table. "Well, come on boy scout. Let's go save the world. Let's get this ironed out. We go to Claude first."

Lily just naturally followed behind Dev. His hand reached back and she grabbed it. "Come on. You'll be safer with us than on your own. God knows what this one and my brother have planned."

"I'm thinking it isn't a wedding gift for us, maybe some pottery?" Ari turned back and offered Lily a limp smile.

As they walked through the crowd, Ari asked several museum officials if they had seen Claude. He was directed to Claude's office.

Albert and his wife were standing at the beginning of the long hallway. "Lily, is everything going well?"

Lily came to a halt which made Dev stop in his tracks. "Actually, Albert, we are going to visit Dr. Barbin. Could you possibly grab a couple of security guards, ones who have guns? Give us five minutes and then come down to her office, please?"

Albert's eyes grew as big as plates. He smiled. "Surely, this is an American joke?"

Lily grabbed his hand. "This is very important. Something may be very wrong in the museum. Please do this."

Dev began to pull her away. "We can handle it. Don't involve him."

"Albert, please." She followed after her husband.

Albert's wife was perplexed. "Is everything well with that woman?"

"I'm not sure." He thought about Lily's request. Several other staff members were acting strangely this evening. Dr. Barbin's assistant Henri was speaking with one of the United States Embassy officials. They were whispering about a shipment. There were no shipments into the museum this night, nor many other nights. He knew. He had been in charge of incoming deliveries years ago. "I think I will do what she asks. There is no harm in being careful."

Ari knocked on Claude's closed door. He heard voices, one was Claude and the other was a man. Perhaps it was Remy, the little man who attempted to push Dev around last night? He nodded back at Dev as he opened the door. "I believe we have everyone in there."

Claude stood behind her desk. She was pale. She was looking toward the other side of the room.

Dev and Ari saw Claude, Remy, and then they followed her glance. There was another man in the office. It was Khalid. Everything had just changed.

Chapter Twenty-Four

*D*ev shoved Lily completely behind him serving as a barrier between her and the others. It was too late to leave her out in the hallway. Khalid had just lit a small cigar.

"Ah, please come in. We can have our own party here," he said softly.

Dev couldn't take his eyes off of Khalid. It was like seeing the devil in the flesh. His attention was soon drawn away by the Embassy official with the gun.

"Close the door, Agent Pierce. You really shouldn't be here, but now it is too late," he commented cooly.

"So, you have it under control, Remy?"

Ari shook his head. "Always the boy scout," he muttered.

Dev understood, but it didn't make it any better. *Shit. I knew Remy was involved. So he's double-crossing Claude. He probably got a better offer from Khalid.*

"Oh, I have it under control. Claude was just about to give me the diamonds she owes me, and the other gentleman was overseeing the transaction. Then, I'm off to Switzerland."

Ari took a few steps ahead and sat casually on Claude's desk. "That's not very bright. Oh sure, you'll be able to sell some diamonds and gain access to your bank account, but I believe the United States and Switzerland have extradition agreements. I would've picked some other place, maybe somewhere warm. Brazil is nice this time of year, and you could enjoy Carnivale in just a few months."

Dev followed Ari's lead. "Personally, I love the islands. Why not go for your own island? You've already trashed a good career. You've failed your friends, your country, and you'll never be invited to another embassy event."

"Think of all the parties you'll miss," Ari added.

"You're an idiot, Ari. You and Pierce's brother have your own operation going. I wouldn't be so glib right now. Claude, the diamonds, now." Remy pointed the gun directly at her.

Ari was facing Claude and Remy. Dev watched Khalid. The terrorist was forming circles in the air with his smoke. Lily began to cough.

"Claude, you have a choice now. You can redeem yourself," Ari said calmly. "We understand why you did what you did."

The usually composed Claude Barbin had tears forming in her eyes. "It's too late, Ari." She looked over to Remy and then to Khalid. "Please, just let my friends leave the room, you double-crossing jackass."

Khalid laughed. "Claude, I'm disappointed in you. You've always been so tough. You've always put your mind to it, and sometimes used your body to acquire what you needed without any consequence. Apparently, it is time to pay up." His eyes ravished her as though she were a piece of meat.

Lily's eyes locked with Claude's. Her new friend mouthed I'm sorry as the tears fell on her cheeks.

Ari looked toward Dev. He knew they both had guns, but in this tight space it wasn't wise to push Remy. Dev's face and body were relaxed. This was the Major Pierce he knew. Without any words between them, they were developing a plan. Already, the new husband had managed to tuck Lily near a bookcase away from the line of fire.

"I know you, don't I?" Khalid asked calmly as he took a couple of steps near the desk. He was directing his question to Dev, but he was also looking past him at Lily. He knew exactly who the American was, and he knew his wife as well. But this game was amusing.

"Yes. It's been a few years."

"Ah, Afghanistan."

"And Syria," Dev added.

"You have a brother who has been on my trail. He is like a hound dog. He is currently very busy with the Ambassador, thanks to Remy. But he is very tenacious. As I recall, you were as well." He touched Ari's back. "And this one is too. Have you joined together? Have you formed your own private detective business? It's a shame, Ari, that you just have never been as good as the others. It must be your pedigree, or lack of it."

Ari laughed. "Oh, *mon Dieu*, I've embraced the fact that I'm a mutt. As for Pierce, I can't stand the man. He plays by the rules and always does the right thing. We idiots tend to not play well with others." Lily heard the sudden deadly tone. He flashed a smile and looked over the desk. "Are the diamonds in that little bag, Claude? I'd love to see them."

Lily was holding her breath. *What was Ari doing, and where was Albert with the cavalry?*

Claude pushed them near him. Ari winked at Dev. "Diamonds have such movement in the light. I'll just take a little peak."

Dev shoved Lily back farther into the wall in anticipation of what was to come. Her elbow banged into a bookcase. As soon as Ari grabbed the bag and looked inside, he threw it at Remy's gun, and Dev tackled Khalid to the floor, punching him out in one blow. By the time Dev rose up, Ari had Remy disarmed and in an arm hold. Claude fell into her chair, but came up with the dislodged gun. Lily was in an action movie. She stayed in position, taking it all in. She was just happy that for once she wasn't the bait.

"Claude, could you call security, or are they involved in this too?" Dev yelled. "Where the hell is my brother?"

The door was pushed open, guards rushed in, and Jackson finally arrived. Albert was at his side. He smiled at Lily. "I brought them, Lily."

Lily sighed. "Thank you, my friend." She much preferred her friend to the ones she saw in front of her. You needed a program just to keep track of who you might want to trust. Claude began to explain, but Ari told his own story, in fluent French. His story had Remy as a madman, someone who just broke. Perhaps he had been overworked. *Whoever thought an embassy official was overworked?* Lily had to laugh at that one. In the meantime, a guard helped Khalid up into the chair and checked his jaw. Lily remained stuck to the bookcase. She watched the scene play out in front of her.

Dev glanced in her direction several times as he talked on his phone to someone. He winked once, hoping to quell her fear. Lily faintly smiled. What had she gotten herself into? Would her world be this crazy for the rest of her life?

Was it too late to get an annulment? She'd call Father Dan as soon as possible.

No, you won't Lily! This is more excitement than you've ever had, and you're doing it dressed in a designer gown.

Lily heard voices down the hallway. She glanced out and saw two Marines surrounding a man in a tux. There were more men behind them. They weren't all going to fit in this small office.

"Which one of you is Agent Pierce?" The formally dressed gentleman looked around the room. He glanced back at Lily and smiled. She was now clinging to her new friend, the bookcase. She would name it Benny.

"I am, sir."

He nodded in Dev's direction. "I've heard a lot about you from your brother. I'm Ambassador Tillman. The Marines will take Remy off your hands. We have been watching him for months now, and INTERPOL wants to talk to him as well."

"The Ambassador happened to be at the gala tonight, lucky for us," Jackson Pierce explained as he pushed his way forward. "And he always brings in the Marines."

"I've never seen anyone arrested by full-dressed Marines. Very classy," Ari stated. "Of course, you Americans always know how to make an entrance. It's a little John Wayne, don't you think?"

Jackson glared at Ari. "And the Mossad doesn't do drama?"

"We are usually stealth-like. You never see us coming."

Lily rolled her eyes. Ari saw her expression and winked.

There was just too much testosterone in this tiny room. Lily breathed in deeply. It was all just too much. She would attempt invisibility by turning to face the wall of the room.

Her attempt at a vacation in her mind was definitely not working. She turned to breathe in more air. She hadn't felt like this since the time she was stuck in a hotel elevator with a wedding photographer, a portable bar, and one unfortunate guest of the bride. Oh, and she was carrying two boxes of flowers! Abby wasn't going to believe what happened tonight. But tonight there were just too many people in this small room.

She watched Dev do his thing, Ari continued quibbling with Jackson, the Ambassador was checking his watch, and the Marines were holding Remy tightly. Claude remained seated in her chair, her head in her hands. The terrorist in the corner had been revived and was mending his jaw. He was showing a paper to one of the museum's security guards. The guard was nodding and extending an arm out to guide him from the room.

"Wait a minute. Where is he going?" Dev asked loudly. "This man is wanted by so many people, and he is suspected in a shooting last night."

"We can't hold him, sir. He has diplomatic privileges, and he is a guest of the President of France. He is also a benefactor of the museum."

Ari's smile faded as he joined Dev in blocking Khalid's exit. "He is a murderer and terrorist." Ari's entire demeanor changed in a second. He was no longer a clown in a sharp tux. Lily was fearful of this Ari.

The guard continued to shake his head. "Please, look at his papers." He extended the document to Ari and Dev.

Dev read it quickly, then passed the document to Ari.

"I can't believe it, but there is nothing we can do."

Ari shook his head. "So, he is free again?"

Khalid grabbed the document. "Still. Still free and there is nothing you two can do about it. Again. I will not press charges against this man, but we will meet again."

Ari managed a smile as he came close to his nemesis. He whispered so only Khalid could hear. "We will meet again, in some dark alley. I'll be the one you see when you take your last breath."

Khalid threw his head back with a peculiar laugh that filled the room. "Such the drama queen, Ari. I've been so close to your family, your sister in Paris and before that, well you remember Tel Aviv."

Ari held up his hands in front of him, as if to surrender. "I do remember. That was many years ago, and yet I can describe every detail of that day. And that is why I will never forget what you have done to so many."

Khalid moved closer to the door, but turned to face Ari once more as if he had remembered a parting thought. "Your little girl was so beautiful, and she had those curls down her back. I'm sure you think of her often, but I remember your wife. I'll never forget her beauty, how captivating she was, so alluring."

Before Khalid could continue Dev grabbed the surging Ari by the waist. "Don't. He's just trying to hurt you."

"He is succeeding," Ari admitted through grinding teeth.

"Don't let him ever succeed in anything. That's how we will take him down," Dev assured him.

Khalid looked over at Lily. "Perhaps I will come to America to visit. It would be so nice to see old friends. I believe there were four of you, no there were five." He glanced in Claude's direction and then turned his attention back to Lily. "Yes, the fifth was killed. Apparently, it is very dangerous to be friends with all of you. Be careful, *madame*."

The Marines pushed to exit the room with Remy.

Khalid stopped them to pat their captive on the shoulder. "You are a sad man. Good riddance and goodbye."

Lily watched as Remy seemed to wince from Khalid's hand on his shoulder. Something was very odd about that. She stepped back as Khalid came closer to her.

As he exited, he looked toward Lily and smiled. "Mrs. Pierce, I believe, it was a pleasure. Hopefully, we will have more time when we meet again."

Dev moved his body in between his wife and the terrorist. "You need to leave now."

Khalid nodded and pushed his way out of the room.

"Dev, just let it go," Jackson said as he came to the other side of Lily.

"Just let the man go who killed hundreds of Americans, killed my friends, and women, and children? He killed Tom, he killed Ari's wife, and daughter. This time I will, Jackson. I can't promise anything the next time."

Lily slid her arms around her husband and buried her face into his tux coat. "When can we leave?"

"Soon," Dev whispered as he held her.

"And you'll throw your life away if you go after Khalid," Jackson muttered.

"Jackson, you will never know and neither will Khalid. If he comes after Lily, I will end him. No one will ever know."

"I may get to him before you, Dev," Ari said as he slid near Lily. She patted his shoulder. *My, there was a story with this one. His pain was still so fresh.*

Dev looked at the team before him. Lily was his sidekick, but Ari and Jackson were an unusual pair who needed to be dressed down. "You two owe me a very large explanation. I feel like I've been played during this elaborate game you developed. I don't like it. I'll be debriefed at the United States Embassy tomorrow, and if I find out you put Lily in danger, there will be hell to pay. My only consolation, and it is a sick one, is your game has ended, and you just allowed Khalid to walk out as a free man."

Lily looked up into Dev's face. His voice had been different, so very cold. She didn't take his words as threats, she understood them as promises of what would happen.

Jackson shook his head. Dev never did understand him. He turned to the Ambassador and in minutes the man and the museum's guards were gone. Ari, Claude, Dev, Jackson and Lily remained. Lily could breathe again.

"I bet the Ambassador is hitting the crab claws." Ari was attempting to lighten the mood. He could see the vein in Dev's neck pulsating. "Lily, we should hit the dessert buffet."

Lily remained in Dev's arms, but she pulled away slightly to look up at her husband. She saw someone alien to her. She didn't doubt that he would kill for her, to protect her. She looked beyond Dev's arm to faintly smile at the ever-charming Ari.

"If we leave now, we could pick up a couple chocolate mousse puff tarts," Lily joked.

"Yes, the ones with the little raspberries on top?" Ari asked.

"Oh yes! That's them."

Lily saw Claude feign a smile. Her very thin hand wiped away more tears and half of her mascara. Lily thought she looked like a broken woman, no respect remaining, left in fear and abandoned by truth and pride.

The new Mrs. Pierce pulled out of her husband's arms and walked over to her French friend. She pulled a tissue from her small clutch and began to wipe Claude's face clean. "That's much better. Now you look like my friend."

Claude breathed out, stood and grabbed Lily in a hug. "I'm so sorry for ever placing you in danger. I was foolish. Remy began threatening me, and so I brought him in. Bernard was difficult enough, and so I brought Jackson into the operation. He brought in Ari. The FBI and INTERPOL thought they could use the tulip bowl as bait to pull Khalid out of the shadows, but then Remy and he began to work together. There was another man I never met. He is the muscle and the organizer. It all went to hell when Khalid had diplomatic privileges. I was reckless all for what, art? An old piece of pottery?"

She stopped explaining to look at Dev with pleading eyes. "I was in over my head. I couldn't place Lily and you in danger, but once you told me he was on your plane, I thought you could help with Bernard. Jackson's idea to bait Khalid gave me a way out."

Dev's voice filled the room. "It seems as though you've been reckless for a long time. You've cost people their lives."

Lily and Claude faced each other eye-to-eye. "You've told him."

"Yes," Lily whispered. "But I have a feeling they all know."

"Then I must face them." Claude kissed Lily on each cheek and turned to face the remaining three men. "I did what I did. I was saving art; I was saving history. I won't deny what I did. I can't bring Tom back. I wish I could."

"His parents were devastated when they heard how he died," Dev shouted.

"Then you will tell them the truth now, and you will have his record changed. I know you. You will do that."

Ari smirked. Devlin Pierce, always the Boy Scout.

"I can't, damn you. They are both dead now. They died thinking their son was a drug user, that he basically committed suicide. I understand saving remnants of early civilizations but not at the expense of live human beings of the present and those of the future." Dev's voice was clear and full of emotion.

"I can't undo what I've done."

"No, but you can stop what is going on in this museum tonight. All the drugs--why did you allow all of that?"

Claude's eyes grew wide. "What are you talking about?"

Before Dev could continue, Lily stepped in. "We found drugs in the pillars, and in the urns with the flowers."

"I don't understand." Claude fell back into her chair in disbelief.

"I checked another pillar down the hallway after Ari told me what Lily discovered. It has packages of something stuck up the inner layer," Jackson added. "I was going to confront you after the gala."

"Seriously, I know nothing."

Lily sat on the edge of the desk by Claude and opposite Ari. She could see his little deviant mind at work.

"So, Claude, if you know nothing about all of this, who planned the flowers and the decor," Ari questioned softly.

"Well, I turned all that over to Henri, my assistant."

Ari smiled. "Ah, the one who is always in the background. He may be Khalid's little spy. And who, and why was Khalid invited?"

Claude nodded. "*Mon Dieu.* Bernard and Henri suggested he be invited. Henri knew Khalid in Beirut years ago. Bernard mentioned he knew Khalid through the Notte family's connection to the tulip bowl."

Ari looked up to Dev. "You know what I'm thinking, don't you, boy scout?"

"It was never about all of this. It's about that old bowl. Bernard could always get him the bowl and just hand it to him, but Khalid always liked a show, and what better way to ship in millions in drugs?"

"With Khalid, it is always about something else. He had to try to kill Bernard. The man knows too much of Khalid's plans." Ari hit his head in frustration.

"And Bernard discovered the tulip bowl, probably with the help of one of Khalid's associate's help. After the plan was struck, Bernard brought the bowl to UNESCO's attention, to Claude's," Jackson added. "He is going after the damn artifact. Claude, you and I will be discussing your little operation later, but right now we need to alert those guards."

Claude picked up her phone and began to direct security back to the viewing area.

"Will he do it in front of everyone?" Lily looked over to the three men who all answered a resounding "yes".

"And he'll get away with it because we are schmucks," Ari added.

"Hmm, schmuck? Hebrew, Yiddish or Arabic?" Lily smiled.

"American. I'm beginning to talk like them. Pretty soon I'll be saying y'all. I'm continuing to practice, Lily."

Dev finally unclenched his fists, and his vein diminished in size. "You will never say y'all. If you ever do, I'll hit you."

"Frankly, Pierce, you have become more aggressive than I remember. It must be something acquired after you marry, *n'est-ce pas?*"

"They have the bowl surrounded. There are now two layers of guards and some of the guests are suspicious." Claude laid her phone down on the desk to wait for the next move.

"Let them be suspicious. I'm going down there," Jackson announced. "Anyone else? Claude, I suggest you remain here."

"I'm in," Ari added. "I'd like to see how the other Pierce works." He patted Dev's shoulder. "This one has become so mean."

"What about you, brother?"

Dev looked over at Lily. His eyes gave her an answer she wasn't expecting. "We are going back to the hotel. You go have your fun, secret agents. Three really is a crowd with you two."

Lily bowed her head in thanks and prayer. She kissed Claude on each cheek and promised they would see her before they left Paris. Lily wasn't actually sure that would happen, but it was a good promise to make.

"Well then, *au revoir,* Lily." Ari blew her a kiss. Lily playfully grabbed the air kiss and placed it over her heart.

"Ari, we will always have drugs and a dinner buffet," Lily joked.

Ari threw his head back in laughter as he walked down the hallway, followed by a much more resolute and serious Jackson.

"Will you be alright, Claude, if Dev and I leave?" Lily touched another tear that had just fallen and wiped it away with another tissue.

"*Oui.* I just want to sit here at my desk and wait. I'm sure your husband has called someone in to take care of me." She looked toward her friend and saw deep eyes, sad eyes. "You two go on. Drink champagne, walk back to the hotel, and salvage what is left of your honeymoon." The woman was done.

Lily joined Dev and shoved his shoulder. "Say something to her."

Dev's left eyebrow lifted. Exactly what was he supposed to say? *Hey, everything is fine. You helped get our friend killed, but it was for something important like a two thousand-years-old vase. No problem, we're good.*

"Claude, we will see you before we leave. INTERPOL will take over the drug investigation and one of their supervisors will be here in minutes to talk to you. I'd suggest an attorney, unless INTERPOL knew all along what you were doing. I'm sure I'll never know. I just need a little time, well a lot of time, to digest all of this."

"I understand, Devlin." Her soft voice included an unspoken apology.

"Sometimes we all do things we aren't proud of, and I understand that completely, but my heart is a little battered tonight. Art and history are worthy of saving, but acquiring those items and paintings through diamond and drug trades isn't something I'm willing to do. What is the greater good? I don't know. I just know what I can and can't live with, how I have to live in order to sleep at night. Goodnight."

He grabbed Lily's hand in his and raised it to his lips. "Let's get out of here."

Neither one of them looked back at the sad woman, sitting at the very large desk, surrounded by art, old pottery and several Egyptian sculptures. She was small among those items. She was tired from all the secrets. She was indeed finished.

Dev reached the main foyer and grabbed two glasses of champagne. He handed one to Lily as he downed the liquid. She was busy watching the rain that was falling. It wasn't heavy, just constant.

Dev had already grabbed another glass. "Rain? Really?"

"We could wait until it clears? I can't get this dress wet."

"I want out of this place. Drink your champagne. I'll be back."

Lily took a sip and stopped. Champagne and she were not having a loving relationship with each other lately. Ever since Claude had taken her shopping that day. Poor Claude.

Lily saw a passing server and placed her glass on his tray. Drinking champagne and watching the rain while standing in the Louvre was just too, too much. Dreams were made of such events in your life. *C'est magnifique!*

Soon Dev returned with an umbrella. "Here's the plan. I'm going to carry you, and you are going to carry the umbrella over yourself and me."

Lily shook her head negatively. "No, you are not carrying me."

Dev lowered his head, his forehead touching hers. "Yes. I am. No grumblings."

"But you don't know how much I weigh."

"I have a pretty good idea by now, honey." He winked. Lily blushed.

"Fine, but if you blow out your back it's not my fault." Dev grabbed her hand and began pulling her down another hallway.

"Come on. We're going to the farthest exit down here and then we'll go out. It's the closest to the hotel."

There was an armed guard at the door, but he smiled when he saw the couple.

Dev shrugged his shoulders. "The rain, we need to leave here to get to our hotel. We need to get to our hotel." He winked at the man.

The man understood completely. He'd been in love once, well many times with many different women. There were those times the rush of love resulted in a rush to the nearest hotel. He opened the door and wished them a very good night.

"So, how does this work?" But before Lily could say anything more, her husband picked her up in his arms.

"Umbrella, please. That's your only job, darlin'." She opened it and held it over them. He began to run through the rain with his precious cargo.

In a matter of minutes, they were at the hotel and in the main lobby. Dev lowered Lily slowly and grabbed the umbrella, shaking out the rain.

"That went well." Lily looked at his back. He was drenched.

"I hope you can get the deposit back on that tux."

He tossed his hair. "But we saved the dress. Let's get something in the bar, maybe an Irish coffee?"

"Coffee? Oh yes, please." Lily sighed. She didn't care if she stayed up all night. She needed that warm liquid to sort out everything she'd seen and heard tonight.

The darkened bar was filled with the light sounds of a piano. The man at the keys was playing a romantic song. Dev sought out a secluded small table against the wall. Lily slid in first into the red crushed velvet booth, and Dev sat next to her.

"Is it bad to order Irish coffee in Paris?"

Dev smiled. "I'm not sure. Maybe we just tell them we want coffee with whiskey, a little whipped cream--"

"*Oui, monsieur*, an Irish coffee for you?" The server was hovering over them.

"I guess you can order an Irish coffee," Lily answered.

"And for you, *madame?*"

"*Un creme, s'il vous plaît.*"

"*Oui, madame, merci.*"

Dev removed his soaked jacket. He looked at his wife. "My, my, we have become very French in a few days."

"We have become very tired of being very scared of everything. I was afraid to go with Claude to find a dress. I was afraid to go to a gala. I was intimidated and afraid of your friends and your brother. I was afraid tonight. And, I'm tired of finding drugs everywhere."

Dev took her hand in his and kissed the inside of her wrist. "The DEA needs you."

She watched his lips place feather-light kisses up her arm. "I could replace Mort."

Dev's head shot up. "How is Morticia?"

"Very happy living with Abby. They are a great couple. I texted Abby a few days ago. It seems as though the shop and she are doing well together."

"How's Jeremy? Has anyone heard lately?"

Lily sighed. "He's great. Tom stopped by the shop before I flew out and said the boy is excelling at school and in his extra duties."

Lily shivered causing Dev to place his arm around the back of her shoulders. "Better?"

"Yes, much. That was wild tonight." She paused as their coffees were placed on the table. "What will happen to Claude? I mean, will she lose her job at the museum? What are they going to do about all those drugs?"

"I'm not sure about any of it. That's for them to sort out.

I'm sure Claude will still have a job saving artifacts and old sites. There are those who will do anything to preserve the past. Besides, Claude may be working on some scale with INTERPOL. Remy will be brought up on charges. I'm certain about that. Our dear friend Khalid will probably be stalked by our other dear friend, Ari. The drugs will probably be confiscated by the French government."

"What about Jackson?"

Dev took a drink and scowled. "Jackson does what Jackson does. He's on loan from the FBI division of arts and antiquities. We have reciprocal relationships with many countries, and he is a professional when it comes to art. I always wondered how his art degree would serve him in his life. He has done well. This partnership with Ari has me baffled, but I'm sure there's something. I just can't believe he owes Ari a favor."

Lily turned her head to the side to consider her new brother-in-law. "Maybe Ari owes him the favor."

"I hadn't thought about that scenario. That could happen, not sure how, but it could."

"So, you are DEA, and he is in the FBI? Wow. You two just couldn't be plumbers or architects?"

Dev smiled shyly. "Just that overachievement thing, and liking a little danger, and hating a desk job."

Lily remained quiet for a few minutes. "What about Ari? He never gave any indication he had a wife or a daughter when we talked."

Dev tightened his arm around her shoulders. "He's never shared, but I heard the story from a contact in Israel. Khalid and he are actually related, but as you heard, he has a complicated lineage. Ari's wife and child were specifically targeted. The day of the attack was on the little girl's second birthday. Khalid apparently planned it so that Ari survived, but was near when it happened. He is a sick--" Dev stopped short of describing his true feelings for the terrorist. "He likes to make it personal."

Lily took a drink of her very tasty coffee. She loved the fresh cream in it. "Husband of mine, what is in store for us tomorrow?"

Dev kissed her cheek. "We are going to sleep late, then maybe shop? I'm sure you have a few more places you just have to hit."

"Yes, please. Tonight, I heard someone say it might snow. If it really does, can we just go for a walk in one of the gardens or across one of the bridges? I've always had this fantasy about taking a walk in the snow in Paris."

Dev growled. "Is that the best fantasy you can come up with?"

"Yes, because my reality lately is pretty over-the-top."

Dev laid money on the table and stood up. He grabbed his jacket and reached his hand out for Lily's. "Come on. I have some fantasies of my own to fulfill, and now that you've had caffeine, I'm thinking you can stay up all night."

Lily playfully retreated from his hand. "I'm not sure I want to go with you. You get me in all sorts of trouble. In fact, Ari is tame compared to you Pierce brothers."

Dev smirked. "It seems you find your own trouble, Mrs. Pierce."

When he winked, she laid her hand in his. On the way up in the elevator, their hands were stuck firmly together.

They were shoulder to shoulder. Lily leaned her head on his arm and yawned.

"Lily, you had caffeine, you can not be sleepy."

Dev's wife saluted him with her left hand. "Yes, sir. I will not be sleepy for at least another hour."

"Make it two." Lily's mouth gaped open at his command. He was saved by the door opening and the appearance of another couple waiting to enter the elevator. Dev pulled her slowly down the hallway to their corner room.

As soon as Lily entered, she kicked off her shoes and began to remove jewelry. Dev threw his jacket on the chair and continued through the room as he removed his tie, cufflinks, shirt, shoes and socks. He began to unbutton his tux pants when Lily plopped on the sofa and looked at him. She had a very unusual look, one that reminded him of his mother for some bizarre reason.

"What, Lily?"

"Well, I was thinking and then I was wondering something. Why did you give up so easily tonight? I mean, you always want to be part of the chase, don't you? I've seen you grimace in pain when we were in Key West, but you were there in the hunt. You couldn't be stopped. But you gave up tonight. You let Jackson and Ari go, but you stayed."

Lily's eyes were boring a hole through him. Dev smiled. His wife was one smart cookie. He walked over slowly to sit next to her.

"Jackson and Ari do a fine job. It wasn't my jurisdiction after all. They didn't need me. Besides, they played me, the entire bunch. I don't play well with others when they sacrifice me that way and place you in danger."

Lily brought her legs up and turned her body to face her bare-chested husband. She laid her hand on his shoulder. "The other day, Claude had you look at some materials in her office. You have been in some sort of a loop. So why give up?"

"Damn, can't you let it go?"

"Have you met me, Dev Pierce? I have to know everything, especially if I can't be in charge of anything. I was definitely not in charge of this chaos tonight. There is no possible list I could make to organize this mess." Lily didn't look at him. She studied a scar on his left arm. It seemed as though she found a new scar from some injury on a daily basis with this man.

"Fine. It is a mess, but tonight I learned how to back off. I made that decision when I saw how afraid you were, again. I have gotten you in some real messes, and this one was out of control. When I was holding you, when it was all over, I decided we needed to get out. You are all I need," Dev murmured. He grabbed her other hand and held it. "I also needed to get back to our honeymoon."

"It hasn't stopped you before, your work in our relationship. In fact, our relationship has always been entwined with your work. So, what don't I know?"

Lily cuddled closer to him. He laughed out loud. "You are too smart for your own good. What you don't know is--" He paused as if he was going to offer up the secret to the largest magic trick in the world. Instead his head lowered, and he kissed her full on the mouth. His lips lingered on hers as though he was attempting to keep her quiet.

After he was finished, he stood and lifted her up against his body. "You don't need to know everything. Knowing everything is not always a good thing. Now, come with me." He began to pull her to the bedroom.

"And why do I want to do that?" He never turned to face her until they arrived at their destination.

Dev spun her around and began unzipping her dress. "Because you need to get out of this dress and into that bed. If you don't, I will throw you in it."

Lily turned around and walked out of her dress. She laid it softly on one of the chairs. "You wouldn't dare, Dev." She saw his twinkling eyes. *I can't say no to those eyes, ever.*

"You really want to go up against me, wife? It's a very small room, and I can catch you very easily."

Lily smiled. "That's true. You are the one that goes running every morning. I might as well surrender right now."

"You've become so French!"

"Oh, that was bad. I'll only surrender to you."

Dev had enough of the games and headed toward her, but Lily took a dive into the bed. "No need to attack. I'm in the bed."

"Where'd you learn to do that?"

"Years of practice. Anytime in a hotel, I always do a dive onto the bed. It's just something I do, even when I'm alone. There was this one time, I dove, and I bounced. I ended up on the floor."

Dev leaned over laughing. "I have never laughed with anyone as much as I do with you." He undressed and slid in beside her. "You have a few more articles of clothing to remove, including this."

"Watch it, mister. This little foundation garment has kept this body in check all night. It won't be pretty if you remove it. Parts might go all over the place."

He kissed her neck. "Oh, I'm counting on that." His whisper was passionate. Dev reached over and turned out the light. "Could you do one favor for me tonight?"

Lily turned and kissed her husband. "Anything." As soon as the word left her lips she regretted it. Anything with him could mean absolutely ANYTHING.

Dev moved on top and began to lower one strap and another, making sure to lay a kiss where the material had been. "Please don't look at the Eiffel Tower while we make love. I feel like I'm in competition with an inanimate object. I'm not sure I'd be the winner."

Lily patted him on the back. "I can do that, as long as you keep me completely entertained. When I get bored, I look at the tower, and I begin to make lists in my head. You know like, get Abby her own box of macarons, make sure I get some more of that lavender soap, and I want to get a photo on that one bridge I love so much."

"Alexandre III."

"Yes, that's the one. Do you think your dad would like some wine? We can get that at the airport, right?"

"Lily?" Dev looked up into her face.

"Yes?"

"*Fermez la bouche.*"

"That sounds lovely, but I think I remember you just told me to shut my mouth."

Dev kissed her forehead, her nose and then lightly

pecked her lips. "*Oui*. Just stop. I want you, all of you. No tower, no lists, no talking. It's just you and me. *Je t'aime*."

Lily blinked twice. What had she gotten herself into? Possibly heaven? No nightmares tonight.

"And that means you love me. That is so nice."

As Dev made his way down to remove the foundation of woven elastic, Lily was finally quiet. It was definitely time to get back to the honeymoon. But she was almost too quiet. She wasn't asleep, was she?

He slowly looked up. She was still awake, but she had her head turned slightly. "You're watching the damn tower." He added a growl.

"It's so pretty, Dev. I have you and the Eiffel Tower. What more could a girl want? Could you do me a favor?"

Dev rolled over on the other side of the bed. "Sure," he answered exasperated.

Lily left the bed to remove the remainder of the killer underwear and hopped back in quickly. It was getting cold in the room.

She leaned over him and took in the view. There was just enough light in the room to see those eyes and full lashes, that jaw, and muscular neck. She touched his chest. It was solid, but she didn't mind sleeping on it.

"What was the favor?"

"My, you are Mr. Impatience. Actually, you already did it."

Dev was now totally confused. First, she wouldn't shut up, then he was uprooted in her affections by an original eyesore on the landscape of Paris, and now her vagueness was infuriating. "What did I do?"

She leaned over and kissed him. His arms took her down on top of him. When she broke from the kiss, she whispered, "You got on your back. Now I need a full two hours, soldier."

Dev attempted to remain serious as he pulled his arm away from her body to snap a salute. "Yes, ma'am. I'll get right on that, ma'am."

Their combined laughter was replaced by whispers of each other's name. Afterward, they fell asleep in each other's arms. Their final vision before slumber took them away was of that beautiful tower.

Back at the Louvre, Jackson and Ari were watching a bowl. Two super agents on the international level were watching a blasted bowl. The bowl had not moved. They were doing a fine job of watching. The guards had been doubled, and the United States Ambassador was regaling the crowd with a story about his first trip to the famous museum. He'd lost his wife somewhere around the Mona Lisa and found her three hours later in the gift shop. Jackson rolled his eyes.

"I've heard that damn story at least three times on this mission alone. The man needs to get some new material."

Ari continued to scan the room. "He'll have a new tale if Khalid makes his move." Ari's eyes targeted the figure on the farthest side of the room, near the main exit. Khalid stood with arms folded. He was smiling at Ari.

"I see him," Jackson muttered as he followed Ari's line of sight. "He seems very relaxed, too much even for him."

"I'm baffled. I don't know what his next move will be, nor ours."

"Who's the bodyguard next to him? He looks American or German."

Ari sighed. "Brad Keeting, CIA. At least he was CIA when we all knew him. Dev knows more about him. I believe one of your brother's friends had a thing with him, something about a tank."

"Ah, it was the priest."

Ari laughed out loud. "A priest?"

"Well, in fairness, he wasn't a priest when he pranked Keeting. The man didn't think it was too funny. I don't know much more than that."

"I like the priest."

Jackson glanced at his partner. "You know him. Do you remember Dan? He's a priest now."

"Really? He and I drank Arak for hours one night."

"What does that taste like?"

Ari's head tilted as he watched Khalid begin to move out of the throng of people. "Anise, what you might know as the taste of licorice. I liked him."

"So, what do we do about him?" Jackson pointed toward the moving figure.

"Absolutely nothing. We can't do anything until he makes a move. We've done all the leg work. INTERPOL has their eyes watching everything. We just stand here watching a bowl."

Jackson touched his earpiece and spoke quietly. "The target is on the move. We're staying here with the Ambassador and the bowl. We'll need cleanup tonight for all the drugs in this place, and has anyone found Henri Dupont?"

Brad Keeting looked back toward the two international agents. "They just don't know what to do."

"They most certainly do," Khalid stated. "Don't doubt that we are being followed. They are not idiots. I may want their deaths, but I do not underestimate them."

"Then should we go after Pierce tonight? Our men say he is back at the hotel." Brad Keeting wanted to do something. Walking away was just not his style. Besides, he became nervous while doing nothing.

"No, Agent Keeting. Leave him be. He is on his honeymoon. We can give him a few months to enjoy his little wife." Khalid continued to move through the crowd, smiling at many of the gala benefactors. Several shook his hand and thanked him for his monetary support of the arts.

Brad Keeting wasn't happy with the instructions, rather the lack of them. "But it would be easier here in Paris, tonight. It'll be more difficult when he is back on his home turf."

Khalid ignored him until they stood waiting for his limousine. He had a plan. He didn't want to hear excuses or arguments, especially not from an American. "It will be done when I say. I want him with his friends. I want them to suffer together. Maybe I meet their wives first. Yes, that would make it all real to the soldiers." He stopped and relished in his plans. "Keeting, you must have patience."

"Oh, I can have patience, I just don't like waiting. They are all out of the Army now. I ran into Pierce over a year ago. You need to know he works for the DEA now, tracking drugs."

Khalid smiled. "Then our paths will definitely cross. Civilians are so much easier to track down." His driver arrived, and the two men entered the large vehicle. "My that was a nice night, but it is too early to retire. Tell the men to be ready in one hour. Make sure Henri is ready. We have a long night ahead of us."

Chapter Twenty-Five

1. Take photos of the hotel
2. Pick up one piece of art for the house
3. Abby's chocolate and macaroons, never enough chocolate
4. Maybe buy a scarf?

"Are you sure you have enough chocolate? I think Switzerland and Germany may still have some left, but France is tapped out thanks to you, honey." Dev asked as he held up the two shopping bags in his hands. Lily and he had just spent the entire day shopping. He needed a drink. A nice cognac would warm him and calm his nerves. The woman could shop. She was deliriously happy. Dev had to admit he was happy too; he'd never had that much fun shopping. But the good time was over as they entered the hotel.

"Agent Pierce, I've been waiting for you." The man who greeted them as they entered the foyer was nicely dressed, but Dev only noticed the American flag pin on his lapel. "I have a message for you from the State Department." The man extended an envelope in Dev's direction.

Dev handed the bags over to Lily. "Honey, why don't you go on up? I'll be there in a few minutes.

Lily's smile decayed, dying in reality. She reached up, kissed him on the cheek, and grabbed the bags. "I'll call for the Marines if you aren't up there in fifteen minutes." Insolently, she glared at the man and turned toward the elevator. Over her shoulder, Lily saw Dev take the envelope and follow the interloper into the bar.

She made her way back to their room, dropped the shopping bag and removed her boots. She sat down on the window seat and looked down on her Paris masterpiece. From the stone streets to the Tuileries below her, Paris was beyond belief. She was in love with a city. Well, she was also in love with a wonderful man. For the first time in her adult life, she wasn't worried about her future, her paycheck, or even her self-confidence.

Had it been fifteen minutes yet? She also didn't have a watch on for the first time in years. *Now, what was going on? We're supposed to leave tomorrow afternoon.*

Lily sighed. She wondered what Abby was up to. Was she really settling into the daily routine of running a flower shop with her boss?

"Stop it," she said out loud. "Where are you, Dev?"

As if he heard her question, her husband entered the suite. "I'm here. Everything is fine." He made his way to her and kissed the top of her head. "Looking at my rival?"

"Yes. Paris and I are in love. We've been meaning to tell you."

Dev chuckled. "I knew that since the first night when you preferred looking at the tower instead of your husband."

Dev headed toward the sofa and took off his shoes. He stretched his long legs out over the small coffee table. Lily rose and sat down next to him, stretching out her own legs to touch his.

"Dev," she said as she looked into his eyes seriously, "I won't give up Paris, and I'm not going to divorce you either. You'll just have to live with this relationship."

Dev laid his arm around his wife and pulled her close. "That's fine until we visit Rome or London. We are not adding any other city to this marriage.

"Agreed." Lily was resting her head against his chest. She looked up into his eyes. "Are you going to tell me about your visitor?"

"He was from the State Department, via the Embassy. He was updating me on some things, and we also have a stop before we leave tomorrow. Bernard Notte remains in a coma, but he is safe in a military hospital, well as safe as possible. We need to meet Claude back at the Louvre. It'll be a good thing to say goodbye."

"Are you angry with her?"

Dev's chest rose and fell deeply. "More disappointed than angry. I have no words for what happened with Tom and now all her dealings with drugs and diamonds."

"And do we know what will happen to her?"

Dev rubbed his wife's back slowly. "Apparently, she is still at the museum so I'm not sure anything will. INTERPOL and UNESCO may have some sort of arrangement. I'm not asking. Frankly, I'll be happy to get back to my own drug dealers, less intrigue."

Lily pushed back and kissed him on the cheek. "Very funny. Less intrigue, right. At least my encounter with the Notte family is all over for now."

"Unless the matriarch starts dealing." His smile elicited a shove from his wife. "Seriously, if Bernard survives, he'll always be looking over his shoulder for Khalid. He'll also have major prison time, hopefully. Now, I have reservations for dinner at a fantastic restaurant tonight. I'm going to knock your socks off with romance and food."

"That sounds wonderful, but I'm not wearing any socks."

"Then we'll have to remove some other item of clothing." He reached out for Lily as she quickly stood up.

She shook her finger at him. "You are very good at that."

"Among other things. We have time before dinner for me to show you my proficiency."

As Dev came toward her like a stalking tiger, she headed to the bed and plopped down. *This was a honeymoon!*

That evening, Lily enjoyed her last bite of chocolate mousse. It was the final course, following french onion soup, cheeses, escargot, and her favorite confit de canard. *Who knew duck could taste so good? But escargots are just too slimy. Garlic and butter make them better, but those items make everything better. The candlelit dinner was a dream.*

"It's getting late. We should probably get back to the hotel." Dev finished paying the bill and asked for their coats.

"Shall we walk back?" Lily wanted one more opportunity to relish in Paris' light. The November skies were pitch black, but the city glittered. The darkness couldn't hold a candle to the glowing romance she was living in.

"I insist." Dev helped her with her coat. "You are going to love it outside."

"I'm not sure about that. I'll need a coffee or hot chocolate to help thaw me out, but I just want one more walk at night."

Dev led her through the restaurant and then stopped her short of the door. "Close your eyes."

"What?"

He turned her around. "Close your eyes, and I'll lead you out. I have a surprise for you."

"Devlin Pierce, you are a very weird man. Fine, I'll close my eyes, but don't let me run into anyone or anything." *She did trust him, didn't she?*

She felt the cold air on her face. He had his hands on her shoulders and his face near hers. "Paris has one more gift for you. Open your eyes, Lily."

Lily felt something wet on her face as she slowly opened her eyes at his direction. Her eyes became wider. It was snowing in Paris, and it was beginning to accumulate. "Oh my goodness."

Dev stole a kiss on her cheek and gathered one of her hands in his. "Nothing else? Could it be that snow makes you speechless?"

Lily swept away a tear. "It's like magic." She leaned her head up to see the flakes in one of the city lights. "This is one of my dreams."

"Any others?" Dev couldn't stop watching the awe and joy on her face. She was like a child sometimes, and maybe that's what drew him to her. He did need to lighten up, to enjoy the life he had. They had both been workaholics who were just looking for that perfect partner in crime and in love. "I hope I can make all your dreams come true, Lily. I really do." He brought her gloved hand up and kissed it.

Lily Pierce was silent as she watched him romance her. *How did I get so lucky?* The entire day had been perfect. It was hard to believe that tomorrow they would be heading back to the United States, to Dev's home.

Her husband and she walked hand-in-hand across her favorite bridge. There was no mention of any secret agents, terrorists, family or even any sort of intrigue. She heard distant police sirens. *We aren't involved, thank God.* There was only talk of their life together. There was even mention of beginning a family as soon as they could. They weren't getting any younger.

There was music playing out into the street from a small club. Dev pulled her in, and they sat at a table in a dark corner. Her husband was very good at enticing her to be very bad. He nuzzled her neck and caressed her shoulders slowly.

"Are you trying to seduce me?"

"Is it working?" he whispered.

"You know I'm a 'given', don't you? I'm a sure deal. There's no reason to persuade me. We are married."

"Ah, but if I don't keep you happy, you'll stay here with Paris."

"Devlin, you had me at chocolate, and you paid for it."

Dev laughed. "Let's go back to the hotel."

"I thought you'd never get to that."

Later that night, Lily woke from a nightmare. She was breathing hard from the dark dream. She had seen a figure in the shadows. The man reminded her of Khalid. He was coming after her. Then he turned, and he was headed toward Father Dan, then JT, then Paul and finally, the terrorist pulled out a gun and shot. The shadows cleared, and a spotlight was on the body laying on the ground. It was Dev, his eyes closed and blood staining his shirt. She turned to face the terrorist, and he was raising a glass of champagne in her direction.

She slowly moved from the bed and grabbed the hotel's robe. The room was cool again. She turned on one of the lamps in the corner of the sitting area and shuffled to her favorite seat. Lily looked out the window and saw her beloved tower. It was the last time she would see it. Even her obsession with it could not warm her; that nightmare had left her heart cold. She grabbed her shoulders. She was shaking from fear and the lowered temperature.

"Lily, honey, come back to bed." Dev's voice was filled with sleep. *What was she doing in that window seat?* "You'll freeze over there."

She fled her view and walked quickly back to the bed. His body warmed the sheets. Lily moved her cold feet onto his legs.

"Geez, Lily. Are your feet always cold?"

"I guess so."

"That's something I should've known before I married you, but we haven't really spent a winter together." He pulled her closer and rubbed her back. "You are so cold. What were you thinking about over there?"

Why did he have to be so darned perceptive? "I was just thinking."

"Oh no. That means you were probably making lists."

Lily didn't smile. He was attempting to be charming. "I wasn't. I was just thinking."

Dev softly lifted a curl that had drifted down into her eyes. He could tell she was thinking, thinking hard. But maybe he saw some fear, or was she just cold? "Honey, is everything alright? Are we alright?"

Lily nodded and shut her eyes. Tears were forming. Her lids shut tighter in a vain attempt to stop the leakage. She failed. Dev's finger swept the tear from her cheek.

"I don't know what is bothering you," he whispered, "but I know that whatever it is, we, you and me, we can conquer it together. We always do. I used to think I worked very well in a team, a team of three, five or more, but you and me, well we are the best together. You've taught me that."

She nudged her head under his chin and took her position on his chest. "Just hold me."

Her husband wound his arms around her back and held her close. He stayed awake until he heard her even breathing. He didn't understand the dragon she was fighting, but he would carry the sword to protect her at any cost. Holding her close, intimately in his arms, was the best job he'd ever had. This marriage thing was pretty good. Hopefully, it would survive the reality of every-day living and the huge changes she would have once they arrived back in the United States. She was coming from brides to boredom in Alexandria, Virginia.

<h1 style="text-align:center">Chapter Twenty-Six</h1>

1. Make sure everything is packed
2. Thank Claude for the dress shopping
3. Follow Dev's lead when seeing Claude
4. Make sure purse is cleaned out so I have no contraband
5. Do I have my passport? Can I feel my passport?
6. One more look at the Eiffel Tower
7. Say goodbye to Paris, hello to Washington, D.C.

Lily could see that Dev was hesitant. She knew he hid any nervousness at all times, well maybe except for their wedding day. He did seem a little different that day. She knew his tells and he had used them during the service, including running his hand through his hair and tugging at his watchband a couple of times. She wouldn't say he was nervous as they entered the Louvre one final time, but she would say he was on guard.

They were led by one of the security guards through the side entrance, through the hall where once stood flower urns and columns filled with drugs, to the exhibit hall where the tulip bowl sat in captivity.

"Well, at least Khalid didn't succeed in capturing the old bowl," Dev murmured to her. His hand was secure around Lily's. He tightened his grip as he saw Claude standing near the exhibit. She smiled slightly. Her eyes were red.

The French woman took a few steps towards them and

opened her arms to embrace Lily. She seemed to be holding on for dear life to her new friend. "I'm so sorry, Lily," Claude whispered into her ear. "I don't know how I can ever make it up to you."

Lily patted her back. "You gave me a wonderful day trying on designer dresses. We had one beautiful day."

Claude pulled back. "We did, didn't we? Maybe someday we can have another?"

Lily nodded. "Yes, of course." The women stepped back from their embrace. Claude stood as a prisoner awaiting a verdict and sentencing from Judge Pierce.

"What can I say to you? Will you ever forgive me for all of this? For Tom?" Claude's voice caught as she said their dead friend and love's name. Lily was holding back tears. She could see Dev swallowing hard.

"There's nothing to say. You did what you thought was right for what you wanted." His gaze tore through Claude. If he was Superman, his x-ray eyes would have obliterated the woman.

"I've done some things I am not proud of, but for good reasons."

Dev nodded. He understood doing bad things for the greater good, but usually when he acted on that skewed principle it was to save a life, not a piece of art or an old clay bowl. It had been in the heat of battle, not at a restaurant in Paris. He had to live with his decisions, now Claude would have to live with hers.

"May we talk a little? I have those files for you to take back to the United States. I also want to show you some of the footage from the other night, of Khalid."

"Fine. We have a little time, but I promised Lily lunch and one more look at her new love, the tower. Then we have a flight out." He looked over at his wife. "Will you be fine here?"

"Sure. The bowl and I are old friends. Go do your job." Surprisingly, he mouthed the words 'I love you' before heading off with Claude. Lily was alone with the bowl, state of the art security, and two armed guards. Alone was a state of mind.

The bowl was intriguing. Dev had explained to her on the way over Khalid's infatuation with the artifact. The terrorist was a descendant of one of the houses of the Ottoman Empire, and the original sultan who created the bowl. It had been a wedding present for a bride. They had three sons together before his dear wife became disenchanted with him. She'd fallen in love with an infidel who had come in search of the empire's beloved tulip bulbs. It had been a long story, but Khalid had come down from the line of one of those sons. The wife had been killed, beheaded, along with her lover. But the bowl was smuggled out by the infidel's brother. The family had searched through the ages to get it back. Khalid had supposedly picked the gala as a grand gesture of redemption and reclamation. He'd failed, again.

Lily studied the color, the intricacies. If she'd seen it in a thrift store, she would've just walked on by, but here in the museum, in a place of honor, it almost glowed with majesty and power. The bloom itself was beginning to fade, but the leaves remained vibrant.

Wait a minute, there's not two leaves. And where's the little bud? Lily walked carefully around one guard, smiled and examined the bowl from another side. Perhaps they had displayed it differently? Maybe they had removed it from the display to a more secure location and had set it facing in a different direction?

She saw the next side. Just one leaf, just a bloom. She walked over to the next side. There was a bloom, a bud and a stem. Finally, she made her way to the very last side of the guarded area. There was a bloom, a bud and only one small leaf.

"*Mon Dieu,*" Lily whispered. One guard turned his head to casually glance at her. She was cursing in French! *No, no, no, Lily, you have to be incorrect. This little discovery could make us miss our plane. As much as I'd love to stay in Paris, I'm getting sick of this spy stuff. Dev is right. Bring on the simple drug dealers.*

To ease her conscience, she walked around another time. She pulled a piece of paper out of her purse and began to take notes of the details. She drew each side with the notation. Even the gold around the rim was not as bright. Sadly, this wasn't the same bowl she saw last night, and that had been before any liquor. Wait, she hadn't had anything to drink for a few days now. Her taste buds were just off.

"Somehow I just knew you'd be here."

No, not more spies. She turned to see the handsome face of her new Israeli/Arab friend. "Hello, Ari."

"*Madame* Pierce. We must stop meeting like this or your husband will become suspicious. We will have to plot another place for our rendezvous in the future." He smiled, and she almost melted. He was wearing a black turtleneck with a grey leather jacket. He was casual in jeans and what looked to be boots of some kind.

"Ah, but will there be a future?" She shoved her pen

and paper into the purse and held onto the shoulder straps to keep her hands from shaking. She wasn't sure if the nervousness was from her discovery or this dangerous man. Her husband was dangerous, but he was comfortable; this man was dangerous and dangerous.

"Are you saying goodbye to our old friend?"

Lily stepped away from the exhibit and over to Ari. "You could say that. Dev is in with Claude, something about everything."

Ari held his head down briefly as if in embarrassment. "Yes," he answered as he lifted his eyes to meet hers. "That was a mess."

"Apparently, it still is. I'm assuming you didn't catch your prey last night."

"No, we did not, but we protected this lovely bowl. No Khalid, but we have pottery. That wasn't a very good trade."

Lily bit her lip. This was way above anything she had ever done or experienced in her life. She had a dilemma that no one had ever prepared her for. Not one teacher, nun, priest, nor her mom and dad had ever taught or warned her about terrorists, super agents, FBI agents, DEA husbands, art thieves, and the occasional drug dealer or smuggler. What should she do?

Ari made the move. He'd noticed her shaking hands, her step back from his step forward. She could be cold. The snow had been unexpected last night and seemed to remove any warmth Paris had with its blanket of white. Lily was still not permitting him in her personal space, although last night they'd become friends over food and conversation. "Lily, what is wrong? What do you know that I don't?"

Lily shifted her weight from one foot to another. She needed to decide right now what would be the better good? "You failed on both counts."

Ari blinked twice. "What are you talking about?"

"You didn't catch your terrorist, and you didn't protect the tulip bowl."

Now his eyes widened in disbelief. "You are mistaken about the bowl. It is setting right there." He pointed defiantly toward the secured item.

"No, I'm not." Her resolute statement shook him.

"Lily, this isn't a game or the newest Tom Cruise movie. What are you talking about?" Ari's demeanor turned deadly serious. Now, he was danger personified.

She pulled her notes and sketches out of her bag and handed it to him slowly. "I keep track of little details. That talent makes me a good wedding florist. We make sure our clients get what they ordered. I remembered last night the leaves on the bowl, the bloom and the small bud. The design isn't the same. Someone has switched the bowl. Either the one last night wasn't authentic, or this one is a fake."

Ari studied her drawing then stepped closer to the artifact. He began to walk slowly around the exhibit, studying her drawings and comparing it to the bowl. He pulled out his phone and pulled up a photo. He looked up at Lily and then back down to his phone. As he came around to the final side to join Mrs. Pierce, he looked again at his phone and back to the bowl. "Shit."

His profanity was loud enough it echoed slightly, and both guards turned to face him.

"I'm beginning to curse in French. You do it in English?" Lily smiled slightly.

He was shaking the paper at her. "You little minx. Why do you have to be so observant?"

Lily was feeling threatened. Perhaps Ari wasn't a good guy? She began to back away as he came closer, but soon ran into a solid structure, her husband.

"Ari, what is your problem?" Dev moved in front of Lily immediately.

"This, her." His frustration was palpable.

Ari waved the paper in Dev's face as he came forward. He stuffed it into his hand.

"What am I looking at?" Dev saw the notes, the drawings as he unfolded the paper and understood immediately. "He did steal the bowl?"

Ari swept his hand through his hair. "We need to hire Lily. She sees everything, everything we do not see. How on earth did he do this?"

Dev pulled Lily around to his side. He held her close with one arm. "You are good, honey. Any ideas?"

Lily laughed nervously. "You are kidding, right?"

"Nope. Any ideas?"

"Show me the real bowl photo," Lily requested, pointing at Ari's phone.

He happily handed over the phone as if to relinquish control. "This is the real thing. This photo was from when it was authenticated in Turkey two years ago. That's the same bowl we saw right there last night." He pointed back at the exhibit.

"Then this isn't the real bowl. This is the fake." Lily handed back his phone.

"Give the woman a prize." Jackson Pierce's voice did echo. Both guards straightened up in surprise.

"Good morning, brother. Here to see us off?" Dev shook his brother's hand as he joined the group.

"No, but I'm happy to see you both before you leave. I'm here because I viewed the footage from the cameras outside and inside the museum last night and this morning. By the way," Jackson lightly touched his brother's shoulder, "great move out the side exit."

Dev smiled, Lily blushed.

"Imagine my surprise to see some movement around three in the morning. We had cleaners coming in to remove the columns, the flowers, anything with drugs. They were to take them to a secure location that INTERPOL set up through the French police. Flowers and columns were removed. Hell, everything was removed. Apparently, not one guard was overseeing the CCTV within the museum, because well, maybe they were paid off, or maybe because they all looked just like INTERPOL security. I've just returned from the secure location, and the storage area is empty. We ran facial recognition on the group and found several most-wanted international burglars and a couple of terrorists.

"Let me guess, Khalid was one of them," Ari suggested. His voice was controlled. He shook his head in disgust. "This museum is one of the world's most secure locations. The man walks right through the front door with an invitation and then he sneaks back in later to steal an artifact."

"What are you talking about?" Jackson was stunned.

"Your new sister-in-law has realized that this bowl," Ari stopped to point at the fake, "is not the real thing."

"No. I didn't see that on the film."

"All they had to do was slide it into one of the urns with the flowers, or even in one of the columns. They could've cushioned it with the drug packets." Lily had explained it all like a professional.

Jackson looked at Lily and blinked twice. He ran his hand through his hair, and Lily smiled. *Hmm, it is a family trait!* "Dev, where did you find her?"

The proud husband brought his arms around his wife. "I just walked into her shop one day."

"We've lost everything." Jackson began to walk and mutter.

"Not exactly everything," Dev whispered to his wife.

"What? What did you say?" Jackson came closer to the couple.

"There's drugs in some of the paintings and frames that Claude received from Bernard. You'll have to test everything, but you might be able to track those items back to some heavy hitters in the international drug trade. I just looked at one frame and smelled meth, you know that ammonia kind of smell? I wouldn't doubt it if you could trace fentanyl back to the Chinese. They put that stuff into everything when shipping into the country. One of my team found it in a guy's underwear once. They may have it in the paint."

Lily patted her husband's face. "You are so smart."

"I'm more concerned about the idiot with it in his underwear," Ari added, finally a smile coming to his face.

"Thanks, brother." Jackson handed a memory stick to his brother. "You'll need this when you get back to D.C. By the way, Henri was seen on the video. He let them in. He checked into the Louvre before the gala and then never left. We had security searching for him while the gala was still going on, but he had a great hiding place--he apparently hid in an unopened packing crate for a future exhibition. He's in the wind now. As for the security team, we found three dead a few blocks from here and three more tied up at the storage facility. Another six INTERPOL agents were massacred within the facility. The trucks that were used were abandoned near George Pompidou Centre. They are currently checking all their art."

"The French government won't be happy with two museums closed today," Ari said softly.

"No one is happy," Jackson admitted. "We have diamond contacts being rounded up. Claude will be debriefed. She had been working with INTERPOL, but they didn't authorize all of her antics. The Swiss are working with us to open Notte's accounts. We will know more, but it will take months, if not years, to unravel this mess."

Ari and Dev looked up to the very ornate ceiling. "Not only did he get away with an item he has been obsessing over for years, he also managed to ship drugs into Europe without any ramifications. He's gotten away with everything." Dev was incredulous. "Obviously, others are involved."

"A lot of payoffs went into this operation. All the guards here at the museum will be questioned." Jackson looked over to Lily. "Your Mr. Bernard Notte was just the tip of the iceberg. He double-crossed everyone and racked up a small fortune. I've already found a few items we've been looking for in Brussels. I'm headed there today."

"What about Remy?" Dev questioned.

Jackson shrugged. "He's dead."

Ari, Lily and Dev shouted, "What?"

"Remy was poisoned"

"Khalid did it," Lily announced. "I knew it." She punched Dev's shoulder. "Khalid walked by and touched him on the shoulder blade. I saw Remy wince. I just knew he had done something. It was probably some sort of contact poison like what the Russians did to that poor man in England." *Jessica Fletcher would be so proud of me right now.*

All three men looked at the florist from Kansas City. They were spellbound by her deduction and her blandness. But Dev winked.

"That's my wife."

Jackson shook his head. "I'll have them check that area of his body, but you are probably right. Khalid likes to get rid of any loose-ends. He'll probably go after Notte when he can. By the way, I checked the video outside the café the night of his shooting. Dev, you were right. Apparently, Khalid needed to shut him up before he talked to Ari or myself again."

"Now that everything is solved and nothing is settled, my wife and I are going for one more meal in Paris. Then we have a flight to catch," Dev announced. "I'll leave the super spy stuff to you two gentlemen."

Dev hugged his brother and mentioned something about Christmas. He looked toward Ari and nodded.

Ari took a few steps to Lily. "It was an honor, *madame.*" He lifted her hand to his lips and kissed it lightly. "Perhaps we will meet again."

Lily looked at his impish face as he lifted his eyes. He was smiling. He took a glance at Dev, knowing full well that the man was glaring at him. "I love making him squirm, don't you, Lily?"

Lily giggled. *Giggling, really Lily?* "I do. It makes him more human."

"Less a boy scout?"

Lily bent her head to his and whispered, "Yep."

Ari stood straight and released her hand. "Devlin, always a pleasure."

"Sure." Dev placed his arm around his wife's shoulders and ushered her away. "We are leaving now, wife."

As they walked away, Lily turned back. "It was nice meeting you, Jackson. I guess we're in a hurry. Ari, we will always have the buffet." Dev was rushing her out of the museum. "Honey, do we have time for me to go downstairs to the shops?"

"Nope. We are in a hurry to get out of here before you find some drugs, solve a murder, find a long-lost artifact, make new friends with an undercover Mossad agent--"

Lily continued to giggle. Dev was still listing various scenarios of sleuthing. It was definitely time to go home.

Jackson and Ari watched in amusement as Dev Pierce pulled his wife out of the museum.

"I've never seen him happier," Ari commented.

"I know, right? I would never have picked Lily for him, but she's perfect. She's challenging."

"She's fun. He needs some fun in his life after all he has been through."

Jackson nodded. "We've all been through a lot over the years."

The two men began to walk toward Claude's office. Ari stopped Jackson midway down the hallway. "I need to thank you for your generosity two years ago."

Jackson nodded knowingly. "No need. You saved my brother once or twice."

"But this was my little sister, the baby of our family. I've raised her since our parents passed away. She was being a teenager at a concert in Paris when those terrorists attacked. And you saved her."

"I happened to be in the right place at the right time, that's all."

Ari shook his head. "No, you saved her. I knew you were in Paris. I called you, and you found her. It was heroic."

"Aw shucks. She's really sweet, nothing like you." Jackson smiled.

Ari patted him on the back solidly. "That's the last time I give you credit for anything. I think I like Dev better."

"Really, the boy scout? You loathe him."

"I loathe him less than I loathe you."

Jackson began to walk toward Claude's open door. "That's not possible. You have no command of the English language."

"Do too."

"Do not," Jackson answered.

"Brussels?" Ari questioned.

"Yes."

"Maybe I'll join you."

"That's not necessary." Jackson scowled.

"Actually, it is. I'm tracking down a painting that was last seen in Bruge. It is a piece of stolen Nazi art."

Jackson's interest was piqued. "Is the family still around?"

"A granddaughter. She lives in Tel Aviv. She likes me."

"Of course she does," Jackson murmured. "Hopefully, I won't run into you."

"I thought you might take me on the flight." Ari flashed a smile.

"You thought wrong, Ari."

The quibbling, as if they were brothers of some variation, continued as they both attempted to enter Claude's doorway at the same time. The suave, dangerous agents were stuck like Laurel and Hardy.

"Let me go in," Jackson demanded.

"No, you let me go in."

"Just move your arm." Jackson shoved to the right.

"You just punched me." Ari shoved to the left. "Americans."

"Really? You want to go there? How many times have we saved the French, the English, the Israelis, the Saudis? Do I need to go on?"

"I speak for the Saudis now. We didn't need your help in the first Gulf War. We needed you to protect our oil fields. We don't like to get our hands dirty. We also needed you to protect that wonderful mall in Kuwait. Thank you for that."

"You're welcome. It's too pricey for me. The FBI doesn't pay me that kind of salary."

"That is a shame for you."

Claude Barbin stood watching the comedy. She had been frightened of her future, but now that she knew the boys would be the ones to finish taking her statement, fear was replaced by laughter. She hadn't laughed in a very long time, well except with Lily. She was missing her already.

Chapter Twenty-Seven

"How much more chocolate did you buy?" Dev asked as he handed Lily's duty-free bags to the flight attendant.

Lily watched her every move. "Where is she taking those?"

"You look like a pet when a favorite food bowl is removed. You won't need them during the flight, and she will place them safely in storage. I'll remember them when we get off the plane."

"You better, buddy." Lily still had the magazine she'd purchased.

"Are you really going to read that?" Dev saw a couple of the headlines. Some celebrity's wedding was featured on the cover.

"I like weddings." She wiggled her nose at him. "Remember?"

Dev settled into his seat beside her. "I do remember you like weddings, especially your own."

"By the way, this return flight will be the perfect time for you to tell me about all of your devious plans with Gretchen, Abby, and members of my family. I still want to know how you put it all together?"

"I made lots of lists, Mrs. Pierce, and I used a copious amount of post-it notes." He'd turned his head close to hers and was smiling.

She kissed him quickly. "I do love a man who uses post-it notes."

"I'll tell you all about it, somewhere mid-Atlantic."

She flipped casually though her magazine. She yawned. "I am so tired. Going back from a trip always seems to take so much out of me. Besides, I had to stand in the long line while my husband was checked in privately, in the short line. I'm sure it had something to do with all the adventures we just had?"

"Actually, it was about a certain item I have in my possession, my souvenir."

Lily looked into his eyes. For a second she couldn't figure it out. The realization showed on her face. "Oh. So I have to stand longer in the line for my chocolate purchases," she lowered her voice, "than you do with a gun?"

"Chocolate can be dangerous."

"Right, it melts."

"There is that. There are those bad guys who are allergic. You could take out an entire gang with your wicked chocolate bar."

Lily yawned again. "I am so tired."

"Well, honeymoons will take a lot out of you, besides, we did try to save the world." He winked. Her heart melted.

"There is that. But we failed."

Dev gathered her right hand and kissed it. She seemed to like it when Ari did it. "Sweetheart, you didn't. You found the drugs, you realized that Remy was poisoned by Khalid, and you discovered the fake bowl. You were better than the professionals."

"But I want to leave it to the professionals. I don't want to ever discover drugs again, anywhere. I don't want to meet drug dealers or smugglers, art thieves, or even international police of any kind."

Dev frowned. "What about me?"

"I want you. You, I will keep."

"That's comforting to know."

"But, if we go back to Paris let's just stick to the restaurants and shops. I'm not sure I'm ready to go back into an art museum for a few years."

Dev chuckled. "You know, today you would've made Jessica Fletcher proud."

Lily pretended to wipe a tear from her eye. "That's the nicest thing you've ever said to me."

His laughter stopped as soon as the final preparations for take-off began. She did make him laugh.

The flight seemed to go by very quickly with several meals served, Dev's tale of the wedding planning, one movie watched (the latest Tom Cruise action movie), a nap, and plans for the future. They agreed she should redecorate the master bedroom. By the end of the discussion, Dev suggested she make any changes she wanted. It was her home too.

It was, wasn't it?

As they landed in Virginia, Dev held her hand. "Well, we're here."

Lily looked out the window and then back at her husband.

They were definitely there. Her new life was ahead of her.

She sighed out loud. She leaned over and kissed his cheek. "I'm finally home."

Notes From the Author

I hope you enjoyed The Tulip Terror. I had a great time writing it, and enjoyed remembering a special trip I once took to Paris. Lily certainly seemed to love the city despite the new characters she meets and the circumstances she faces. She is becoming a danger magnet, just like Abby said!

Paris is the ultimate "foodie" city (all of France has amazing food) where you can experience crêpes from street vendors and over-the-top Michelin rated dinners. The coffee (don't expect them to refill your cup) is so good you really just want to sit at a café all morning with a warm cup in your hand. One of my favorite places, Angelina's, has the best hot chocolate. They bring you a cup of melted chocolate and a container of whipped cream, real cream. You mix it together and you are transported to heaven, seriously it is heaven. I enjoyed duck and fresh olives. Butter is really butter, and bread is its own food group. Don't even get me started on the cheese. Fromage forever!

During my special Paris trip, we rented a flat not too far from the Cathedral of Notre-Dame. I began writing The Tulip Terror before the devastating fire of 2019. I can not explain on paper what the Cathedral was like, when you walked up to it, and stood inside. There really are no words that are adequate, and so I cried as I watched the fire take the spire. We always used to light a candle there, just like Lily did.

Once again, the wedding stories are based on real events, except for the largest wedding in the story. Were you surprised that Lily didn't plan her wedding, except for the selection of her dress? And how much do you love Devlin Pierce? His plans really proved how much he really cares for her and needs his wife in his life.

In every adventure, we are pulling back a layer of Devlin Pierce. He has some intriguing friends, and enemies. Our Lily is becoming her own force of nature. She is finding her way, and maybe she discovers a new path.

One more interesting item--the fleur-de-lis has been used by the monarchy in France for centuries. It is translated as "flower of the lily" and it is also a design for boy scouts. Lily and Dev are both represented by its meanings, but I never did plan it that way!

So what is next for our lovable couple? The Sweet Pea Secret will be out soon. Lily and Dev will each have to face their pasts while continuing to plan their future. We have realized they both like to plan out everything. Sometimes, you can't plan for every little thing; life happens and when it does, the post-it notes are thrown in the trash. You can't make a list when you're busy fighting for your life. What we do know is Lily and Devlin Pierce will do it together, and together they can't be stopped.

The end is just the beginning for Lily and Agent Devlin Pierce. Watch for their next adventure in The Lily List Mystery Series.

C.L. Bauer offers a peek into the flower and wedding world she knows well in her hometown of Kansas City, Missouri.

Visit www.clbauer.com or email clbauerkc@gmail.com.

Welcome to Lily's!

C.L. BAUER

C.L. Bauer grew up and lives in Kansas City, Missouri. Her first novel The Poppy Drop, A Lily List Mystery was well received by the top 100 Books of Independent Publishers when it launched in 2018.

The Lily List Mystery Series features the highly organized, post-it note, and list making florist Lily Schmidt. Readers have enjoyed the adventures of the mystery loving woman and the wedding stories that are highlighted in these novels. Ms. Bauer draws on true events from her family's wedding and event flower business. With over one hundred years of serving families on their special days, Clara's Flowers has received numerous awards in the wedding world, including "best of" and "legacy winner" for service and design.

C.L. Bauer's first love of writing provided an early career in journalism. During high school, she began as a sports reporter, became an editor in college, and continued professionally in every writing medium including advertising and creative direction.

The author enjoys her family, travel, a good book on a rainy day, bulk post-it notes, and meeting her readers. She can always be swayed to feast on Mexican food, watch a hockey game, and drink the occasional fruity libation. If you've read her novels, you already know she loves Kansas City during the holidays.

You can reach C.L. Bauer on all forms of social media including her author pages on Facebook, Instagram, Twitter, Amazon, and Goodreads. Please review this and any of C.L. Bauer's published works. They are widely available for purchase in print and e-book forms. She's available for book club discussions virtually or in-person.

As always, happy reading!

Sign up at www.clbauer.com for this author's newsletter, promotions, pre-order information, free chapters, and upcoming publications. Contact C.L. Bauer directly at clbauerkc@gmail.com.

Coming in 2021...A Lily List Mystery Exclusive! Can't get enough of your favorite characters? The Exclusive novels feature more adventures with Lily's friends. Mysteries, murders, and more romance are coming your way!

www.ingramcontent.com/pod-product-compliance
Lightning Source LLC
Chambersburg PA
CBHW070618100726
47907CB00007B/1789